Bremen Public Library
Bremen, Indiana
7-10

W9-ASK-866

BLOOD
RANSOM

Bremen Public Library
Bremen, Indiana

MISSION HOPE
SERIES

BLOOD RANSOM

LISA HARRIS

ZONDERVAN®

ZONDERVAN.com/
AUTHORTRACKER
follow your favorite authors

ZONDERVAN

Blood Ransom
Copyright © 2010 by Lisa Harris

This title is also available as a Zondervan ebook.
Visit www.zondervan.com/ebooks.

This title is also available in a Zondervan audio edition.
Visit www.zondervan.fm.

Requests for information should be addressed to:

Zondervan, Grand Rapids, Michigan 49530

Library of Congress Cataloging-in-Publication Data

Harris, Lisa, 1969-
    Blood ransom / Lisa Harris.
       p.   cm.
       Includes bibliographical references.
       ISBN 978-0-310-31905-4 (pbk.)
       1. Americans--Africa--Fiction. 2. Slave trade--Fiction. 3. Human trafficking--Fiction.
    4. Africa--Fiction. I. Title.
    PS3608.A78315B57 2009
    813'.6--dc22   2009037495

All Scripture quotations, unless otherwise indicated, are taken from the Holy Bible, *New International Version*®, *NIV*®. Copyright © 1973, 1978, 1984 by Biblica, Inc.™ Used by permission of Zondervan. All rights reserved worldwide.

Author's disclaimer: "While *Blood Ransom* is a work of fiction, including the setting I chose to use, modern-day slavery is very real. Drawing from my own experiences across Africa over the past twenty years, my goal in writing this book was to weave current issues facing this vast continent into a riveting story that depicts not only these adversities, but also its beauty and hope."

Any Internet addresses (websites, blogs, etc.) and telephone numbers printed in this book are offered as a resource. They are not intended in any way to be or imply an endorsement by Zondervan, nor does Zondervan vouch for the content of these sites and numbers for the life of this book.

All rights reserved. No part of this publication may be reproduced, stored in a retrieval system, or transmitted in any form or by any means — electronic, mechanical, photocopy, recording, or any other — except for brief quotations in printed reviews, without the prior permission of the publisher.

Published in association with Hartline Literary Agency, Pittsburgh, Pennsylvania 15235.

Cover design: Laura Maitner-Mason
Interior design: Christine Orejuela-Winkelman

Printed in the United States of America

10 11 12 13 14 15 • 23 22 21 20 19 18 17 16 15 14 13 12 11 10 9 8 7 6 5 4 3 2

To all my friends
scattered across the beautiful African continent.
I will forever hold a piece of you in my heart.

And they sang a new song with these words:
"You are worthy to take the scroll and break its seals and open it.
For you were slaughtered, and your blood has ransomed people for
God from every tribe and language and people and nation."

Revelation 5:9 NLT

BLOOD
RANSOM

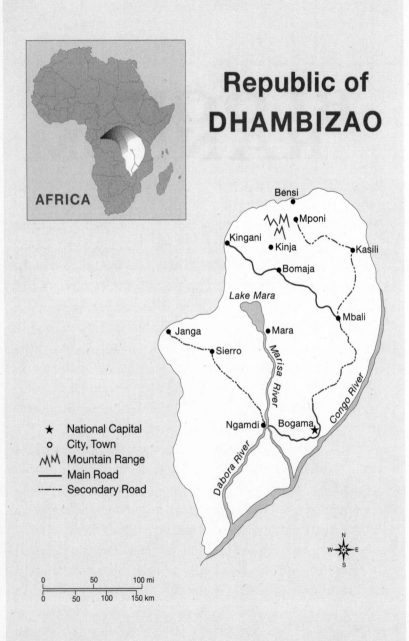

Republic of
DHAMBIZAO

AFRICA

★ National Capital
o City, Town
ΜΜ Mountain Range
—— Main Road
----- Secondary Road

Bensi
Mponi
Kingani
Kinja
Kasili
Bomaja
Lake Mara
Mbali
Janga
Mara
Sierro
Marisa River
Congo River
Ngamdi
Bogama
Dabora River

N
W E
S

0   50   100 mi
0   50   100   150 km

PROLOGUE

A narrow shaft of sunlight broke through the thick canopy of leaves above Joseph Komboli's short frame and pierced through to the layers of vines that crawled along the forest floor. He trudged past a spiny tree trunk — one of hundreds whose flat crowns reached toward the heavens before disappearing into the cloudless African sky — and smiled as the familiar hum of the forest welcomed him home.

A trickle of moisture dripped down the back of his neck, and he reached up to brush it away, then flicked at a mosquito. The musty smell of rotting leaves and sweet flowers encircled him, a sharp contrast to the stale exhaust fumes of the capital's countless taxis or the stench of hundreds of humans pressed together on the dilapidated cargo boat he'd left at the edge of the river this morning.

Another flying insect buzzed in his ears, its insistent drone drowned out only by the birds chattering in the treetops. He slapped the insect away and dug into the pocket of his worn trousers for a handful of fire-roasted peanuts, still managing to balance the bag that rested atop his head. His mother's sister had packed it for him, ensuring that the journey — by taxi, boat, and now foot — wouldn't leave his belly empty. Once, not too long ago, he had believed no one living in the mountain forests surrounding his village, or perhaps even in all of Africa, could cook *goza* and fish sauce like his mother. But now, having ventured from the dense and sheltering rainforest, he knew she was only one of thousands of women who tirelessly pounded cassava and prepared the thick stew for their families day after day.

Still, his mouth watered at the thought of his mother's cooking. The capital of Bogama might offer running water and electricity for those willing to forfeit a percentage of their minimal salaries, but even the new shirt and camera his uncle had given him as parting gifts weren't enough to lessen his longings for home.

He wrapped the string of the camera around his wrist and felt his heart swell with pride. No other boy in his village owned such a stunning piece. Not that the camera was a frivolous gift. Not at all. His uncle called it an investment in the future. In the city lived a never-ending line of men and women willing to pay a few cents for a color photo. When he returned to Bogama for school, he planned to make enough money to send some home to his family — something that guaranteed plenty of meat and cassava for the evening meal.

Anxious to give his little sister, Aina, one of the sweets tucked safely in his pocket and his mother the bag of sugar he carried, Joseph quickened his steps across the red soil, careful to avoid a low limb swaying under the weight of a monkey.

A cry shattered the relative calm of the forest.

Joseph slowed as the familiar noises of the forest faded into the shouts of human voices. More than likely the village children had finished collecting water from the river and now played a game of chase or soccer with a homemade ball.

The wind blew across his face, sending a chill down his spine as he neared the thinning trees at the edge of the forest. Another scream split the afternoon like a sharpened machete.

Joseph stopped. These were not the sounds of laughter.

Dropping behind the dense covering of the large leaves, Joseph approached the outskirts of the small village, straining his eyes in an effort to decipher the commotion before him. At first glance everything appeared familiar. Two dozen mud huts with thatched roofs greeted him like an old friend. Tendrils of smoke rose from fires beneath rounded cooking pots that held sauce for evening meals. Brightly colored pieces of fabric fluttered in the breeze as freshly laundered clothes soaked up the warmth of the afternoon sun.

His gaze flickered to a figure emerging from behind one of the grass-thatched huts. Black uniform ... rifle pressed against his shoulder ... Joseph felt his lungs constrict. Another soldier emerged, then another, until there were half a dozen shouting orders at the confused villagers who stumbled onto the open area in front of them. Joseph watched as his best friend Mbona tried to fight back, but his hoe was no match against the rifle butt that struck his head. Mbona fell to the ground.

Ghost Soldiers!

A wave of panic, strong as the mighty Congo River rushing through its narrow tributaries, ripped through Joseph's chest. He gasped for breath, his chest heaving as air refused to fill his lungs. The green forest spun. Gripping the sturdy branch of a tree, he managed to suck in a shallow breath.

He'd heard his uncle speak of the rumored Ghost Soldiers — mercenaries who appeared from nowhere and kidnapped human laborers to work as slaves for the mines. Inhabitants of isolated villages could disappear without a trace and no one would ever know.

Except he'd thought such myths weren't true.

The sight of his little sister told him otherwise. His mind fought to grasp what was happening. Blood trickled down the seven-year-old's forehead as she faltered in front of the soldiers with her hands tied behind her.

No!

Unable to restrain himself, Joseph lunged forward but tripped over a knotty vine and fell. A twig snapped, startling a bird into flight above him.

The soldier turned from his sister and stared into the dense foliage. Joseph lay flat against the ground, his hand clasped over the groan escaping his throat. The soldier hesitated a moment longer, then grabbed his sister's arm and pulled her to join the others.

Choking back a sob, Joseph rose to his knees and dug his fingers into the hard earth. What could he do? Nothing. He was no match for these men. If he didn't remain secluded behind the cover of the forest, he too would vanish along with his family.

The haunting sounds of screams mingled with gunshots. His grandfather fell to the ground and Joseph squeezed his eyes shut, blackness enveloping him. It was then, as he pressed his hand against his pounding chest, that he felt the camera swinging against his wrist. He stared at the silver case. Slowly, he pressed the On button.

This time, the world would know.

With a trembling arm Joseph lifted the camera. Careful to stay within the concealing shade of the forest, he snapped a picture without bothering to aim as his uncle had taught him. He took another photo, and another, and another ... until the cries of his people dissipated on the north side of the clearing as the soldiers led those strong enough to work toward the mountains. The rest — those like his grandfather, too old or too weak to work in the mines — lay motionless against the now bloodstained African soil.

In the remaining silence, the voices of two men drifted across the breeze. English words were foreign to his own people's uneducated ears but had become familiar to Joseph. What he heard now brought a second wave of terror ...

"Only four more days until we are in power ... There is no need to worry ... The president will be taken care of ... I can personally guarantee the support of this district ..."

Joseph zoomed in and took a picture of the two men.

A monkey jumped to the tree above him and started chattering. One of the beefy soldiers jerked around, his attention drawn to the edge of the clearing. Joseph froze as his gaze locked with the man's. Someone shouted.

If they caught him now, no one would ever know what had happened to his family.

Joseph scrambled to his feet as the soldier ran toward him, but the man was faster. The butt of a rifle struck Joseph's head. He faltered, but as a trickle of blood dripped into his eye, he pictured Aina being led away ... his grandfather murdered in cold blood ...

Ignoring the searing pain, Joseph fought to pull loose from his attacker's grip, kicked at the man's shins. The soldier faltered on the uneven terrain. Clambering to his feet, Joseph ran into the cover of the forest. A rifle fired, and the bullet whizzed past his ear, but he kept moving. With the Ghost Soldier in pursuit, Joseph sprinted as fast as he could through the tangled foliage and prayed that the thick jungle would swallow him.

ONE

Natalie Sinclair fingered the blue-and-yellow fabric that hung neatly folded on a wooden rod among dozens of other brightly colored pieces, barely noticing the plump Mama who stood beside her in hopeful anticipation. Instead she gazed out at the shops that lined the winding, narrow paths of the market, forming an intricate maze the size of a football field. The vendors sold everything from vegetables and live animals to piles of secondhand clothing that had been shipped across the ocean from charities in the States.

Natalie stepped across a puddle and turned to glance beneath the wooden overhang at the stream of people passing by. Even with the weekend over, the outdoor market was crowded with shoppers. Hip-hop-style music played in the background, lending a festive feel to the sultry day. But she couldn't shake the uneasy feeling in the pit of her stomach.

Someone was following her.

She quickened her steps and searched for anything that looked out of place. A young man weaved his bicycle through the crowded walkway, forcing those on foot to step aside. A little girl wearing a tattered dress clung to the skirt of her mother, who carried a sleeping infant, secured with a length of material, against her back. An old

17

man with thick glasses shuffled past a shop that sold eggs and sugar, then stopped to examine a pile of spark plugs.

Natalie's sandal stuck in a patch of mud, and she wiggled her foot to pull it out. Perhaps the foreboding sensation was nothing more than the upcoming elections that had her on edge. All American citizens had been warned to stay on high alert due to the volatile political situation. Violence was on the rise. Already a number of joint military-police peacekeeping patrols had been deployed onto the streets, and there were rumors of a curfew.

Not that life in the Republic of Dhambizao was ever considered safe by the embassy, but neither was downtown Portland. It was all a matter of perspective.

And leaving wasn't an option. Not with the hepatitis E outbreak spreading from the city into the surrounding villages. Already, three health zones north of the town of Kasili where she lived were threatened with an outbreak. She'd spent the previous two weeks sharing information about the disease's symptoms with the staff of the local government clinics, as well as conducting awareness campaigns to inform the public on the importance of proper hygiene to prevent an epidemic.

In search of candles for tonight's party, Natalie turned sharply to her left and hurried up the muddy path past wooden tables piled high with leafy greens for stew, bright red tomatoes, and fresh fish. Rows of women sat on wooden stools and fanned their wares to discourage the flies that swarmed around the pungent odor of the morning's catch.

Someone bumped into her from behind, and she pulled her bag closer. Petty theft might be a constant concern, but she knew her escalated fears were out of line. Being the only pale foreigner in a sea of ebony-skinned Africans always caused heads to turn, if not for the novelty, then for the hope that she'd toss them one or two extra coins for their supper.

Her cell phone jingled in her pocket, and she reached to answer it.

"When are you coming back to the office?" Stephen's to-the-point greeting was predictable.

"I'm not. I'm throwing a birthday party for you tonight, remember? You let me off early." A pile of taper candles caught her eye in a shop across the path, and she skirted the edge of a puddle that, thanks to the runoff, was rapidly becoming the size of a small lake.

Stephen groaned. "Patrick's here at the office, and he's asking questions."

She pulled a handful of coins from her pocket to pay for the candles. "Then give him some answers."

"I can't."

Natalie thrust the package the seller had wrapped in newspaper into her bag and frowned. Patrick Seko, the former head of security for the president, now led some sort of specialized task force for the government. Lately, his primary concern seemed to revolve around some demographic research for the Kasili region she'd been compiling for the minister of health, whose office she worked for. Her expertise might be the prevention and control of communicable diseases, but demographics had always interested her. Why her research interested Patrick was a question she'd yet to figure out.

The line crackled. Maybe she'd get out of dealing with Patrick and his insistent questions after all.

"Stephen, you're breaking up."

All she heard was a garbled response. She flipped the phone shut and shoved it back into her pocket. They'd have to finish their conversation at the party.

"Natalie?"

She spun around at the sound of her name. "Rachel, it's good to see you."

Her friend shot her a broad smile. "I'm sorry if I startled you."

Natalie wanted to kick herself for the uncharacteristic agitation that had her looking behind every shadow. "I'm just a bit jumpy today."

"I understand completely." Rachel pushed a handful of thin braids behind her shoulder and smiled. "I think everyone is a bit on edge, even though with the UN's presence the elections are supposed to pass without any major problems. No one has forgotten President Tau's bloody takeover."

Natalie had only heard stories from friends about the current president's takeover seventeen years ago. Two elections had taken place since then and were assumed by all to have been rigged. But with increasing pressure from the United States, the European Union, and the African Union, President Tau had promised a fair election this time no matter the results. And despite random incidences of pre-election violence, even the United Nations was predicting a fair turnover under their supervision — something that, to her mind, remained to be seen.

Natalie took a step back to avoid a group of uniformed students making their way through the market and smiled at her friend. After eighteen months of working together, Rachel had moved back to the capital to take a job with the minister of health, which meant Natalie rarely saw her anymore. Something they both missed. "What are you doing in Kasili?"

"I'm heading back to Bogama tomorrow, but I'm in town because Patrick has been meeting with my parents to work out the *labola*."

"Really? That's wonderful." Her sentiment was genuine, even though she happened to find Patrick overbearing and controlling — as no doubt he would be in deciding on a bride price. She hugged her friend. "When's the wedding ceremony?"

Rachel's white teeth gleamed against her dark skin, but Natalie didn't miss the shadow that crossed her expression. "We're still discussing details with our families, but soon. Very soon."

"Then I'll expect an invitation."

"Of course." Rachel's laugh competed with the buzz of the crowd that filed past them. "And by the way, I don't know if Patrick mentioned it to you, but Stephen invited us to the birthday party you're throwing for him tonight. I hope you don't mind."

"Of course I don't mind." Natalie suppressed a frown. Stephen had invited Patrick to the party? She cleared her throat. "Stephen just called to tell me Patrick was looking for me, but it had something to do with my demographic reports. Apparently he has more questions."

"Patrick can be a bit … persistent." Rachel flashed another broad smile, but Natalie caught something else in her eyes she couldn't read. Hesitation? Fear? "I'll tell him to wait until they are compiled. *Then* he can look at them."

Natalie laughed. "Well, you know I'm thrilled you're coming."

She would enjoy catching up with Rachel, and she had already prepared enough food to feed a small army. It was Patrick and his antagonistic political views she dreaded. She'd probably end up spending the whole evening trying to avoid them both.

"I'm looking forward to it as well." Rachel shifted the bag on her shoulder. "But I do need to hurry off. I'm meeting Patrick now, but I'll see you tonight."

Natalie watched until her friend disappeared into the crowd, wondering what she'd seen in her friend's gaze. It was probably nothing. Rachel had been right. Her own frayed nerves were simply a reaction of the tension everyone felt. By next week the election would be over and things would be back to normal.

A rooster brushed her legs, and she skirted to the left to avoid stepping on the squawking bird. The owner managed to catch it and mumbled a string of apologies before shoving it back in its cage.

Natalie laughed at the cackling bird, realizing that this was as normal as life was going to get.

Spotting a woman selling spices and baskets of fruit two shops down, she slipped into the tiny stall, determined to enjoy the rest of the day. She had nothing to worry about. Just like the UN predicted, the week would pass without any major incidents. And in the meantime, she had enough on her hands.

She picked up a tiny sack of cloves, held it up to her nose, and took in a deep breath. With the holiday season around the corner, she'd buy some extra. Her mother had sent a care package last week filled with canned pumpkin, chocolate chips, French-fried onions, and marshmallows. This year Natalie planned to invite a few friends over for a real Thanksgiving dinner. Turkey, mashed potatoes, green-bean casserole, pumpkin pie —

Fingers grasped her arm from behind. Natalie screamed and struggled to keep her balance as someone pulled her into the shadows.

TWO

Natalie's heart pounded in her ears. She jerked her arm free from her attacker and fell hard against a wooden post supporting the shop's tin roof. Tiny splinters pricked her forearm as she scraped against the rough wood. Rubbing the tender spot, she peered into the darkened corner behind a fat basket overflowing with ripe mangos to where a young boy hovered in the shadows.

Natalie paused. There was something familiar about his face. High cheekbones, broad nose, and a scar that jetted across his chin before fading at the jawline. He couldn't be more than fourteen or fifteen. She dug through the recesses of her mind. She knew this boy.

He took a tentative step forward. "It's me, ma'am. Joseph Komboli."

Natalie shook her head. "Joseph?"

"From Maponi. I worked for you."

One of my translators.

Joseph Komboli had helped her communicate with a dozen remote villages in the mountains until someone in the government insisted she focus her efforts on the more densely populated segments of the country.

The whites of his eyes stood out against his dark face as he looked up at her. "I didn't mean to frighten you."

23

Natalie reached out her hand to greet him, then noticed a bandage tied haphazardly around his forehead. She tugged him out from the shadows to where light filtered through holes in the tin roof. The cloth was stained with dried blood. "Joseph, what happened?"

"I ... I fell." He picked up a handful of cinnamon sticks and rubbed them between his fingers, all the time keeping his gaze on her face. Slivers of brown bark crumbled and scattered to the ground.

"Hey! You will pay for that — "

Natalie retrieved a handful of coins from her front pocket and thrust them at the angry shopkeeper who'd appeared from out front. Worries of pre-election violence vanished. "You need to see a doctor."

"No ... I can't." He made his way toward the edge of the shop and paused. Raindrops pinged against the metal roof. If they didn't leave now, they'd be caught in an afternoon downpour. "You don't ... understand." His voice cracked. "They are gone. All of them." The patter of rain intensified, as if trying to drown out his voice. "The Ghost Soldiers came ... I managed to escape."

The words hit Natalie harder than a punch to her gut. She'd heard the rumors. Entire villages vanishing overnight, their inhabitants spirited away to work in slave labor camps that confined them to isolated mines in the mountains. All of which contradicted the government's assertion that such rumors were false.

Joseph looked around and took a step toward her, ignoring the stares of the shopkeeper who scrambled to secure her wares from the impending downpour. "They took my family — everyone able to work — and dragged them out of the village. Aina is only seven, and my father ..."

Natalie shuddered at the thought of what a man could do to a seven-year-old girl. But Ghost Soldiers were supposed to be nothing more than rumors ... like stories whispered at summer camp about the boogeyman or other fabled monsters that hid under her bed and in her closet while she slept. And while she wasn't so naïve to think that human atrocities didn't exist here as they did in places like Sudan and Rwanda, the government had told her they had proof the Ghost Soldiers did not exist. Hadn't Stephen tried to convince her of the very same thing?

"But the demographic numbers don't add up, Stephen. What if the rumors are true and people are disappearing from their villages? Hundreds ... Thousands ..."

No. Natalie worked to steady her ragged breathing. Stephen's calm assurances had been correct. *"This is Africa. The government census is an estimate at best. No one verifies the numbers or expects them to be one hundred percent accurate."*

The numbers didn't have to add up. There was no such thing as Ghost Soldiers.

But the gnawing thought in the back of her mind remained. Hundreds of people lived isolated in the mountains never to be counted by the government. If they disappeared, no one would know. Their nomadic existence among the mountainous forests did nothing to prove the existence of the Ghost Soldiers. Or disprove it.

"Ma'am?"

"I'm sorry." Natalie pressed her hand against her forehead. "I parked my car in front of the market. Let's get out of here before we get completely drenched."

"But I can't—"

"I'm taking you to a doctor, Joseph. Period. Then we'll talk."

Natalie grasped Joseph's elbow and steered him through the market, past vendors busy securing plastic tarps over their goods and leaky roofs. She didn't want to admit the fear she'd seen in Joseph's eyes. She'd known him as a bright young man, eager to work and sympathetic to the people she'd come to help. Today a haunted look hovered behind his gaze.

A wave of panic swelled in her chest as she unlocked the passenger door of her car just before the heavens let forth their fury. Conversing while driving was impossible. So was calming her imagination. Instead she wove through the muddied streets and focused

Bremen Public Library

on getting Joseph the medical care he needed. The front tire of her car hit a pothole as she turned the corner, sending a splash of water toward the row of vendors that edged the street. The windshield wipers clicked each passing second with a steady thump that matched her quickened heartbeat.

By the time Natalie reached the clinic, the deluge had ended, leaving behind an eerie silence as the sun poked its yellow rays through the darkened clouds once again. She'd have Joseph's wound stitched up, then take him to a café she knew that served cold soft drinks and decent pastries. She might get home later than planned, but everything, including the food, was pretty much ready for the party.

She glanced at her passenger, praying she'd find a way to make sense of his rambling about Ghost Soldiers.

THREE

Chad Talcott checked the drip of the peripheral IV line that contained a dose of diazepam for the young woman who lay motionless on the mattress. Barely ninety pounds, Hanna's body suffered from a high fever and repeated muscle spasms. He'd diagnosed her with tetanus, caused by the dirty knife used to cut the umbilical cord. It had taken her relatives eight hours to carry her to the clinic and another six for her premature baby to succumb to the disease. And if his fears were correct, Hanna didn't have long. This was the part he hated: death that stole mothers from their families and pushed babies into the grave before they had a chance to live.

He crossed the tiled floor and scrubbed his hands in the stainless-steel sink that hung at the end of a row of ten uniform beds. Three other wards, mirroring this one, comprised the majority of the compound funded by Volunteers for Hope International. Temporarily recruited doctors and nurses from the States, Europe, and Australia worked alongside national staff to make a difference.

Except sometimes a difference wasn't enough.

The remote rural areas, in particular, were problematic. There, women gave birth on reed mats on mud floors with no means of sanitation. Tetanus was far too common when traditional midwives had to cope without sterile instruments. Attempts to ensure all child-bearing women were vaccinated against the disease had improved the situation over the past five years, but there were still too many women living in outlying areas, often inaccessible to aid workers' help.

Chad watched Hanna's chest rise and fall beneath the worn sheet and prayed that she'd make it. The typical Dhambizan woman had ten pregnancies during her fertile years and was fortunate if a third of her children survived. One out of every twenty mothers didn't survive childbirth. If that wasn't enough, malaria and diarrhea were widespread. Water sources ran contaminated when drinking and washing sources doubled as latrines. The list — and suffering — went on and on.

His glance shifted to the woman next to Hanna, and he reminded himself that there was another side.

Malaika wouldn't have survived her difficult delivery lying on a mud floor. At the moment, though, she rested peacefully while her two-day-old baby nursed contentedly at her side. Tomorrow they would both go home.

Chad rubbed his eyes before returning his gaze to Hanna. His father, always the optimist, had seen hope for this country and had stayed twenty years to prove it. But hope wouldn't keep this mother of three alive or tell a grandmother that her only living child was going to die.

Sometimes there was simply nothing anyone could do.

His stomach growled, and he glanced at the lopsided clock hanging on the wall. All he'd found time to eat today was two bananas and a handful of peanuts — not enough to sustain him through seven surgeries and eight hours on his feet.

He nodded to the nurse on the other side of the room. "I'm going to take a five-minute break."

His twelve years living in the country as a missionary kid, along with all his medical training and two years in one of Portland's emergency rooms, hadn't prepared him for work in the Republic of Dhambizao. Just like five minutes of fresh air wouldn't erase the heaviness he felt in his heart or change Hanna's situation. But it would clear his head and help him finish the day.

He slipped through the front door and let the wooden frame slam shut behind him. Beyond the green lawn, bougainvillea covered the eight-foot cement wall surrounding the two-acre compound, splashing orange, pink, and purple against the gray mortar. A breeze brushed against his face but did little to lessen the heavy humidity in the air.

At the side of the building the generator clicked and he turned to look. The power was off ... again. But conditions could be worse. One of his friends worked in a field hospital in Sudan comprised only of inflatable tents. At least the clinic here in Kasili could boast of solid cement walls and a handful of ceiling fans.

As he lounged against the wall, an attractive white woman, her hand at the back of a young African boy, swept across the sidewalk from the small parking area and up the stairs toward the clinic. Chad tugged on the bottom of his navy-blue scrub top. He'd enjoyed few moments of quiet since his arrival eight weeks ago, and the one he'd just found was obviously over considering he was the only doctor on duty at the moment. "Can I help you?"

The woman stopped at the edge of the sidewalk. "This is Joseph. I think he might need stitch — " She stopped on the top stair and took a hard look at him. "Chad ... Chad Talcott?"

"Yes?" He stared into her toffee-brown eyes and his hand automatically reached for the ID badge above his left pocket. Then he remembered he'd left it behind in the States along with Dr. Pepper, Doritos, and the Thanksgiving dinner he'd miss next week. "Do I know you?"

"Natalie Sinclair." She held out her hand. "If I'm not mistaken, we went to the same high school back in Portland."

"You went to Central High? Wow. That was a long time ago."

Worry lines etching her mouth softened. "You don't remember me, do you?"

Natalie Sinclair. He tried to place the name as he shook her hand, but the only image that came to mind was a short, awkward teenager with unruly hair and braces. The woman standing before him was neither short nor gangly. Light makeup, shapely brows, subtle curves beneath her bright yellow sundress . . .

Chad cleared his throat. "I remember the name . . . You helped lead our academic decathlon team to the state championship."

"You have a good memory." She smiled. "And I remember that you were quite the athlete back then."

" '*Back then*' being the key words." Chad laughed. "That was a long time ago. Back home I still manage to run five miles a day and dabble in martial arts, but football's a thing of the past."

She pushed back the lock of damp, coppery hair that had tumbled across her eyes and glanced at the boy. Her smile faded. "Would you mind looking at his wound?"

Chad greeted Joseph in Dha, which brought a look of surprise to the boy's face. He mumbled a response in return.

Eyeing the bloody wrap that covered a wound, Chad motioned them both inside. "Do you speak English, Joseph?"

The boy nodded.

"Well, you happened to catch me during my one free moment all day. Come in and I'll take a look at what you've done to yourself. When did this happen?"

The boy stared at the floor and shrugged. "This morning."

Chad led them inside a small room and had the boy sit on the end of the examination table before pulling on a pair of surgical gloves. "Are you hurt anywhere else?"

Joseph's chin dipped to the tiled floor. "No."

Chad glanced at Natalie, wondering if the boy could speak anything beyond monosyllables. He unwrapped the cloth so he could assess the injury, thankful when he realized it wasn't too serious. "Do you want to tell me what happened?"

"I … fell outside my village."

"How'd you get here?"

"I got a ride."

"Well, that's a start." Chad pulled out what he needed from the supply tray. "I'm going to numb the spot, but the stitches still might sting a bit."

Chad worked quickly, assessing the boy's behavior as he cleaned the wound and began stitching. The boy never flinched a muscle, staring straight ahead at a poster about polio that hung on the white wall.

"There you go," Chad said once he had finished. "Are you feeling any dizziness?"

"A little."

He checked the boy's pupils. "What about a headache?"

"Yes."

Chad dropped his penlight into his front pocket. "You've got a slight concussion, which means you need to rest for the next twenty-four hours."

Joseph reached up and touched the spot with his fingertips. Chad handed him a mirror.

"Not a bad job if I do say so myself." Chad pulled off his gloves, then squeezed some liquid soap onto his hands before turning on the water to wash up.

Joseph jumped down from the table, grabbing the edge to catch his balance. "Can I go?"

"Hey, slow down." Chad poured some water into a plastic cup and handed it to him. "This is more than just a bump on the head, isn't it? You look like a boy with a problem. I'm a doctor and am used to listening and seeing what I can do to fix things. Maybe I can help you." He shot the boy a broad smile as he urged him back onto the table.

Joseph shook his head. "You can't."

Can't or won't let me? You've got to talk to me, boy, so I can help. "Why do you think I can't help you?"

The young man shrugged.

Chad glanced at Natalie. "Do you know what happened?"

"You're right. Joseph didn't just hurt his head." She paused, pressing her lips together. "There's a lot more involved."

Chad caught the panicked look Joseph shot Natalie as he picked up a thermometer from the tray. He placed it under Joseph's tongue for a reading. "Will you do something for me? Stay still until this beeps. I need to talk to Natalie in private, but I'll be right back."

Halfway down the narrow, empty hallway, he leaned against a rough section of the chipped cement wall. Three volunteers from Houston were arriving in two weeks to paint the buildings and do general repairs. He was already looking forward to the spruced-up work environment, some spiritual encouragement, and perhaps a few Snickers bars.

Natalie glanced up at him. "You've got great bedside manners."

"I learned from the best. If you remember, my father was a doctor."

Natalie smiled. "I remember seeing him at school functions. He always had a handful of root-beer candies in his pocket and wore that handlebar mustache."

Chad laughed at the memories. "He died seven years ago. I still miss him."

"I'm sorry. He was a good man."

It might be nice to reminisce together one day, but at the moment he had a feeling the boy in the exam room needed more than a few stitches. "What about Joseph? Do you know how he hurt his head?"

She stood with her arms folded around her waist, her smile vanishing. "He told me he was returning to his village when it was attacked by Ghost Soldiers."

"Ghost Soldiers?" Chad pinched his nose with his thumb and forefinger and closed his eyes for a second. "There have been rumors of Ghost Soldiers for years, Natalie, but their existence has never been proven."

"Joseph says he has pictures."

"Did you see them?"

She shook her head. "He told me he dropped the camera while trying to get away."

"So there's really no evidence of what happened."

Her voice rose a notch. "The evidence is that he watched his mother and father and sister being forced from their village by gunpoint, and those who weren't strong enough to work were murdered. He's got a concussion from the butt of a rifle from one of the soldiers. Isn't that enough evidence?"

"From the reports I've heard, no one has ever been able to substantiate the existence of any kind of hidden, modern-day slave trade in this country."

"All it would take would be a few well-placed bribes and the truth vanishes." She gnawed on the edge of her lip. "But what about this? For the past seven months I've been doing some demographic work for the minister of health and asking a few questions. While I can't confirm anything yet, my research points to the fact that entire villages have vanished."

"Many of these people are nomadic — "

"I know. And that's the official response from the government. But you and I both know that the country's potential for wealth is enormous. With its vast quantities of gold, diamonds, and other natural resources ready to be taken by the highest bidder . . ." She paused for a moment. "I know this is hard to believe, even for me, but what if he's telling the truth, Chad?"

He still wasn't convinced. "The government's financial motivation to exploit its people is valid, but I've followed the politics of this country for the past decade. The president seems to have finally realized that it's in his interest to go along with the United Nations.

Following the rules of the game brings in millions in extra aid relief for his people."

"Or gives him another place to skim off a large portion for himself." She pointed at the room where Joseph waited. "You're the doctor. You saw him. The boy's traumatized."

He held up a hand. "Don't get me wrong. I've seen enough horror in this country to last me a lifetime. Little girls raped by their uncles, kids missing limbs because of landmines, women forced to sell themselves to feed their children ... and that's just the beginning. You can add AIDS, polio, and other outbreaks."

She jutted out her jaw and took on a determined stance. "Then what's so hard about believing in the Ghost Soldiers?"

"Do you really believe in them?"

"I wasn't sure until today. Joseph's a bright young man. He has no reason to lie."

"But with no proof ..." Chad looked away, trying to make sense of it all.

There was another, more realistic, possibility.

He lowered his voice to ensure Joseph couldn't hear him. "Have you considered that he might think you're his ticket out of here?"

Natalie's brow furrowed. "What do you mean?"

"I grew up here, and I've seen it dozens of times. Joseph speaks English, which means he's educated. He meets you, a compassionate foreigner with the financial means to buy his way out of here to something better. What Dhambizan doesn't dream of living in Chicago or Dallas with a decent job and enough food on his table for his family?"

Natalie threw up her arms. "He's not after me for a handout. He didn't even want me to bring him here."

"I'm not saying that he's lying." He clenched his jaw. He hadn't wanted to start an argument, but it was a possibility that had to be addressed. "But what if he took advantage of an opportunity?"

"He told me about his sister, Aina. They dragged her away, Chad.

Along with his mother and father. They shot and murdered his grandfather — "

"Just consider the possibility. A story like his could go a long way in helping him receive political asylum in the States."

He'd seen enough of Africa to know that there was often a fine line between truth and lies, and that embellishments were more often than not rolled into the facts. And there was nothing Natalie could do to change things even if the existence of the Ghost Soldiers was proven to be true.

"I have to consider the fact that he's telling the truth." She rubbed her temples with her fingers. "But I'll also concede that the upcoming election has me on edge."

"Which is all the more reason not to overreact."

"Maybe." Natalie started walking back toward the exam room. "I need to get going. I was planning on throwing a party for my boss tonight at my house, but I can still make sure Joseph rests tonight."

"And then?"

She stopped and shrugged. "I don't know. The authorities are occupied with the upcoming election. I doubt they have the time or resources to investigate Joseph's story."

He reached out and gently squeezed her forearm with his fingers. "Don't get involved in this, Natalie. If you have to, call your boss or your senator back home — or forget about it for all I care. But don't get involved."

A hint of anger registered in her eyes. "You've turned cynical."

He dropped his hands to his sides. "No. I'm a realist. I decided to return because of my love for the people. It's the corruption and suffering I hate. And as much as I'd like to take it all away ... realistically, I know I can't."

"Joseph mentioned something else too." She stared down the hall at the examination room. "He overheard two of the men speaking in English. They inferred that they'd be in power in four more days, that President Tau would be taken care of, and that they had the support of this district behind him. Which sounds to me like the election's being set so the opposition wins."

"The election is rigged?" Chad's stomach muscles clenched. "That's hard to believe. The UN has an election committee in place to ensure something like this doesn't happen. Forget about this. Just go home and make sure Joseph gets some rest."

"I'll go home." She turned and caught his gaze. "But if Joseph is telling the truth, then the lives of a whole village — and perhaps the entire country — are at stake."

FOUR

"So what are you saying, Patrick? That the United Nations is using the Republic of Dhambizao as a poster child for fair and peaceful African elections?" Natalie set another bowl of homemade salsa on the wooden table next to the vegetable tray and frowned.

As she'd expected, Patrick Seko had waylaid the conversation to fit his own political agenda, leaving little openings for topics other than the country's upcoming elections. But while she hadn't wanted a political debate at tonight's birthday celebration, if Joseph was right and there were plans of a presidential takeover, it wouldn't hurt to find out everything she could about the election. And Patrick was the perfect place to start.

"'A poster child.' I like that." Patrick picked up a handful of fried plantain chips and popped one into his mouth. "And yes, that's exactly what I'm saying." His tall, burly stature hovered over Rachel's tiny figure as she stood beside him finishing a plate of curry and rice. "And if something does happen to go wrong, we blame it on the election committee. Either way, we come out looking good."

"Another violent election won't make anyone look good, Patrick, and you know it." Stephen balanced his plastic plate on his lap and picked up his drink from the floor beside him.

"Stephen's right." Natalie scooped a spoonful of the salsa onto her plate. "I'd like to know what kind of security measures are being implemented so history doesn't repeat itself."

Patrick grinned, clearly in his element. "I can assure you there is nothing to worry about. Troops are out on the streets in force from here to the capital, and if necessary, the UN has promised to employ extra reinforcements to ensure there are no serious security issues."

One of Natalie's other guests stepped forward. "But do you actually think that the UN's extra security is going to make a difference in the end for the people of this country?"

Patrick's smile faded. "I'm sorry, Miss ..."

"Gabby Mackenzie. I'm a journalist from the States in town for a couple days."

Natalie turned to Gabby, who'd contacted her recently for help in finding a translator and lodging while in the country. From what Natalie had since learned about her, the up-and-coming journalist wasn't likely to be afraid of taking on a tough interview, the wilds of Africa, or Patrick, for that matter.

"What exactly are you implying?" Patrick asked.

Gabby kept her gaze even. "I've spent the past three weeks talking to dozens of investors and government officials from Lusaka to Dar es Salaam to Bogama, and while there are some who, I admit, want to help the people working for them, others are obviously exploiting their workers and pocketing the profits. So my question is how will having a new president, or even another term with the current president in this country, change things for the thousands of people being exploited?"

Stephen dropped his fork onto his plate. "I believe our current president has promised to continue to fight against foreign and local investors involved in the exploitation of workers."

"I've heard the promises." Gabby obviously wasn't done making her point. "But the workers are the ones who pay the price — sometimes with their lives — while foreign investors pay paltry wages and pocket the huge profits."

"I'm assuming you have a solution to this problem?" Patrick asked.

Gabby set her empty plate on the edge of the table as if ready to take on the challenge. "For starters, business and foreign investors have to be held accountable, instead of allowing their workers to perform under such despicable conditions. Nor should governments accept every offer promising schools and roads when in exchange they are stripped of their natural resources — "

Shaking her head, Gabby took a step back and caught Natalie's gaze. "I'm sorry. Tonight's supposed to be a celebration, not a time for me to stand on my soapbox."

Natalie couldn't help but be impressed with the woman's passion. "I don't think anyone here is beneath a good debate. Isn't that right, Patrick?"

"Well said, but for now ..." Patrick held up his Coke for a toast. "To Stephen and the Republic of Dhambizao. May both have many fruitful years of productivity — and peace — ahead of them."

"I hope you're right." Stephen held up his drink, smiled, and took a sip.

While the group dispersed to help themselves to more food, Natalie poured more peanuts into the glass bowl.

Gabby helped herself to a small handful. "I appreciate your inviting me here tonight. I've never been able to turn down a good homemade meal or a political debate."

"Then you're at the right place." Natalie chuckled. "At least for the political debate part."

Gabby laughed. "I don't see anyone complaining about your food."

"Just know you're welcome anytime you're back in the country. Are you still leaving in the morning?"

"I've got an early flight to the capital in the morning and one more meeting before I fly back to DC."

"I am intrigued by the premise of your article." Natalie pressed her lips together, wondering how much — if any — of Joseph's situation she should bring up. As a journalist, Gabby would want solid proof. Something Natalie didn't have. "I've seen how the workers are treated in several of the outlaying mines, but what if … what if there was more involved than simply low wages and dangerous working conditions?"

Gabby cocked her head. "What do you mean?"

"Have you ever heard of the Ghost Soldiers?"

"What exactly are Ghost Sol — "

"So I see you're not the only one asking questions about the Ghost Soldiers, Natalie."

Natalie spun on her heel to face Patrick. "Gabby and I were discussing the article she's writing."

Patrick swirled the ice in his glass and shot her a smug grin. "Perhaps you should join the ranks as a reporter."

Natalie frowned at the sarcastic suggestion. "I'm quite happy to leave journalism to the experts like Gabby."

"Sound advice, don't you think, Miss Mackenzie?" He turned back to Natalie. "Of course, I would have thought a potential hepatitis epidemic would have you too busy to worry over unverified rumors of Ghost Soldiers."

"So what do you think about these rumors, Patrick?" Natalie ignored the man's hard stare, wondering what Rachel saw in him.

"I've been investigating them."

"Really?" That would explain his interest in her demographic reports and the questions they raised. "And what have you discovered?"

"That the villagers are 'disappearing' because they are nomadic. You can't expect accurate counts when over ten percent of the population lives deep in the mountain jungles and has little contact with the outside world. I say the Ghost Soldiers are nothing more than rumors spread by the opposition to discredit the president."

"Do you have proof they don't exist?" Gabby asked.

"Of course I do."

No doubt laced with lies and exaggerated facts.

Someone buzzed at the front gate. Natalie glanced at the door and made a mental note to finish the conversation at a later date. "If you'll both excuse me."

She set her uneaten food down on the edge of the kitchen counter and took the chance to slip away from both the conversation and her tumultuous thoughts. Hurrying down the front steps, she tried to shake off her simmering anger. She'd come here to help an impoverished people, and the fact that most of the government leaders were more interested in lining their own pockets than confronting real concerns like people's lives made her furious.

She stopped at the edge of the sidewalk and looked up at the night sky. Stars hovered above her — thousands more, it seemed, than the view she'd had from her apartment balcony back home in Portland.

The heavens declare the glory of God, and the skies proclaim His handiwork.

Breathing in the sweet scent of jasmine that crept along the outside wall, she willed her nerves to settle down. Sometimes the natural beauty of this place was the only proof she could see that God even existed here.

Chad stood at the gate.

"Hi." She shot him a broad smile as she unlocked the gate. "I'm glad you came."

"I'm glad you invited me."

Natalie felt a blush creep across her cheeks. He'd changed from his scrubs to blue jeans and a khaki T-shirt and looked relaxed. His hair was curly like she remembered from high school, cut short in the back and left a little longer on top. The time that had passed since she'd last seen him in the States had given him a mature confidence, along with a few gray hairs.

He might not agree with her stance to do whatever she could to help Joseph, but as she left the clinic she'd decided to invite him anyway on the premise he might enjoy a home-cooked meal and meeting a few people. Truth was after eighteen months of living in Dhambi-zao, there was always a certain wave of security that encircled her when meeting another American. Which was the same reason she'd invited Gabby.

He stepped inside the compound, and she shut the gate behind him. "Sorry I'm late. I was tied up at the hospital longer than I expected."

"No problem. Hungry?"

"Starved."

"Good. I've got hot curry and rice, fresh fruit, and chocolate cake."

Chad patted his stomach. "Then I'd say you're the answer to my prayers."

An hour and a half later, Natalie opened the gate to let out the last of the guests. Except for Chad. He stood behind her, the porch light illuminating his boyish grin, and shoved his hands into his front pockets. "I'm not exactly in a big hurry to get home to my empty room. Need some help cleaning up?"

"Are you volunteering to do my dishes or trying to talk me out of getting involved with Joseph?"

He shot her a sheepish look and followed her back into the house. "Maybe a little of both."

"At least you're honest. Which is more than I can say for some people around here." She grabbed a pile of plastic cups and headed for the kitchen, thankful that the slight awkwardness between them at the clinic had vanished.

"From what I could tell, everyone seemed to enjoy themselves."

"As long as Stephen had a good birthday, then I'm happy. He can be cranky at times, but overall he's a good guy." Natalie rummaged through the cupboard for some pain medicine to take the edge off the headache that had been brewing behind her temples since her conversation with Patrick. "And I always enjoy catching up with friends."

Chad started scraping dishes into the trash. "I haven't had a chance to ask you what you're doing here. You had an interesting assortment of guests. The former head of security to the president, a government nonprofit liaison, an American journalist, and a nurse, for starters."

She swallowed the pills with the last of the punch. "You learned all that in the space of an hour and a half?"

"People intrigue me."

Natalie smiled. She liked a man who wasn't all about himself. "I'm working to prevent the spread of communicable diseases. Stephen — the nonprofit liaison who works alongside the minister of health — is my boss, in a roundabout way. Technically I work for an organization out of the States, but I'm pretty much at the disposal of what they want done here in the field."

"Disease control. That's pretty important work." Chad turned on the tap and started rinsing the dishes while she worked to clear the leftover food from the adjoining room. "Is that how you met Joseph?"

"Yes." She covered the leftover cake and set it in her small fridge. "One of the main methods of disease control, as I'm sure you know, is vaccinations and education. During school holidays he worked a number of times as my translator in some of the more remote villages."

Chad stopped to look at her. "How is he?"

"Asleep in the back room."

"That would be the medicine I gave him. I thought it might help to calm him down."

Twenty minutes later, Natalie glanced around the living room and kitchen and smiled. "Well, that was painless. And quick. I appreciate your help."

Chad hung up the wet dish towel he'd been using. "I suppose I should head home now."

Natalie didn't stop to think about what she wanted to say. Chad might not agree with her involvement, but if she was going to help

Joseph, she needed advice from someone she could trust. "You know I'm not going to just forget about what happened out in the village."

He shot her a half smile. "I suppose you don't come across as someone who'd simply walk away, but that doesn't change how I feel. Working in health care in a third-world country has its own risks, but getting tangled up in the corruption that could be underlying a government is an entirely different story."

She shook her head. "So I do nothing? Just allow Joseph's family to rot away in some godforsaken mine?"

"You make it tough to ignore."

"Good. I've got a comfy wooden swing in the backyard that the previous renters left. It's perfect for brainstorming, if you're not in a hurry to leave."

Chad shoved his hands into his back pockets. "I think I'd like that."

FIVE

Chad pushed his foot against the hard ground and let the swing sway gently back and then forward. Twelve hours ago he would never have imagined himself relaxing beneath the night sky. After two months of intense work at the clinic with little time off and no social life, the distraction was good. The company even better. And the second helping of chocolate cake wasn't too bad either.

He took another bite of the sweet dessert and savored the flavor. The food the clinic served could never compare to this.

But that didn't change the fact that Natalie was putting herself in the middle of something that could turn out to be extremely dangerous. Government coups and rigged elections weren't something to get involved in.

He wasn't ready to tackle that subject. Not yet, anyway.

"Why Africa?" he began. "From the looks of things you could have about any job you wanted."

Natalie laughed. "So why some hole-in-the-wall city like Kasili, Dhambizao?"

"Yeah."

"Is it too cliché to say I wanted to make a difference in the world?"

He took a sip of his coffee. "I suppose I could say the same. There's something about working here that helps make up for at least some of the problems in this world."

"Which is why I can't forget the look on Joseph's face when he told me about his family."

He toyed with a bit of cake. Maybe he was really no different than she. He hadn't been able to forget the faces he'd known growing up here.

"So why did you come back to the RD? Everyone heard how you and your family escaped during the last election. It must have been terrifying."

He scraped a glob of frosting from the plate, then licked his fork. "I've asked myself that very question a time or two since returning here. I had nightmares the first few days as memories from the coup flooded back, and I still jump every time a taxi backfires."

Thinking about it, Chad flinched. He could still hear the gunfire that had echoed around them the day of the coup ... Women screaming as they ran through the streets with their children ... Safety had seemed elusive. But, somehow, they'd made it out alive.

He pushed aside the losses of that day and focused instead on Natalie's question. "They need me here. I speak the local language, which gives me an advantage above other volunteers. But mainly I came for the same reason as every other person who hops on a plane to take part in some grand humanitarian mission."

"Do you think we really do?"

"Make a difference?"

She nodded and even in the shadows of the backyard, he caught the sadness in her expression.

Chad combed his fingers through his hair wishing he could avoid the question. But it was one he knew they both had to deal with every day. "Tonight I lost a patient. Her name was Hanna, and she was twenty-four years old. She was the only sibling still alive out of one brother and two sisters, and she had three small children of her own. She gave birth to a baby in a mud hut twenty miles from here. A traditional midwife did what she could, but with no sterile instruments tetanus set in. In the end it killed both her and her baby."

"I deal with preventing death, so I don't have to face it too often." She brushed back a wisp of hair and furrowed her brow. "I can't imagine seeing all the suffering you do."

Chad gnawed on his lower lip. Her insight was legitimate. As a doctor, he'd learned to remove himself emotionally from the situation in order to deal with the grim realities of life and death, but even that ability didn't completely numb him. Losing someone always hurt, just like saving someone always strengthened his determination to stay in the game.

He reached down to set his empty plate and fork on the ground beside him, surprised at how talking about the young woman helped ease the sorrow he felt over her death. "I have another patient named Malaika. She gave birth two days ago at the clinic. She would have bled to death in the village, but we were able to save her. I never quite get over losing a patient, but every one I save helps to remind me that it's worth the risk. And that, I suppose, makes it worth being here."

Natalie ran her index finger around the rim of her mug. "How long did you commit to stay?"

"Six months. How about you?"

"Two years." She looked up at him, her dark eyes intense. "Do you ever question where God is in all of this?"

"Yeah." He'd asked God that very question tonight when the nurse told him Hanna was gone. "I never could understand my father. He was an optimist who could look beyond the situation and see God's greater work. All he ever tried to do was serve God by helping one person at a time. I've always wanted to be like him."

"Not a bad philosophy. But what about you? Where do you see God in all of this?"

"Truthfully? Sometimes I'm not sure what role God plays." His frankness surprised even himself. "I told you I wasn't cynical, but maybe I am."

"I wouldn't say that." She stretched out her legs. "I'm sorry to have gotten so serious, but it helps to be able to talk with someone who understands. I know God wants me here, but sometimes the burden of what I have to deal with gets too heavy."

"I know exactly what you mean." He smiled at her because he liked her honesty. He liked the familiarity of her American accent, the fact that they shared the same faith, and even the Oregon Ducks mug she drank her coffee from. They were all things he was comfortable with — a part of home and their shared background.

"I know you think I'm wrong, but I can't stop thinking about Joseph, his father and mother, and his little sister. There's got to be something I can do."

He wondered if the nightmare of living through the last coup was his real reason for not wanting to get drawn in. "We don't know who's involved, or who we can trust. If this district is mixed up in all this, like Joseph said, that means there's likely to be bribed officials or sympathizers on every level in this area."

"So I just sit back and do nothing, like you said?"

He glanced at his watch. It was getting late, but he wasn't ready to end the conversation. Surely there was an answer here somewhere. "Have you thought any more about what you're going to do about Joseph?"

"I don't know. He can't go back to his village. I suppose I could help him get to the capital. He stays there with his uncle during the school year."

"And the Ghost Soldiers?"

Natalie blew out a short breath. "Patrick told me tonight he has proof that the Ghost Soldiers are nothing more than rumors from the opposition party to discredit the current government."

"Do you believe him?"

"I want to, but I also can't forget what Joseph told me ... Something happened, Chad. Something horrible."

Part of him wanted to assure her everything was going to be all right, but that was one guarantee he could never make. Losing his best friend, Stewart, to gunfire during the coup all those years ago had taught him that. "I still don't think you should get involved, but call me if you need to, okay?"

She nodded, and they both sat quietly for a few moments as the swing rocked back and forth. Somewhere in the night a cricket chirped, and an owl hooted in the trees above them. A radio played next door, its static reception crackling across the breeze. Poverty, hardship, and death surrounded them both, yet somehow life went on. Babies were born and grew up to have babies of their own. People found ways to survive in conditions his friends back home couldn't understand.

Maybe God was still here . . . somewhere.

He cleared his throat and shifted to the edge of the swing. "Thanks for tonight. I enjoyed myself immensely, but I think I'd better go. Five o'clock is going to come sooner than I want."

"Thanks for staying."

He caught her smile and felt a sense of peace wash over him. "You're welcome."

With a start, Natalie sat up on the lumpy couch in her living room and stared at the figure standing above her. "Joseph. You scared me to death."

"I'm sorry. I . . . I need some water. Please."

"Sure."

Natalie stumbled across the living room, still half asleep. She shook her head, trying to forget the dreams that had haunted her. Even in sleep, she couldn't shake the implications of Joseph's story.

She poured him a glass of filtered water from the fridge, then leaned against the counter while he drank it. When he finished, he set the cup down in the sink and caught her gaze.

"I need you to take me to my village."

"Your village?" She ran her fingers through her tangled hair, still hearing Chad's warnings. He was right. She shouldn't get involved. "I don't know, Joseph."

"Everything I told you is true. My sister and parents were dragged up into the mountains ... the dead bodies." The tone of his voice pleaded with her. "I need you to see it. I need you to believe me."

"I want to help you, Joseph, but — "

"They will kill my father." His hands dropped to his sides. "He has TB."

"Tuberculosis?" Joseph's words pierced her heart. "I didn't know."

"He can't work in the mines. Maybe a few days ... but in the end ... when his strength leaves, they will kill him. Like they killed my grandfather."

"I don't know what to say except that I'm so sorry."

"Then you will take me to my village? You will see what I saw and help me find my camera? I need the photos. I need to save my family."

Natalie rubbed the back of her neck. Photos would prove to Patrick, Stephen, and even to Chad what had happened. And would help substantiate Joseph's claims that the Ghost Soldiers existed.

Natalie nodded. "We'll go in the morning."

SIX

Joseph stared out the window of Natalie's two-door car, the thick forest a blur of green as they headed into the mountains. The first few kilometers outside the city had been dotted with dozens of pedestrians making their way along the edges of the tarmac road. Donkeys pulled wooden carts. Women balanced firewood on their heads. Children played in the ditches using old tires and bottles as toys.

As the elevation had increased, fewer people lined the pothole-filled road. Now all he saw besides the trees were occasional small villages where goats and chickens roamed free between circles of mud huts.

He glanced at Natalie, who stared straight ahead, her knuckles whitened from gripping the steering wheel. Perhaps he wasn't the only one dreading what lay ahead.

He clicked his tongue against the roof of his mouth. "I heard someone talking about the Ghost Soldiers last night at your house."

Her frown deepened. "I thought you were asleep."

"I was afraid to sleep." Darkness had brought renewed terror as it dragged his mind back to his village. The morning sun peeking over the crest of trees had done little to remove the fear.

Natalie loosened her grip and wiggled her fingers. "I spoke about

51

them with Patrick Seko, who used to be the former head of security to the president. Now he's heading up a specialized task force, and apparently one of his jobs is to find the truth behind the rumors."

His heart sank at her admission. "So you believe they are only rumors."

"I didn't say that — "

"But you don't believe it's true."

"I believe you, but I need proof, Joseph. Patrick said that the soldiers are nothing more than rumors spread by the opposition to discredit the president, and with the elections being held in three days, that's what most people are going to believe." She shot him a quick glance. "But don't worry. I brought my camera, and if nothing else, I'll be able to photograph what's left of the village. They'll be evidence of what happened."

Like his grandfather's body. A chill slid up his spine. "And then?"

"I'll take the photos to a few key people. I might not like Patrick, but I don't think that even he would try to sit on the truth."

Joseph wanted to grasp onto the optimism in her voice, but her stoic expression deterred him. His people had been too often forgotten. In school, he'd read of the atrocities men had acted out against each other. How would the proven existence of the Ghost Soldiers change anything in his country? A large profit was enough motivation to wipe out the consciences of those in charge.

Natalie shifted gears and glanced at him. "We're close, aren't we?"

"Yes." Joseph jutted out his chin. "Just beyond that tree. We will walk from there."

The back tires crunched the gravel as Natalie slowed down and parked the car along the edge of the road. Joseph squeezed his eyes shut, suddenly regretting his decision to bring her here. He'd hoped to wake up this morning and find out that everything he'd seen yesterday had been nothing more than a horrible nightmare. But dawn hadn't erased the vivid images impressed in his mind. Nor their reality.

Taking in a deep breath, he forced himself to get out of the car. The potent scent of the forest assailed him. Yesterday it had welcomed him back as one of its own. Today he felt like a stranger. Even the familiar hum of birds and animals urged him to turn around and run.

He wiped away a trickle of moisture from his neck. The humid air grew thick in his throat, and his breathing turned shallow. A picture of his sister surfaced in his mind's eye. Wide brown eyes, tangles of black braids, bright smile. And his father ... They had to find him before it was too late —

No.

He pushed away the fear that threatened to leave him immobile. He could do this. He had to do this for his family.

Natalie slammed her door shut with her hip and slung her bag over her shoulder. She threw him an oblong object that he caught in midair. "What is it?"

"A granola bar. You hardly ate anything this morning." Natalie stood at the edge of the road, ripped the plastic wrapper off her own bar, and took a bite.

Joseph chewed on the grainy bar, missing his mother's cooking prepared over the fire every morning. Before he'd left home to attend school in the city, it had been his job to walk the three kilometers to the river to haul water for drinking, bathing, and cooking. Days had been filled with similar chores. Gathering firewood, tending to the few livestock they possessed, and watching after his younger sibling.

A twig snapped and he glanced up. Natalie had already started down the worn path toward his village — or what remained of his village. Broken pots, lifeless bodies, smoldering fires ... He wasn't ready to see it all again. Returning meant facing what the Ghost Soldiers had taken from him.

Knowing he had no choice, he swatted at the insect buzzing at his ear and hurried to catch up. Wind rattled the limbs of the trees. A parrot whistled in the distance while a bush rat dashed into the undergrowth. Fifteen minutes passed. Then thirty. Dozens of shades of green from the abundant plant life faded into a dull gray ...

Aina emerged from the forest.

Joseph stopped. His sister smiled at him in her tattered dress, faded by the African sun.

Mbona stepped out from behind another tree and waved.

Joseph smiled and hurried toward them. The musty smell of leaves and sweet flowers captivated him, then began to mingle with the stench of death. Rifles appeared on the backs of men with black masks. Joseph looked up and caught a glimpse of sunlight filtering down through the thick vegetation. The flat crowns of the trees spun above him ...

Something brushed against his shoulder.

"Joseph, are you all right?"

He looked up at Natalie, then glanced back into the forest. Aina and Mbona had vanished. Blinking his eyes, he spun around, frantic. They had just been here. He stared past the branches of the evergreen trees. Past the bushes and ferns. Vines and roots twisted before him. He turned around in slow motion. He had to find them.

"Joseph?" Her fingers gripped his forearm. "Are you all right?"

He pushed away the vision, smearing his damp hands against his pants, but said nothing.

Natalie paused and rested her hands against her thighs to catch her breath. "We don't have to do this. We can go back — "

"I have to find them." He rushed ahead of her, then stumbled over a thick vine. His right hand scraped against the rough bark of a tree as he righted himself. Blood pooled at the spot, then dripped down his palm. "I am the only one who can save my family."

The trees began to thin as they approached the village. He listened for sounds of life, laughter, even screams, but there was nothing. Only the sound of his heart pounding within his chest.

SEVEN

Natalie stood in the center of the empty village and squeezed her arms around her waist. When she and Joseph had arrived at the tranquil scene, she'd braced herself for the emotional impact of seeing firsthand what the Ghost Soldiers had left behind. Instead there was nothing pointing to the chaos of yesterday. No signs of the struggle Joseph had described. Only a compound of empty huts sitting in the morning sunshine.

"I do not understand." Joseph's voice cracked beside her. "They are gone. Their bodies … my grandfather … There's nothing left."

Natalie's lungs contracted. "Joseph —"

"They shot my grandfather here. I saw it. And Aina … they took her … I never saw my mother …" He stumbled away from her toward the edge of the compound. "I must find the camera."

While Joseph searched for the camera, Natalie gazed across the familiar compound. Eleven months ago, she'd visited this village. Women had welcomed her in their bright dresses made from fabric they'd managed to secure from the city. She had given free vaccinations to the children and taught them how to thwart diseases such as hepatitis that could run rampant in a village.

Lifting her camera, she started snapping photos of the quiet scene.

Today no women chatted around the cooking pots; no laughing children played beneath the shady mango trees. Gone were the old men playing an unending game of *kari* at the edge of the compound while shooing away squawking chickens and lazy dogs.

But where were the bodies Joseph had glimpsed, laying on the damp African soil? All that remained was an eerie quiet that seemed to reverberate louder than the forest itself. Had someone come in and whisked away all signs of life? Or were Chad's gut instincts on target, and there was nothing more to the story than a young boy's vivid imagination?

"Don't get involved in this, Natalie. Tell Stephen, leave it to the local authorities to investigate. Call your senator back home if you have to, or forget about it for all I care. But don't get involved."

Don't get involved.

Chad's words played over and over in her mind. He was right. She shouldn't even be here. If Joseph was wrong, she'd done nothing more than plop herself in the middle of the jungle where she could be attacked by mysterious soldiers who kidnapped and killed villagers or bitten by a venomous snake. Neither sounded very smart.

And if Joseph *was* right? How in the world could she deal with such brutal realities in a corrupt third-world country? She'd signed up to bring relief to the people, not to get involved in the political arena.

Natalie held up her hand to block the sun that cast rays of light across the brown earth. Two dozen mud huts, with their neatly thatched roofs, surrounded her. Pathways between them had been swept, grass cleared, and firewood piled along the sides of the huts. Crossing the soft ground, still damp from the rain the day before, she searched for signs of a struggle. Dozens of random footprints scattered out before her, but she couldn't be sure whose they were. The rains could have washed away the villagers' footprints.

But not a group of soldiers who had returned to cover up their handiwork.

Trying to ignore the lump of fear swelling inside her, she glanced beyond the eastern edges of the village to where neat rows of corn and manioc had been planted during the first rains. Beside them bamboo, tied together with homemade rope, formed bins to keep stalks of dried maize from last year's harvest out of the reach of animals. Pulling out one of the yellowed stalks, Natalie crumbled the dry husk between her fingers. How many hours of work had been put into planting, watering, and cultivating this vital crop? Without constant care, the crop would be ravaged by animals or burnt by the midday sun. Why would the villagers leave all this work unless it was under force?

Natalie made her way past one of the huts, its mud walls decorated by a band of dark brown around the bottom, and snapped another photo. Twelve feet away sat an open smoke-stained kitchen. Clay water pots lay in one corner beside a stack of rusty plates. Nearby, a hollowed-out gourd was filled with dried cassava. She crouched down in front of the fat, black pot and lifted the wooden spoon to reveal a sauce that smelled of tomatoes and piquant peppers. The embers below had long since grown cold, leaving behind nothing but a mound of gray ash.

She stood and rested her hands against her hips. Something wasn't right. While it might be true that Joseph's tribe migrated when food sources like wild game dissipated, leaving healthy crops behind or a pot full of sauce untended wasn't normal.

A flash of pink caught her eye. Skirting a pile of firewood, she leaned down and pulled out a worn cloth doll from the edge of the sticks. Two tiny black-beaded eyes stared back at her. The mouth had been made from red thread stitched in a zigzag pattern. One shoe was gone, and the dark face was streaked with mud.

Natalie squeezed her eyes shut. She remembered the young girl and her doll as if it were only yesterday. Her faded red dress had barely reached to her thighs, and her dusty brown feet had dug their toes into the soft earth as she'd grasped the cloth treasure and stared up at Natalie. Around them, the village had stirred with life. The tangy smell of sauces being cooked in their black pots for the evening meal drifted across the compound with the afternoon breeze. Mothers nursed their babies. Children sauntered back from the dusty trails with water held high on their heads. It had been her job to help them improve their lives.

The little girl had tugged on the skirt of her dress as Natalie knelt down and greeted her in Dha. *"Eh fo banda."*

"Eh fa."

Natalie had taken the ragged doll and smiled at the girl, wishing she had something to give her.

Something snapped in the brush. Natalie opened her eyes, pulled away from the vivid memories. She ducked against the frame of a low doorway and stared into the bush. Another twig cracked and a pig rushed by, squealing as it disappeared behind one of the huts.

She pressed her hand against her heart and let out a slow breath of relief. Clasping the doll between her fingers, she peeked inside one of the dim huts. A mattress covered with a frayed pink sheet sat in the corner of the room. A table and chair on the other side. Even without the photos for proof, it didn't take much for her to believe Joseph's story.

Outside the dark living areas, the bright sunlight blinded her. A family of monkeys howled in the distance, and Natalie shivered at their jabbering. She skirted the perimeter of the village, stopping at the empty clotheslines.

Three feet in front of her was a patch of blood.

Natalie pressed the doll to her chest and swallowed the tears that threatened to erupt. Maybe if she brought Chad up here he would have some ideas of what to do, who to talk to. Something had to be done.

"I found it! Now you'll believe me."

Natalie spun around at the sound of Joseph's voice.

The young man bounded across the level ground with the camera, stopping in front of her when he saw the doll. For a moment the significance of the camera was forgotten.

"Where did you get that?"

Natalie shrugged and pointed toward one of the huts. "It was lying on the ground."

"It's Aina's."

His sister. Natalie felt her stomach clench. "I'm sorry. I — "

"What if I never see them again?" He grabbed the doll and crushed it against his chest.

"I don't know, Joseph. I don't know."

There was nothing she could say. No words that could erase the emptiness she knew he was feeling. Except for one thing.

"They're not rumors, are they?" she whispered.

"No."

He handed her the camera. She flipped open the small square screen and scanned the photos one by one. A man in black with a rifle in his hands jabbed an older woman ... A villager grasped a child's hand ... A group of women, their hands raised to the heavens, were prodded toward the forest ... An old man lay motionless on the ground ... A soldier gestured with a grin on his face ...

"You were right about all of this, Joseph. The Ghost Soldiers are real." Natalie swallowed hard. No longer did they have only the word of a local village boy. "Now we've just got to get someone else to believe us."

Something rustled in the bushes. Natalie turned and saw a flash of light.

Joseph grasped her arm.

Why would they return? There was no reason, unless someone had followed them here. She tried to push away the fear. "There was a pig running around a few minutes ago. It's probably just an animal."

He didn't look convinced. But neither was she.

"We've got what we need. Let's go." Natalie shoved the camera into her backpack, grabbed Joseph's hand, and started running.

EIGHT

Relief flooded Natalie as she pulled into the parking lot of her office compound, thankful for the security of the high walls and the electric barrier that surrounded the property. Such safety measures had become the norm in a city riddled with burglaries and petty crime. She waited until the automatic gate clicked shut, then stepped out onto the brick drive. The gardener raked leaves in the corner of the compound. Voices drifted across the yard from people passing on the street. Strange how life continued as if nothing had happened.

Beside her, Joseph raced up the front steps of the one-story building. The walls of Kalambali Square, with its chipped and worn exterior, held offices for two nonprofit organizations as well as a branch of the government health headquarters.

Inside the office, she nodded as she swept past the receptionist, who seemed more intent on filing her nails than the stack of papers lining her desk.

"Is Stephen in?"

The secretary shook her head. "He should be back any minute."

"Please tell him to come see me when he returns. It's very important."

Her tiny office at the end of the narrow hallway held little more than a desk, two chairs, and a few items she'd brought in to brighten up the space. A collage of photos hung above her desk beside a wilted plant that needed water. She glanced at the pictures of her parents, taken at her father's sixtieth birthday party.

They hadn't been thrilled with her decision to move to the RD. Since retirement, becoming grandparents had topped their wish list. But up to this point, neither she nor her brother, Sean, had managed to supply them with a bundle of joy. Sean had married an attorney set on making partner by the time she turned thirty-five.

At least no one would be sending them a notice of her death today.

Natalie shoved open the window to let in a breeze, then waved Joseph onto the extra chair. Pulling the memory card out of the camera, she prayed it would work with her photo printer. She'd told her parents she didn't need the expensive piece of equipment and had only used it twice; anything more than a computer or laptop seemed an extravagance in a country where people struggled to find enough food. For the first time, she was glad they'd insisted on the purchase.

Joseph sat on the edge of the chair. "Is it going to work?"

"I think so." Natalie drummed her fingers against the desktop as she waited for the first photo to emerge. When it did, she shuddered. The camera had captured the mocking expression of one of the men in black. "I'll make two copies. That way I can give a set to Stephen and keep one for myself. And I want Dr. Talcott to see these."

She pulled her cell phone out of her purse to call Chad, then paused. What about Gabby? Her journalist friend's connections with the media might be enough to get something done. Even the RD would make a humanitarian effort in order to avoid bad publicity.

She logged onto her online account, typed in the password, and punched out a quick e-mail to Gabby. After attaching three of the photos, she pressed Send, then erased the message in the Sent box and emptied the trash. There was no need to take any chances at this point.

Chad was next. She punched in the number he'd given her and waited for it to ring. The call failed.

Natalie frowned. Great. The lines were down ... again. She dropped the phone back into her purse. More than likely they'd be up again soon, but for once she wished things would work when she needed them.

Another photo fell into the tray. One of the soldiers was pushing someone onto the ground. She pressed her lips together, afraid she was going to be sick. Joseph's fingers tightened around the edge of the desk. They both needed a distraction. "Tell me about school."

Joseph seemed to understand her desire to talk about something other than the images they'd just seen.

"There are many students and few teachers, but I want to keep learning, so I study hard. That is what the camera was for — a way to earn extra money for books and something to send to my family." He ran his finger along the edges of the chair. "And maybe a chance for University. That is ... was ... my mother's dream."

A sullen look crossed his face. There was simply no way to avoid the subject.

Natalie squeezed his shoulder. "I'm so sorry."

"It is our life. I do not expect it to be easy, but this ..."

The last picture finally dropped into the tray. Natalie separated the pile of color photos. They would be enough to convince someone of what was happening.

The front door slammed shut. She dropped the second set of copies into Joseph's backpack and zipped it shut.

"Stephen?" She heard the familiar gait of his heavy boots before he stopped at her office.

He leaned into the doorway looking anything but pleased to see her. "Where have you been? I've tried to call you all morning. You didn't leave a message as to where you were going."

His normal fatherly concern was overbearing today. "I guess you didn't notice that the cell phone tower is down again."

"It was working fine an hour ago." He frowned. "Next time at least leave word where you're going. I'm responsible for your well-being."

Natalie grimaced. Obviously she wasn't the only one whose pre-election nerves were hanging from a thread. He wasn't going to be happy when she told him she'd been running through the jungle instead of teaching preventative health measures in the relative safety of the city.

"I took Joseph up the mountains to where his family lives."

Lived.

The veins in Stephen's neck pulsed. "I told you to leave it alone. There's no such thing as Ghost Soldiers."

"Don't be so sure." Natalie watched his face, gauging his reaction. Disbelief? Fear? She wasn't sure at this point. "They're real, Stephen, and I have proof."

Stephen ran his hand across his short black hair. "Natalie, leave it alone. Sometimes you have to overlook things — for the good of everyone."

"For the good of whom, Stephen? A little girl ripped from the only home she's ever known? A grandfather killed because he's not strong enough to work?" Her heart thumped. She wanted to scream at the way everyone tried to bury the problem. "How does that work for the good of everyone?"

"I've talked to Patrick — "

"Maybe Patrick cares more about his position as a government official than looking at what's really happening out there."

"He assured me they were only rumors — "

"Look at these." Natalie began dropping the photos one at a time onto her desk in front of him. "Then tell me if you still think the existence of the Ghost Soldiers is nothing more than a rumor."

NINE

Stephen set down his briefcase and moved over to Natalie's desk, picking the photos up one by one. The familiar pang of guilt wrenched through his gut. There was no denying the story the pictures told — the faces of the victims wouldn't let him.

For a moment, he was back on one of the street corners of the capital, seventeen years ago, on the eve of another presidential election. All public meetings had been banned. Hospitals were paralyzed as doctors and nurses went on strike. Curfews were imposed and food was virtually nonexistent.

He'd lost Camille that day, and his heart had never completely mended. Maybe if he'd believed her, believed that together they could make a difference in changing this country, things would have turned out differently. He'd prayed every night since then that God would let him relive that one moment over and find out. But God apparently wasn't in the business of redeeming lost souls. And his was certainly lost.

You're a coward, Stephen Moyo.

"Stephen?"

At Natalie's voice he jerked his head up. "What did you say?"

She leaned against the wall cabinet, irritation evident in her gaze.

64

"I said, what do we do now? You have the contacts in the government. We can't just look away and pretend this didn't happen."

"Maybe not, but I don't want you involved either. I've got to think."

But not here — it felt like the cement walls were closing in on him. Ignoring Natalie's surprised look, he shoved the photos into his briefcase and walked out.

As he stalked down the hallway, he forced the past away and focused on the present. The question was what was he going to do? He didn't believe Natalie. He couldn't. Even the blatant proof he carried couldn't erase his doubts. Patrick had assured him that there were no grounds to the circulating rumors.

Still, he envisioned the horror on the face of a young girl in the photos. Something was wrong. Very wrong. What would Patrick have to gain in covering up something like this?

Unless he was somehow involved . . .

Stephen pushed the implications aside and instead threw open his office door.

Natalie was right behind him. "I won't forget what I saw."

"I'm not asking you to."

"I mean it, Stephen. You can't just walk away from this."

He froze at his desk, letting his briefcase crash to the floor as her words reverberated in his mind. A fresh flood of memories . . .

You can't just walk away from this.

Camille had said the same thing to him. She'd stood in front of him, the wind whipping against her long skirt. Ebony skin. Wide smile. Broad cheekbones . . .

He couldn't shut out the image.

Gunshots had echoed in the distance, and the smell of death hung heavy in the air. She hadn't cared that the odds were against her. She'd found the courage to stand up for what she believed.

And he'd lost her.

Natalie rested her palms against the desk beside him. "What are we going to do, Stephen? This points to the reality of a modern-day slave trade —"

"No!"

"No? What do you mean, no?"

He rubbed a bead of sweat from his forehead as he moved around the desk and slid into his seat. This was why he'd left his last post. Leaving the corruption seemed easier than confronting it.

Coward.

"Stephen?" Natalie's persistent voice wouldn't leave him alone.

"I don't know. I might be able to make a few phone calls," Stephen relented, gripping the edge of the desk with his fingertips. Yes, he could do that much — make a few phone calls.

She dug the photos from his briefcase and handed them to him. "Then call them. Please. We need to know if anyone recognizes anyone in the photos."

Stephen stared at his telephone. The image of Camille wouldn't let go of him. He didn't have to get involved, but he also couldn't just do nothing and let it happen again. He'd make a call or two. Then it was someone else's job to do something.

He started digging through his desk, trying to clear his mind enough to remember where the business-card holder was stashed. Normally he was more organized — He let out a sigh of relief. The holder was sitting in the third drawer where he always kept it.

Natalie pressed her back against the wall. "I'm taking Joseph back to my house. Promise me you'll call someone when the lines are up again."

He nodded.

"Good. And give the pictures to Patrick when you see him again. Surely that's enough evidence to convince him he's wrong."

"Are there any other copies of the photos?"

She clinched her fists at her sides. "I have my own set somewhere safe."

Somewhere safe.

He hadn't felt safe for years. It was as if he'd been thrust into some cloak-and-dagger game without knowing who the players were. He didn't want to ignore the plight of an entire village — or, for that matter, the possibility of countless others. But he knew the dangers of getting involved. He'd never make a difference anyway. Chances were it was all about money. Money had always been the root of this country's destruction. Dhambizao was rich in natural resources — gold, diamonds, zinc, and other prized minerals — and there were lots of megacorporations willing to pay to get to them. More than enough motivation for power-hungry officials to line their own pockets while ignoring the toll it took on their people.

He didn't know which side of the fence President Tau sat on, but in the long run it didn't matter. There would be no investigation. Never would be. The best thing Joseph could do was to count his lucky stars he hadn't been there when the village was ransacked. At least the boy still had a chance.

Trying to ignore the photos, Stephen clicked open the document he'd worked on earlier that day and started typing. Work was the one thing that could make him forget. About Joseph's village, about the election ... about Camille.

He'd barely gotten started when he heard voices down the hall and recognized Patrick's voice. Five minutes later, Patrick sauntered into Stephen's office, tugged on the edge of his suit jacket, and sat on the edge of the desk. "Natalie told the secretary that you have something for me."

"Apparently you were wrong." Stephen slammed the pictures onto his desk, then pushed them toward Patrick. "Looks to me as if these prove the existence of the rumored Ghost Soldiers. Or whatever you want to call them."

"Where did you get these?"

"The boy with Natalie, Joseph Komboli, took them. Ghost Soldiers attacked his village."

Patrick looked through the photos slowly, as if trying to digest what he was seeing. He flipped through them a second time. "You haven't shown these to anyone, have you?"

Stephen shook his head. "I saved them for you. I figured you were the one who could do something about the situation."

"You did good." Patrick leaned over and patted him on the shoulder. "I suppose neither of us have forgotten … well … Camille, for one."

Stephen cringed at the veiled threat and bit his lip rather than say something he'd regret.

"Where did Natalie go?"

"I don't know. She said something about going home."

"She has another set?"

"She's got a second printed copy and the memory chip in the camera."

Patrick leaned closer until Stephen could smell the foul odor of his breath. "I'm counting on you, Stephen. Counting on you to make sure Natalie stays out of this. We have to stick together, you know."

Stephen forced a smile, but he knew the people Patrick worked for and his gut told him that giving the photos to Patrick was no different than throwing them into the incinerator. And that looking away this time would cost him more than losing the woman he loved.

TEN

Natalie listened to the hum of her car as it idled at the stoplight. She tapped on the steering wheel and waited for the light to turn green. Kasili, like most of the larger cities in the country, was a startling contrast of two worlds. Modern, though neglected, office and apartment buildings on paved roads bordered unlit dirt roads and rows of traditional mud huts. Where she sat, hawkers stood along the side of the roadway, walking from car to car with everything from mangos to clothes hangers to sunglasses. A blind beggar stood at the street corner holding a bowl in his outstretched hands. It was the same man she'd given coins to for the past six months.

She pulled up her ponytail and wiped the back of her neck with her hand. Yesterday's rains had left the air humid, and the cramped, stuffy quarters of her non-air-conditioned car didn't help either. But with incidences of carjackings on the rise, keeping her windows rolled up in the city had become a necessity.

Natalie gulped down the last of her water, dropped the empty bottle onto the seat between her and Joseph, then pressed on the accelerator as the light turned green. She needed time to clear her head and figure out what to do now. Stephen might have promised to make

69

some phone calls, but she knew that wasn't enough. The rest of the world didn't have time to deal with the problems of the RD.

For now, they'd go back to her house, eat a bowl of leftover curry with some chocolate cake, and see if she could come up with a plan. While a slab of cake might not solve today's problems, it certainly couldn't hurt.

She glanced over at Joseph's solemn expression. They both needed a break from the emotional impact of what they'd seen.

Natalie paused at another red light. But as it flickered to green, glass shattered behind her. She gasped and jerked around to see what had happened.

"Your bag!" Joseph fought to unlock his door.

"And your camera." Turning, Natalie saw the thief as he darted away. Short frame, ebony skin, knitted cap ...

Ignoring a honk behind her, she shifted the gear into Park and jumped from the driver's seat. Her black purse dangled between the thief's fingers as he skirted across the road toward the throng of people surrounding the market. A second later he disappeared behind a vegetable stand.

Natalie had barely made it to the curb on the opposite side of the street. She stomped her foot against the sidewalk and returned to the car. It was no use chasing the crook. She'd never find him. His head start had been too significant.

Another car blasted its horn behind her. She slid into the driver's seat and glanced at Joseph. Shards of glass had splattered across the backseat and onto his headrest. "Are you all right?"

He sat forward in the seat to avoid the glass. "I think so."

She drove with trembling hands until she came to the relative safety of the guarded parking lot of a hardware store. "I'm so sorry about your camera, Joseph."

He nodded at his backpack sitting on the floorboard in front of him. "We still have the printed photos in my backpack."

Running her fingers through her hair, she worked to steady her breathing. So much for clearing her head. She couldn't even think. All she could hear was the shattering of the backseat window replaying in her mind like a broken record.

Joseph picked off a shard of glass that had stuck to the collar of his shirt. "You should call the police."

Natalie tried to swallow the lump of irritation rising in her throat. Of all days. She'd had several friends robbed at intersections in their cars, but she had enough trouble to deal with today without having to fill out a police report on items she'd probably never see again. She made a quick inventory of what was missing. A handful of change, her international driver's license, Joseph's camera ...

Joseph's camera.

She felt the acid rising in her stomach. What if this hadn't been a random theft after all? Stephen knew she had an extra set of photos. What if he'd told Patrick? Patrick might deny the existence of the Ghost Soldiers, but if there was a cover-up involved ...

The implication ripped through her like one of the shards of glass on the seat behind her. If Patrick was involved, he'd have had just enough time to arrange a local thug to ensure that no evidence remained of what had taken place in Joseph's village.

No. Surely she was jumping to conclusions. She needed to go home and think.

The jingling of her cell phone made her jump. "Hello?"

"Natalie, it's Chad."

Relief flooded through her as she checked for traffic, then exited the parking lot. "The phones have been down. I've been trying to call you."

"What's wrong?"

"I ..." Her voice broke.

"Natalie —" The line crackled.

"Chad?" *No, Lord. Please. I've got to have someone I trust.* She pressed the phone against her ear and tried to stop the rising panic in her voice.

"Natalie, what happened?"

She breathed out a sigh of relief. "I went to Joseph's village. It's true. The Ghost Soldiers exist, Chad. I have pictures. Proof."

A pause. "I thought you weren't going to get involved."

"I couldn't ignore what Joseph saw." Natalie blinked and tried to see through the tears.

"Maybe not, but this isn't a game, Natalie. Especially if the Ghost Soldiers exist. It's too dangerous."

"Really." Anger seeped through the tears. "I'd say so. Someone just smashed the back window of my car and took my purse with the camera and memory chip."

"Are you in your car?"

"Yes."

"Come to the hospital, and we'll figure out what to do together."

Squeezing the phone against her shoulder, she turned left onto her street. "I'm already here at my house — "

"Natalie, you don't know if it's safe."

"I need to go inside and try to sort through what's going on." She waited for Joseph to open the gate for her before pulling into her driveway and turning off the engine. The front door was shut, and the metal bars were still intact on the windows. Nothing looked out of place.

"Everything looks fine here." She hurried up the porch steps. "I'll be at the hospital in thirty minutes. Forty-five, tops. I promise."

She hung up, then jammed her key into the security gate, thankful Joseph was with her. The small entryway looked undisturbed. Her umbrella hung on the iron coat rack. Yesterday's mail lay unopened on the half-moon table.

She looked farther in. A stream of light shone onto the tiled kitchen floor.

The back door stood open.

"*No, no, no . . .*" Natalie took a step sideways, knocking into Joseph in the process. She looked into the living room. Her couch was tilted forward. Drawers had been pulled out and dumped on the floor. Papers lay scattered across the floor.

Joseph stood beside her, eyes wide, his fingers clutching his backpack. "Who would do this?"

"I don't know." Natalie punched in Chad's number as terror rose in her throat and sucked the air from her lungs.

"Natalie?"

"They've been here." This time she didn't try to erase the panic in her voice.

"Get out of the house, Natalie. Now."

"I'm coming. I've got to grab my passport and some cash in case I can't come back." She rushed toward the tiny garage situated off of the living room, thankful she'd opted not to carry her ID in her purse.

The door to the garage slammed open against the cement wall. Nothing looked touched in this part of the house. Something had scared the intruders away ... unless they were still hiding ...

Pushing the thought aside, she scrambled toward the old sleeping bag and camping chair where she'd hidden a small safe. Her emergency backpack sat next to it. She'd packed it months ago, a "grab pack" with enough food, water, and other emergency items to last at least three days if conditions in the country turned completely sour. Maybe she should bring it along as well.

"Natalie?"

"Just a minute." She laid the phone on the shelf beside her and opened the safe, then picked the phone back up.

"Get out of there, Natalie."

Grabbing her passport and the backpack, she rushed outside with Joseph beside her. "I'm on my way."

ELEVEN

Chad gave Joseph a bottle of Coke, then handed Natalie the cup of steamy liquid he'd insisted she drink despite her protests that the weather was too hot for tea. She needed something to calm her nerves, and other than giving her a sedative, which he didn't think was necessary, this was the next best option.

She'd finally decided to comply and now sat across from him in a hard metal chair in the exam room. Joseph sat beside her, wearing the same trousers and red T-shirt from yesterday. The boy probably didn't own more than two or three shirts, pants, and a school uniform.

Chad watched as Natalie added another teaspoon of sugar from the tray and stirred her drink, the spoon clinking against the edge of the mug. For what she'd been through, she appeared remarkably put together. He'd listened to her story. Twice. Once for a general overview of what had happened and a second time for more details. Both times had left him feeling sick to his stomach.

He couldn't begin to imagine what she'd gone through the past few hours, let alone the distress Joseph must be feeling knowing his family had been kidnapped. Not that he hadn't experienced the throes of terror himself. Hearing her tale awakened memories he'd prefer to leave buried in the recesses of his mind.

She continued to sip her tea. Neither of them was in a hurry to discuss what should happen next. Even he wasn't sure how to proceed. He might deal with clinical issues that did not always follow an exact pattern, but at least he had the skills to make an educated diagnosis. Facing the skeletons of a corrupt country and saving Joseph's family would take more than intellect and contacts. It was going to take a miracle.

He watched as Natalie brushed a strand of copper hair away from her eyes and leaned forward, holding the mug between her fingers and staring at the floor. Somehow, in the past twenty-four hours, she'd managed to draw him in and make him a part of her world.

Natalie set her mug on the desk. "Do you want to see the photos now?"

He'd been avoiding any visual images of the tragedy. Already the scene played out too vividly in his mind. Suppressing his growing desire to forget the entire situation, he reached for the stack of photos as the low hum of the fan stopped. The power was off again. He picked up the telephone with his free hand. Great—no power and no phone. They might as well be on the moon as far as getting word to anyone about the situation. And there was no telling when they would be back on. Outages were becoming more and more frequent, phone service completely unreliable.

Chad flipped through the photos Natalie handed him, and his stomach clenched. She was right. An old woman fell to the ground as a rifle butt struck her from behind ... A young boy attempted to fight back against his attacker ... Dark shadows of blood ... Terror on faces ...

There was no denying anymore that the Ghost Soldiers existed.

He turned to Joseph, his heart wrenching at the boy's loss. "I'm sorry this had to happen."

Joseph fiddled with the half-empty bottle in his hands. "Me too."

Chad gave the photos back to Natalie. There had to be a solution. No one deserved to be ripped away from everything they knew and loved for another man's greed. But that didn't mean Natalie was the one to try to put a stop to the horror.

He leaned forward and rested his elbows against his thighs. "You gave copies of the photos to Stephen, and he's got connections in the government. You need to let him take care of this."

Natalie shook her head. "I don't trust him."

He raked his fingers through his hair. "I know you said you thought he wants you to be quiet about what happened, but you don't really think he's involved, do you? What would be his motive?"

"What's anyone's motive to use slavery as a means for gain? It's pure and simple greed." She caught his gaze. "I never would have thought that Stephen could be involved, but there's a leak somewhere. I told Stephen about the photos and within the hour my purse was stolen and my house was trashed. That's not a coincidence. Either he's involved or it was Patrick, who in turn sent the thugs after us."

"Maybe, but that doesn't get us any closer to a solution."

"That's why I've made a decision." Natalie took a final sip of her tea, then set it on his desk. "I'm going to the capital to follow up on my own connections in the government. Rachel works directly for the minister of health and has access to demographic files that might help us find out where Joseph's family is. There also might be someone at the U.S. Embassy who can help."

He felt a lump rise in his throat. "That's impossible."

"What is?"

"Going to the capital." He sighed. Shouldn't it be obvious? He could think of a hundred reasons that made the trip impossible. Impassable roads, the possibility of getting arrested, the dangers of hitting something—or someone—at night, as well as the additional roadblocks and security due to the upcoming election. And even if she did insist on following through with this insane quest, he could never let her go alone.

He glanced at his watch. It was almost one. The day had been slow, but he didn't get off work for another four hours. He could get Dr. Wrede to cover for him, but was that really a solution?

He decided to reason with her. "You know a trip to the capital is too dangerous, Natalie. If we left now, we wouldn't reach the capital until the middle of the night, even if we could get past the damaged roads and heavy security. And that doesn't even factor in the volatile political situation with the impending election. It's not safe."

She set her bag in her lap and raised her chin. "I'm open to options. What would you suggest?"

Chad frowned. Why did she have to be so stubborn?

Joseph's bottle clunked against the edge of the metal chair. "If I do not find my father, they will kill him."

They both turned to the boy.

"Joseph's right." Natalie blew out a short, hard breath. "His father has TB, and you can imagine what they will do with a man who can't work. And what about the election? You know what happened when President Tau took over. Over four thousand people were killed in protests, police brutality, and the eventual coup. If something's being planned again, there's going to be backlash. I don't want that to happen."

"You know I don't either." That thought alone carried enough motivation to get him involved. "The election is in three days."

Natalie gripped the strap of her bag. "Joseph's father might not have that much time."

Chad swallowed hard. No phone. No power. No safe way to get to the capital. If these were the odds for performing surgery, he'd never make the first incision.

He could think of only one viable option.

He rubbed his jawline and considered the consequences of what he was about to say. A glance at Natalie's determined gaze clinched his decision. "I think I know someone who can help."

TWELVE

Gabby rubbed the tight muscles of her neck, irritated that she'd just lost her chance at a one-on-one interview with Alexis Yasin. She leaned back against the leather seats of the rented vehicle and watched crowded street corners of Bogama whiz by. Months of research and countless hours of digging through red tape had sent her chasing leads through four African countries, but she'd come to the RD specifically to follow a lead on the European investor. While Yasin was only one of dozens of wealthy financiers who had sprinkled their money across the continent, he stood out because of his additional generous disbursements of humanitarian aid. She hoped that made him different from the average investor — whose generosity was too often an attempt to appear genuine while exploiting cheap labor and lax safety laws for monetary gain.

One of her sources, a freelance journalist based in Bogama, had placed the businessman in the country, but all her attempts to track him down the past four days had been futile. Granted, the man was known to avoid interviews, which might account for his evasiveness. But still, she wasn't convinced.

She pulled the file on Yasin from her leather briefcase and studied her notes on the man. Born in 1968 and raised in London by a single mom, he'd received a degree in International Finance in the early nineties. The next record of him was in 1995 when he went on to build his empire from the ground up. Throughout the years, he'd managed to keep a low profile while his bank account rose, undoubtedly into the billions. But while the world saw him primarily as a generous businessman, she'd been able to verify his financial involvement with at least two questionable mining companies in this country — one near the capital and the other outside Kasili.

While there was always the slim possibility he wasn't aware of the substandard conditions at these mines, instinct told her that if she dug deeper, she'd more than likely find yet another man who didn't think twice about using child labor for the sake of his bank account. Fifteen years of living on the continent as a child had not only convinced her to follow in her father's footsteps in the fight for personal freedom for the underprivileged, but it had also had taught her that corruption and injustice often run deep with many who yield any kind of power.

"I'm sorry you weren't able to secure an interview."

Gabby glanced up from her file to the front seat where Adam, the translator she'd hired on Natalie Sinclair's recommendation, sat. "So am I, but I'm not done trying. I need that interview."

Adam yawned. Obviously she wasn't the only one tired of the hectic schedule she'd forced them both to keep. "Are you hungry? The driver says traffic is light and we have time to stop for something."

Gabby waved away the offer. "Thanks, but I think I'd prefer to skip lunch."

A taxi blasted his horn past them as they headed toward the east side of town where the airport was located. She tried to ignore her queasy stomach — the victim of an early-morning street vendor's fare. She'd known better, but memories of *boerewors* in South Africa and *koshari* in Egypt had prevailed. The thought of another three flights and layovers between Central Africa and Washington, DC, didn't help either. But while it was the part of her job that guaranteed a week of jet lag, one didn't stack up awards in journalism by giving in to fatigue — or unwelcome bouts from food that didn't always agree with one's system.

Their driver, Jacob, stopped at a red light. Gabby closed her eyes, wishing there was a way to avoid the long flight ahead of her.

A gunshot shattered the quiet. The driver's window exploded and glass flew across the seats. Adrenalin rushed through her as her gaze darted to the passenger window. A half dozen men surrounded the car.

Oh, God, no ...

The driver's door opened and someone dragged Jacob from the car.

Her father's body flashed before her. Her mind screamed. *No!* It wasn't going to happen again.

Someone pounded on her door, then jerked on the locked handle.

Another shot fired from outside the car.

"Adam!"

"Get down." He shoved her onto the back floorboard, then threw himself behind the wheel. "Hang on."

Tires squealed. The force of the acceleration threw her against the backseat. Hands over her head, Gabby braced herself and prayed for a miracle.

THIRTEEN

Natalie drummed her fingers against her leg and gazed out the passenger window of her car. The hot breeze from the shattered back window ruffled her hair — and her fraying nerves. The silent commute to the airstrip had had her mind whirling in a dozen different directions. When had her modest ambitions of saving the population though vaccines turned into the necessity of liberating a group of modern-day slaves? She was a health care worker, not an abolitionist.

She shot a quick glance at Chad, who gripped the steering wheel as he wove through the crowded streets. His normally serene expression was marred with a concentration that formed creases across his brow.

She pulled on the fabric of her skirt and wadded a section between her fingers. Letting Chad drive had wiped away her last vestige of control — a feeling she feared she was in no position of winning back anytime soon.

A group of schoolgirls stood on the muddy street corner, while the roar of taxis, bikes, and motorcycles filled the pothole-ridden thoroughfare. The normalcy of the scene struck her. Even the upcoming election hadn't put a damper on everyday life. But all of that could change in an instant.

Chad took a right turn off the main boulevard onto a narrow dirt side road outside of town. Half a kilometer later, a hangar and a one-story building came into view. All that stood between them and the airfield was a rundown chain-link fence and a strip of tall grass waving in the afternoon breeze.

They passed a large truck, its black exhaust filling the car with the smell of sulfur. Natalie coughed as she pulled her hair into a ponytail and held it back with a clip from her backpack. There was one question she still had to ask. "What if your friend won't fly us to the capital?"

A shadow crossed Chad's face. "There's a good chance he won't be able to."

Natalie shook her head. "If this doesn't work, we'll just find another way."

He gripped the steering wheel. "I told you about my patient who died yesterday. You can't save them all, Natalie. No matter how hard you try, it's just not possible."

He might be right, but that didn't lessen her resolve. "Then we need to come up with Plan B."

"Better yet, let's pray we don't need a Plan B." Chad parked the car under a short overhang and tossed her the keys. "You two stay here. I'll see if I can find Nick." He jumped out of the car and disappeared into the large hangar to the right.

"You okay back there?" Natalie turned to Joseph, who sat in the backseat, and remembered that neither of them had eaten lunch. "You must be hungry."

He nodded. "A little, ma'am, but I'm fine."

Pulling her backpack into her lap, she dug into the front pocket. "Hope you don't mind living on granola bars today."

"Thank you." Joseph ripped off the wrapper.

Natalie leaned against the headrest as she munched on her stale granola bar. What she wouldn't do for a decent meal to hold her over the next few hours. If she had her way, though, they'd fly straight to Bogama, leaving little chance of squeezing in lunch anytime soon.

The clock on the dashboard clicked off ten minutes, then twenty, and there was still no sign of Chad. She slid out of the car for some fresh air. What had they been thinking? No pilot was going to rush them to the capital without advance notice or adequate funds. Coming up with Plan B was inevitable. If only she had a clue what Plan B was.

Joseph joined her along the side of the car. "He's going to die, isn't he?"

"Your father?" Natalie caught the shadow that crossed his face. "We're going to find him."

"But not before it is too late." He shook his head and leaned against the passenger door. "Last time I saw him he struggled to work in the fields. He will be even worse now."

Natalie's resolve strengthened. There was now no choice of whether or not she was going. If Chad couldn't find a pilot, she'd simply take her chances and drive there herself.

Joseph fiddled with the frayed hem of his shirt. "Dr. Talcott said to pray. Do you believe it works?"

His candid question dug up a layer of fresh guilt. She crumpled the empty wrapper in her hand and shoved it into her skirt pocket. How had she managed to rush through the day without relying on her heavenly Father? Her occasional one-sentence pleadings for help had been far outweighed by worry.

I'm sorry, Lord. "I know prayer works."

His dark eyes seemed to plead with her for answers. "My mother prays to Jesus. My uncle to Allah. My grandmother ... she prayed the ancestors would protect us. But no one was there to save them when the Ghost Soldiers came."

Natalie swallowed hard as the vivid images of the photos flooded her mind. She shuttered her eyes against the mental pictures but knew their poignancy would never disappear. "Who do you pray to?"

"Jesus. When I do pray." He kicked at the gravel with the toe of his shoe. "But today I am not sure there is a God big enough to hear me."

Natalie was struck by the vast implications of his comment. How many people had turned their beliefs away from a God who didn't give them the answers they expected? Away from a faith that shattered in the horror of the night?

"God never intended things to be this way." Natalie winced as her own clichéd words rang shallow. Words tended to fall flat when everything a person knew was gone. "All the bad things men do ruined God's plan for us."

Joseph shook his head. "Then why did it happen?"

"I don't know, Joseph. I just don't know."

A glossy starling flew across the gravel parking lot, its iridescent wings glistening in the sunlight. The Bible claimed that God cared even for the birds of the air. She had to believe that God heard Joseph's family's cries. Yet that conviction was blurred by the fact that some now lay in unmarked graves while the rest were forced to work for another man's gain.

Man's choices don't change who God is.

The words echoed through her mind as the starling flew out of sight behind a cluster of trees. Maybe that was true, but why didn't God intervene more often to stop Man's wrong choices?

Chad emerged from the hangar with a man following him. His broad grin erased some of the frustration she felt. Maybe God *was* about to answer their prayer after all. "Natalie, I'd like you to meet Nick Gilbert. He flies for Compassion Air. He may end up regretting this, but he's agreed to fly us to Bogama this afternoon."

Natalie's lungs let out a whoosh of air before she even realized she'd been holding her breath. She shook the hand of the thirty-something pilot, who wore a pair of shorts and a T-shirt. "We really appreciate this, Mr. Gilbert."

"Call me Nick." Despite his strong southern drawl, the boyish-looking pilot seemed at home in his surroundings. "I was scheduled to pick up a group in the morning anyway, so your timing is perfect. Besides that, I never was one to pass up a goodwill venture if I could avoid it."

"Thank you, sir." Joseph stepped forward to shake the man's hand.

"Why don't y'all come with me?"

Natalie grabbed her backpack from the front seat, hesitating at the broken window. "What are the chances I come back to a stripped or missing vehicle?"

"The overhang should keep any rain out, and I'll warn the security guards to keep an eye on it." Nick eyed the vehicle. "That's about the best I can do, though."

"Then that will have to be enough."

There wasn't time to find another place to store the car, and with the phones down, she couldn't even ask Stephen to come and get it. Besides, she might not completely trust her boss, but she owed him an explanation of her whereabouts. All she could do was try the connection again from the capital.

She pulled a few items from the glove compartment, tossed them into her bag, and hurried to catch up with the men. Inside one of the hangars sat a small plane.

"This is one of our Cessnas," Nick was explaining as she walked up. "We use it for ferrying teams to remote villages, as well as transporting medicines, food, and other supplies." He handed a clipboard to Chad. "I'm going to need each of you to sign this form. Then I'll take care of the official paperwork as quickly as I can so we can reach Bogama before dark."

Natalie eyed the plane. Bullet holes riddled the belly, and it needed a new coat of paint. The road might be filled with police blockades and potholes, but she was no longer convinced that the route by air would prove any safer. "Are you sure it can fly?"

Nick nodded. "Don't let its looks deceive you. Our aircraft might not win any beauty contests, but our mechanics make sure they're in top condition." Chad handed her the clipboard and pen, and she scribbled her name on the signature line. "Time's a-wasting, folks. Let's get this show on the road."

FOURTEEN

The muscles in Chad's shoulders relaxed for the first time all day. All they had to worry about now was catching a taxi to the embassy. The two-hour flight wouldn't give them much time to spare, but if they were late, he had an emergency number he could call once they landed. The phone service in Bogama might not be reliable, but from his experience, he'd trust it above Kasili's system any day.

The Congo River flowed beneath them. Twenty-seven hundred miles of water moved through half a dozen countries with its tributaries, islands, and falls. He leaned against the window and took in the details of the miniature world below. He'd always grabbed any chance he could to fly in a small plane. Instead of soaring thousands of feet above the ground in a commercial airliner through formless clouds, a patchwork of earth spread out below them almost close enough to touch. Trees draped the edges of the gray-blue waters, whose offshoots twisted away from the river. Fisherman effortlessly maneuvered their dugout pirogues along the winding waterways, taking advantage of the river's bounty, while a half dozen crocs sunned along a sloped bank.

A month ago, Nick had flown him to a small village on the western border of the country where an outbreak of cholera had struck.

The two-hour flight had saved a week of travel in a four-wheel-drive vehicle, something time would never have permitted, and in the process, lives had been saved. Now he prayed that this afternoon's flight across the mountainous terrain would be worth it as well.

In the distance, a row of tall mountains broke the horizon. The rugged landscape, with its varying shades of green, surged forward until it came to a stop along the banks of the Congo. A herd of elephants drank at the river's edge, casting shadows against the banks of the water.

He nudged Natalie with his elbow. "Hey, I found you a herd of elephants."

She opened her eyes, the strain of the day's events apparent on her expression. He'd encouraged her to try to sleep during the flight, even if it was only for a few minutes. She'd turned on her iPod and agreed — on the condition he wake her if he saw any animals.

She pulled out her earbuds and leaned across him, leaving a subtle trail of perfume. Another time, another place, he might have toyed with the idea of getting to know her better. But a short-term volunteer position and a serious relationship didn't go together. Besides, by this time tomorrow, they'd both be back to their separate routines.

"Oh, Chad, they're magnificent."

While she dug her camera out of her bag, he glanced across the aisle at Joseph, whose soft snores were drowned out by the roar of the engine. At least he was getting some rest after the emotional trauma of the past forty-eight hours.

A wisp of soft hair brushing against his cheek brought him back to the subject he was trying to avoid. Forget the elephants. Natalie Sinclair was one of the most beautiful women he'd met in a long time. Pretty, smart, passionate . . .

"Do you want to trade places?" he asked.

"I'm fine if you don't mind me leaning over you a bit."

He cleared his throat and stared at long lashes and wide brown eyes before letting his gaze dip to her full lips. He didn't know about her, but she was definitely not in his way.

She snapped another shot. "It's still somewhat debatable how closely they're related, but did you know there are two types of elephants in this area?"

"Really?" He watched her animated expression, enjoying the chance to discover another side of her.

"There are bush elephants and forest elephants. Obviously the bush elephants are found in the woodlands and savannas, while the forest elephants thrive in the denser areas, but the differences go much further than that. There are marked differences in diet, socialization, and even communication."

He folded his hands in his lap and continued to watch her. "Tell me more."

"Forest elephants live in a smaller group setting. Two to four compared with the bush elephant that prefers a much larger herd."

Natalie zoomed the lens of her digital camera and snapped another picture. He couldn't help but smile as she alternated between sharing facts about the animals and taking photos of the landscape.

"One of the amazing distinctions is the documented range of frequency when communicating ..." She stopped midsentence, tilting her head as she caught his gaze. "You're laughing at me?"

He chuckled. "Not at all. I'm thoroughly enjoying our conversation. And you sound as if you know what you're talking about."

She rested against her seat, the photo session over for the moment. "I spent a month between my sophomore and junior years of college working with a research foundation in Kenya. I loved the research, but hadn't decided whether I wanted to work with animals or people."

"Obviously people won out."

She nodded and slipped the lens cap back on before setting the camera in her lap. "It was a God thing, really. I remember sitting on a tree stump in the middle of nowhere, it seemed, taking notes on a family of elephants we were tracking. I was sick with some virus but still determined to survive the rest of the summer. I told God if He wanted me to, I'd return, but I needed confirmation on what He wanted me to do."

"And did you get it?"

She nodded. "The next day we rode out to the Rift Valley. Coming home, we picked up a woman who was later diagnosed with typhoid. It turned out that half the village was sick from contaminated water. So, while I'll always love animals and admire those who work with them, I felt God called me that day to make a difference in stopping disease."

"Have you ever regretted your decision?"

"Nope. You and I both know that we'll never get rich working for a nonprofit organization. But while my work might make a small difference in the scope of things, most days I feel as if I'm making a difference."

"You are."

A slight blush crept up her cheeks and she swept a loose strand of hair behind her ear. "You know, I don't feel like I've had the chance to properly thank you for all you've done. Finding me a plane on little to no notice isn't a small thing."

He felt his heart skip at her smile. "You're not the only one hoping to make a difference in this world."

The plane shimmied. Natalie grabbed his arm for a brief moment. "I'm sorry, I ..."

"Don't enjoy flying?"

"Flying's fine." Her laugh rang hollow. "It's the thought of crash landing that bothers me."

The plane shook again then twisted sharply to the left. This time, Chad grabbed the armrest. "Nick?"

The plane took another sharp turn and all went quiet.

"I need everyone to make sure their seat belts are fastened tightly," Nick shouted. "I'm going to have to make an emergency landing."

FIFTEEN

Trees rushed up at them. Natalie felt her stomach lodge in her throat. They were going to crash —

The force of the landing slammed her body into the seat in front of her. She braced against the cushion and waited for the fatal crack of parts breaking off — or the explosion of the fuel tank — as the plane screeched to a halt. Instead, only an eerie quiet surrounded her.

She shuddered, then drew in a breath, her heart pounding as she slowly sat up. "Chad?"

"Is everyone okay?"

She looked up at the sound of Nick's voice. He turned around in the front of the cabin. His left eye was already turning an angry red shade, but no other outward injuries were apparent.

"I'm okay." Chad stretched out his arms beside her.

Joseph nodded from across the aisle. "My wrist hurts, but I am all right."

Natalie still searched to find her bearings.

"Make sure she's all right." Nick stepped over his seat, which had been wedged forward. "Because of the hills, I can't radio for help, so for now I'm going to see if I can open the door. I don't smell any fuel, but let's not take any chances."

90

"Natalie?" Chad's hand brushed her arm. "Are you okay?"

She arched her back and tried to assess if anything was broken. Her knees had jammed against the front seat. She reached up and rubbed the ache in her jaw. No doubt, she'd be covered with a rash of bruises and have sore muscles come tomorrow, but nothing seemed broken.

"I think so." She drew her hand across a sore spot on her forehead.

Chad had already found the wet wipes in her backpack.

"Let me take a look." He washed away blood with the wipe.

"Ouch, that stings."

"It's just a scratch. Hardly noticeable. Does anything else hurt?"

Natalie shook her head, then stopped. The slightest movement made the pounding behind her temples stronger. "My head."

He pressed his fingers against her neck and checked her pulse. "Any ringing in your ears?"

"No."

"Nausea?"

"No."

Lifting up her eyelid with his thumb, he studied her pupils.

"I'm fine, Chad. Really."

"Then tell me what you remember."

Natalie pressed her eyes shut. She didn't want to remember what had happened or the terror that had accompanied the last five minutes. At least they were all still alive. That was a miracle as far as she was concerned.

Thank you, Jesus.

"Natalie?"

She let out a labored breath. "The engine went out, my life flashed before me, and Nick somehow managed to land the plane without killing us all."

He chuckled and checked her pulse. "What day of the week is it?"

"A not so good one?"

"You certainly haven't lost your sense of humor. The day?"

"Tuesday." She rubbed the back of her neck. "Good enough?"

"For now."

"Do you think there's something wrong? The last thing I need is a concussion."

"I think you're fine, but I'm still going to keep an eye on you."

She caught his serious expression and wished the thought of him watching over her didn't appeal to her so much. She glanced at her watch. Their chance of making it to the embassy in time was over, as were any chances of making a phone call. So much for saving the world. They'd be lucky if they could manage to get back home in time for Friday's elections.

Chad slid out into the aisle. "Sit here for a couple minutes and hold this cloth lightly against the cut. I need to make sure Joseph's all right."

With her hand on her head, she looked around the plane. The Cessna was still miraculously in one piece. From the window, she caught sight of the slow-moving Congo River. Thick brush gave way to the sandy shoreline against the water's edge where they had landed. Another few yards to the right and they'd have ended up in the middle of the river. How had Nick managed to land the plane without hitting a tree or running them into the Congo?

The plane walls began to close in around her. Her temple throbbed. She had to get out. Slowly, she unbuckled her seat belt and rose from her seat. Chad stood beside Joseph, assessing any injuries. Joseph winced as Chad examined his hand.

"I don't think it's broken, but definitely sprained." Chad looked up at her. "Do you see a first-aid kit?"

She rummaged through the cockpit and quickly found the metal box.

Chad pulled out an elastic bandage. "Nothing to worry about, Joseph. This will keep it immobile, and in a few days you'll be as good as new."

Natalie moved to the open door of the plane, her backpack slung across her shoulder.

"Let me finish here, Natalie, and I'll help you down."

Two minutes later, Chad jumped to the ground, then reached up to help her. She slid into his arms, her legs shaking as the reality of what had happened began to sink in. He didn't let go until she took a step back on her own.

How had life gotten so complicated? Yesterday she'd been content to pour her heart into teaching disease prevention and trying to stop an epidemic. Then Joseph showed up. And Chad ... She shook her head. Her mind was too muddled to even think about the implications of where her heart wanted to go. Someday. When all of this was over ...

Chad tilted up her chin and looked her in the eyes. "I want you to promise you'll tell me if you get nauseated, if your headache doesn't go away—"

"I know the symptoms."

"Promise me you'll tell me?"

She shot him a lopsided grin. "I promise."

Nick came out from under the belly of the plane with a frown on his face. "I'm sorry about this, folks. I don't know what to say."

Chad met him halfway. "What do you think happened?"

Nick ran his fingers through his hair. "I'm pretty sure it's a clogged fuel filter. I should be able to fix it, but it'll be dark soon, which means we're not going anywhere tonight."

Chad shook his head. "I don't know how you managed to get us on the ground in one piece, but thank you."

"This plane doesn't need a long landing strip, but all the same, it was a miracle."

Natalie joined them. "Any idea where we are?"

Nick glanced at his flight plan. "One hour and twenty minutes from takeoff puts us roughly a hundred and forty kilometers from

Kasili. And from what I saw from the air, I'm pretty sure we're nowhere near any town."

Natalie set her backpack down beside her. She had enough food and water to get them through tomorrow. After that, her rations would be gone. And there were other problems as well. In another couple hours, the sun would set, leaving them all vulnerable and exposed. A chimp howled in the distance. Natalie shuddered. A tromp through the jungle at any time wasn't an appealing thought.

Joseph stood in the clearing beside the plane, slowly turning in a circle.

Chad walked up beside him. "What is it, Joseph?"

"I know this place."

"What?"

He held up his hand and pointed to the east. "That hill. And there …" He turned back to the river.

Natalie stared at the rocky hill, then turned to the shoreline. Surely it was impossible for Joseph to recognize the uniform terrain that had to be the same for the next fifty kilometers.

Nick rested his hands on his hips. "You really think you know where we are?"

"I have friends in a village not far from here. We could stay the night."

Natalie held up her hand and took a step forward. "Wait a minute. We're in the middle of nowhere, Joseph. Even if you do know this area, the sun will be setting soon and the trees are filled with snakes, monkeys, and only God knows what else. It would be crazy to leave here."

Nick wiped his forehead with a handkerchief. "All of us could use a good night's sleep and something to eat."

Chad folded his arms across his chest. "What about the plane, Nick?"

"It's not going anywhere, and the village might give us a way to communicate with someone back in Kasili. I'm willing to take the chance."

"Natalie?"

Her stomach rumbled at the thought of a hot plate of cassava and sauce. Still ... "Wouldn't it be safer to spend the night in the plane, then look for help once it's daylight again?"

"The village is not far," Joseph promised.

Natalie fiddled with the strap of her backpack. "I don't know."

Joseph took a step toward her. "You have done more for me than I can repay. Please, let me help."

SIXTEEN

Natalie took another look at the airplane, feeling as if she was leaving behind the last link to civilization, then set off after the three men across the damp African soil. Golden rays from the afternoon sun filtered through the forest's green canopy and gave them enough light ... for the moment.

The further they retreated from the river, the thicker the vegetation became. Sprinkled through the trees were open patches of grass, the perfect feeding spot for impala and other buck. The Republic of Dhambizao had one game reserve in the far north. The rest of the country's wildlife existed only where villagers and poachers hadn't driven or killed them off — which didn't dismiss the chance of running across a lion, snakes, or even a rogue male elephant.

She shivered and slowed her steps, studying the edges of the path for snakes and animal tracks. Research treks during college had always been taken in an equipped four-wheel-drive vehicle with guards carrying rifles, never on foot without some sort of security measures. Driving through the bush in a jeep was one thing, but she didn't remember penciling in a foot safari in her day planner.

A *whoop* sounded from deeper in the forest, and she flinched. A second *whoop* answered the call. Hyenas. Fatigue, the lack of food, and the high stress of the day all calculated into her nerves being strung tighter than a *bangoma* drum.

The booming foghorn call of a hippo echoed through the trees.

Natalie froze. "Joseph?"

Their new leader turned and made his way back to where she stood. The hippo called again from the direction of the river, shattering the late-afternoon silence.

"There is nothing to be afraid of, ma'am."

She pointed toward the river. "But that was a hippo."

"Hippos usually stay in the water till night, then come out to graze. We will be at the village soon."

"I realize that they *tend* to stay in the water." Natalie looked at Nick, then rested her gaze on Chad. Both of them were grinning. She threw up her hands in defeat. "Okay, I'm sorry. Let's go."

Natalie focused on the trail as they started walking again. A dung beetle with his prize wandered along beside them. At least she had nothing to fear from him. "You must think I'm a complete wimp."

Chad chuckled at her statement. "Hardly. Even I have to admit I'd rather be sitting over a nice steak dinner in the capital than walking through the bush completely vulnerable."

Vulnerable ... helpless ... defenseless ... She hated feeling this way.

She looked up at the sky, where half a dozen vultures circled in a slow, methodical pattern. "At least I'm not the only one ready to get out of here."

"Don't be so hard on yourself." Chad caught her gaze and threw her a broad grin. "None of us were expecting a tromp through the African bush today."

Or having her back window shattered or her house ransacked or surviving a plane crash in the middle of nowhere. Still, she couldn't help but laugh at how ridiculous their situation seemed. It was as if she'd landed on some TV reality show and the cameras wouldn't stop rolling.

Natalie watched as Joseph made his way along the leaf-strewn path — which had probably been formed over a period of time by hippos or some other large predator — in front of them. He walked slowly, seemingly absorbed with the smells, sounds, and changing colors of the environment around him. The boy might not be a professional guide, but years of living in the mountains of Dhambizao had obviously taught him to recognize certain variances in the landscape that someone like her would never see.

A monkey swung across a branch above her, chattering as it dropped bits of dirt and leaves onto her head. Irritated, she shook away the fallen debris and matched her steps with Chad's. "Back at the airport, Joseph asked me if I believed prayer really worked. He's not sure there's a God big enough to save his family."

"What did you tell him?"

"Some clichéd answer about how God never intended things to be this way and that man's sin corrupted God's original plan." The day's events flickered frame after frame like a PowerPoint presentation in her mind. "It makes sense when you're sitting on a church pew, but perspectives change when life rips everything away from you."

"Simple answers aren't always wrong, though I know what you mean." Chad shoved his hands into his jeans pockets. "It's difficult to understand how so much evil and suffering could exist in a world created by a good God."

"Exactly." Natalie hesitated. She feared to ask the nagging question out loud: why did His promise to work everything together for good often seem to fall short?

Chad kicked a dead branch aside without losing stride. "The one thing I have noticed is how I tend to cry out to God only when things go wrong. One of those paradoxes that doesn't always make sense."

"Like growth through suffering or refinement through the fire?"

"Exactly."

The thought made her look at her own life. She'd seen how her own fairly easy existence had made her depend more on what she could do instead of what God wanted to do in her life. And that those who walked through the fire and found God faithful seemed to be the ones who stood firm in who He was no matter what.

Joseph stopped in front of them, interrupting her train of thought.

Nick tugged on the rim of his baseball cap. "What is it?"

Pressing his fingers against his mouth, Joseph bent down to study the ground. Natalie stepped forward to see what he was looking at.

"Lion tracks." Joseph crouched and stared straight ahead. "They are fresh."

Natalie glanced up again at the vultures she'd seen earlier. A knot swelled in her throat.

Joseph pointed through the tall grass. Barely discernible was a male lion. "There was a kill."

The lion's brown mane ruffled in the breeze as he ripped at the carcass of an impala.

"For now he will eat." Joseph signaled ahead. "We must walk quietly and not run."

Natalie held her breath as fear escalated into pure panic. She'd seen lions in the wild before but was still amazed at the size of the massive beast. A typical mature male measured four feet tall at the shoulder, while his body spanned over eight feet.

Slowly, the four of them edged away from the kill. After another half a kilometer she allowed herself to relax. At least as much as she could relax considering they were walking through the untamed African bush without weapons.

Afternoon shadows began to fall across their path as the sun began its descent toward the horizon. By six, it would be dark, which meant if they didn't find the village soon, all they'd have left to lead them was the silvery glow of the moon.

They turned the bend, and the path opened up to a savanna the size of a football field. Two dozen impala fed on the tall grasses that whispered in the warm breeze.

Joseph quickened his pace. "The village is just ahead."

Natalie felt an overwhelming a sense of relief. Any chance of contacting the embassy today had been eliminated when the plane crashed, but at least they'd be able to eat a hot meal and get a decent night's sleep before regrouping in the morning and figuring out what to do. At this point even the hard ground for a bed appealed to her tired muscles.

The click of a rifle reverberated in the shadows.

Natalie stopped beside a clump of grass and scanned the edge of the savanna. Her heart pounded in her ears. Two men stood at the edge of the clearing, one with a gun pointed at them.

Chad pulled Natalie behind him.

Joseph fell to his knees as the man shouted. "Drop to the ground and put up your hands."

SEVENTEEN

Chad squeezed Natalie's wrist. In deciding to come, he'd promised himself he would protect her. No matter what. A picture of Stewart flickered through his mind, and he fought back the sting of pain. He might not have been able to save Stewart, but he would protect Natalie.

One of the men shouted, his words too rapid for Chad to understand. Impala scattered into the woods around them, rustling through the tall grass as they ran for cover. Beside him, Joseph and Nick put up their hands. Chad followed suit, dropping to his knees while making sure he was in the line of fire between Natalie and the gunmen.

He nudged Natalie behind him. "Stay back."

She made no effort to resist his instructions. "What do they want, Joseph?"

"They think we are after their livestock." Fear laced the boy's words, but his voice held steady. Joseph spoke again to the men, his expression animated as his voice continued to rise. Chad strained to understand the gist of the conversation. *Poachers . . . cattle . . . dead . . .*

A minute later, Joseph rose slowly from the hard ground and motioned the others to follow. "We can get up. It is safe now."

Chad hesitated. "Are you sure?"

The men walked toward them, their rifles now at their sides.

Joseph nodded. "With the elections coming up, most of the police have gone to the capital. They have had many of their sheep and cattle stolen. They only want to protect what is theirs. I told them I go to school with one of their own ... Mbella. They have apologized and said we are welcome."

"Looks to me like they're doing a fine job scaring away trespassers." A ripple of relief, mixed with lingering anger, swept through Chad. He helped Natalie up before letting go of her hand. "Are you all right?"

"Yes." She looked up at him, the fear in her expression evident in the fading pink glow of the sunset. "You know you don't have to protect me."

Chad's brow rose. "Considering all that's happened during the past twelve hours, it seems to me as if you need someone to protect you."

Her grin displaced the rest of his anger. "Perhaps you have a point."

Chad felt his heart quicken. He hadn't wanted to get involved. How, then, had his path so quickly intertwined with hers?

Joseph stepped up beside him and made quick introductions to the two men, who one at a time grasped Joseph's forearm with one hand and shook his hand with the other in their traditional greeting. "They wish to apologize, but insist they cannot be too careful. They have lost many animals to these thieves."

Chad followed the party as they crossed the open field toward the flicking lights of the village. A dozen huts dotted the cleared area. Smoke rose from the cooking fires, bringing with it the strong scent of fried fish and fiery hot sauce. Women sat in front of fat iron pots, stirring with tall wooden spoons, while the men exchanged stories around the fires. Children, their laughter rippling through the humid night, played in the shadows of the thatched huts.

Joseph stopped near the center of the compound. "They have told me that the women will prepare a place for us to sleep after we eat."

By the time darkness had settled in around them, the four sat at a small wooden table enjoying bowls of cassava and sauce. A radio, powered by a car battery, buzzed in the background. Insects chirped. A baby cried. Inside the camp they should be safe until morning. And by that time, maybe he and Nick would have been able to come up with Plan B.

Natalie formed a ball of cooked cassava between her fingers and dipped it into the thick, red sauce. "Have you ever tasted anything so delicious?"

Chad smacked a mosquito on his arm. "Not since your party last night."

She shook her head. "Was that only yesterday? Seems like ages ago already."

"It is hard to believe." He smacked another mosquito, wondering what made him so appealing to the deadly insects. "Nick, you missed the best chocolate cake this side of the equator."

"Stop, please." Nick held up his hand, shaking his head. "The last time I had a decent slice of cake was at my mom's, back in Louisiana nine months ago."

Chad slapped the back of his arm.

Natalie laughed as she dug through her backpack and pulled out a tube of bug repellent. "I'd say we all need some of this, gentlemen."

Nick fiddled with the brim of his baseball cap. "Do you happen to have any pain medicine in there as well?"

A moment later she handed him two tablets. He popped the pills into his mouth and downed them with a sip of the warm Coke they'd been offered.

"I'm impressed." Chad rubbed the cream on his arms. "You really are prepared."

"I had hoped never to encounter an emergency and have to use it, but I can already see that my 'grab pack' is coming in handy." She wiped some repellent on her own arms, then passed the small container to Nick. "I've also got enough clean water to last us through tomorrow. Maybe into the next day if we ration it."

Chad formed another ball of cassava with the tips of his fingers. "How bad's your headache, Nick?"

The pilot shook his head. "Nothing a good night's sleep won't cure. Once daylight hits, I need to try and fix the fuel blockage so we can find a way out of here."

Joseph set down his finished bowl and pushed back his chair. "They have a place for us to sleep. I can show you."

Nick glanced at Chad and Natalie. "Do you mind?"

Chad shook his head. "Considering the nightlife here, I don't think you'll be missing much."

The entire village would be up with the sun. For now, with no electricity, darkness had brought a close to another day.

Natalie handed Nick a small water bottle. "Let us know if you need anything else, Nick."

Chad turned back to his bowl. "How's your head?"

"Fine, actually." She pressed her fingers against the spot she'd hit in the crash. "I was expecting a whopper of a headache."

"Any nausea?"

She shook her head as one of the women came to clear their plates. Chad complimented the woman in Dha for the delicious meal, thankful they were here and not stuck or injured in the downed plane.

"*Tsiko teyo*, Mama." Natalie, it seemed, wasn't to be outdone when it came to language.

The woman bestowed upon them a white, toothy smile before slipping back into the shadows of the hut.

Chad sat back in his wooden chair. "I'm impressed."

"I don't know why." Even in the dim light, he was certain he saw a rosy blush reach her cheeks. "I'm certainly not fluent like you are. Just a few phrases here and there to help me get by."

She pulled a chocolate bar from her bag, ripped off the wrapper, and handed him half.

He grinned. "You are full of surprises, Miss Sinclair."

She laughed and nibbled on the edge of her bar. "While I love their food, it gives me a horrible sweet tooth."

He bit into the chocolate. "Let me tell you, this helps bring a smile to a day that definitely ranks as one of the worst I've experienced in a very long time."

Natalie's own smile faded as she stuffed the wadded wrapper into her skirt pocket. "Do you think the plane was tampered with?"

Her question didn't surprise him. The same thought had played through the back of his mind since their unexpected landing along the Congo River. "They would've had to have followed us from the hospital. And the only time they could have done anything was the ten or fifteen minutes Nick worked on the paperwork to get us out of there."

"Enough time to mess with the fuel tank?"

"Security is nil on a good day, so the possibility is certainly there." He rubbed the back of his neck. "Nick should be able to tell us more tomorrow, but yes. I think someone would have enough time to do some damage."

"At least whoever it was has no idea where we are now." She took the last sip of her drink, then caught his gaze. "Why did you decide to come with me?"

Chad hesitated at her question. There were still aspects of his past he preferred not to talk about. Yet Natalie had somehow managed to waltz into his busy life like a welcome afternoon shower, bringing a short respite from the hot African sun.

"I lost my best friend during the last coup, and as I look at Joseph I see a part of myself." He combed his hand through his hair. "And I suppose, in some odd way, I thought your father would appreciate knowing someone was looking after his daughter."

Her gaze dropped to the table. "Joseph isn't the only one asking why God didn't stop such a horrible event, is he?"

Sometimes he hated the truth. "No, he's not."

There were questions he didn't want to ask. Questions he wished his sometimes faltering faith didn't force him to ask. Where was God in all of this? When Stewart died? When Joseph's family was ripped from their home and dumped into some godforsaken mine in the middle of the mountains?

Chad shook his head. He still believed God was in control — and believed he'd stay firm in his faith no matter what. But that didn't take away the pain of the situation. Or the questions.

Tears formed in the corner of Natalie's eyes, then dropped, and before he could think about what he was doing he reached out and wiped one from her cheek with his thumb. "I'm sorry."

"For what?"

He rested his hand against her cheek a second before pulling away. "For the fact that you've been shoved into an impossible situation."

She sniffed and tried to hold back more tears. "Do you really think the election's being rigged?"

Chad shrugged. "It does tend to be the norm in this part of the world."

"But surely it's not going to be easy to pull off with the UN election committee hovering so closely. At least not completely undetected. Could someone really get away with it?"

"I don't know." He shook his head. "With the resources at stake, the gamble might prove strong enough to take that chance."

"Which means we've got to figure out who's planning to take over and stop them."

Chad's eyes widened. "You're talking about interfering with a major presidential election of a country."

Natalie leaned forward. "I'm talking about saving Joseph's family."

A knot formed in Chad's chest. If she was right, they had less than seventy-two hours to put a stop to what was happening.

EIGHTEEN

Natalie woke with a start. Sunlight poured through the cracks in the wooden shutter, causing her to squint. She swung her arm across the bed and grabbed for her alarm clock. Instead her hand hit the air.

Where was her clock?

Squinting, she looked around the room. Thatched roof ... stack of broken chairs ... wooden dresser with a bright green crocheted covering ...

The events of yesterday rushed back. Joseph's plea for help and the pile of incriminating photos ... The plane crash ... Being held at gunpoint by the villagers ... She closed her eyes, wishing she could wake up back home in her bed in Kasili —

Her eyes popped back open as memories of her ransacked living room shattered that idea. Safety seemed an elusive figure she couldn't hold on to.

Her own dreams during the night had been surprisingly void of the drama surrounding her the past twenty-four hours. The only thing they'd been filled with was a tall, handsome doctor with dark curly hair and blue eyes. She shook her head and pulled the sheet to her chin. There was no time to think about Chad Talcott — or how he made her wish she had time to think about him.

She sighed and tried to recapture the peace she'd managed to find while sleeping. The deep breath made her long for the rich scent of percolating coffee from her tiny kitchen. Instead, all she could smell was the woodsy aroma of the cooking fires.

Turning over on the straw mattress, she tried to stretch out the stiffness in her legs. Her foot hit something hard at the bottom of the bed. Propping herself up on her elbows, she stared at the lump under the sheet. She wiggled her toes, but the lump didn't move. She lifted the sheet and peered beneath the worn covering.

A six-inch lizard stared back at her.

Natalie screamed and scrambled out of the bed, her foot tangling in the sheet. Falling backward, she landed with a dull thump against the hard floor. Air whooshed out of her lungs, and she struggled to take another breath.

"Natalie?"

Her chest burned, and she couldn't move. As the wooden door of the hut swung open, she looked up at Chad from her awkward position on the floor. The sheet was wrapped around her legs, her skirt bunched around her thighs, and she was certain her hair stuck out in at least a dozen different directions. Definitely not the way to make a good impression.

He knelt beside her. "Are you all right?"

"I'm fine." She managed to sit up, thankful she'd opted to wear her clothes to sleep in. She rubbed her left shoulder, which had taken the brunt of the impact. "What were you doing? Standing guard outside my hut all night?"

He shot her a grin. "Nick and I were outside talking. I heard you scream."

She gritted her teeth together and pointed to the bed. "There's a lizard in my bed."

Chad thumped the bottom of the mattress. "It's dead."

Her gaze narrowed. "I realized that after I screamed and crashed to the floor and it still hadn't moved."

Dead or alive, she had no desire to get close to the creature.

Chad folded his arms across his chest, the smirk on his face broadening. "You're bound and determined to trek across the dangerous African bush, but you scream at the sight of a little lizard?"

"Very funny." Natalie threw one of her shoes at him, missing his shoulder by a centimeter. He didn't need to know the extent of her phobia of lizards, snakes, mice . . .

He caught the sandal before it hit the floor, a gleam in his eye despite his deadpan expression. "Watch out. I've been told I can be far more vicious than even a dead lizard."

"Ooh, I'm scared." She couldn't help but laugh. It was one thing she liked about him. No matter what the situation, he seemed to know how to bring out her sense of humor. "Have you come up with Plan B?"

Chad dropped the shoe. "Joseph left to find transport to the capital. We should be able to get there by boat."

"What about the plane?"

"Nick's going to head back there with Mbella, one of Joseph's friends. He's sure he can fix it and fly out of here, but it's going to take some time. He doesn't want to take off until he's certain everything is okay, and there's no way to transmit a message at this point because of the radio's restricted line of sight. If all goes well, he'll meet up with us in the capital for his scheduled pickup and take us back to Kasili once we've talked to the embassy."

Natalie nodded. At least something was working out. "I need to ask Nick to try to contact my boss once he's airborne then."

"I've already asked him to." He turned toward the door to leave. "As soon as Joseph returns we can leave."

"Chad."

"Yeah?"

She pointed to the bed and shot him a pleading look. "The lizard."

Chad moved back to the bed and, after wrapping the lizard in the bottom sheet, slung it over his shoulder. "Anything else, ma'am?"

"No." She ignored his thick cowboy drawl as he slipped out of the hut and shut the door behind him. "Of all the ridiculous situations."

Shuddering at the horrific thought of sleeping all night with a dead lizard, she grabbed her backpack, wishing she had an extra change of clothes. Her skirt looked like it had been trampled by a herd of buffalo, and her shirt hadn't fared much better. If nothing else, a coat of lip gloss and mascara would perk her up.

Natalie brushed her hair into a ponytail, then dug in her backpack for her small cosmetic bag. Her Bible slid onto the dirt floor. She picked up the small black-leather book — a gift from her parents on her twenty-first birthday — and flipped it open to the gum-wrapper marker in the book of Leviticus. Apparently her systematic, daily readings through the Old Testament had vanished somewhere along with the last days of the rainy season when she'd packed the emergency bag.

Leviticus. The corners of her lips drooped into a frown. Maybe that's why she'd stopped reading straight through the Bible and switched instead to passages from the New Testament she'd left on her bedside table. Slaughtering goats and bulls for sin offerings had little to do with her daily life. Or so it seemed.

Floundering for encouragement, Natalie turned to the Psalms. David had been chased by his enemies more than once. Hounded by men who wanted him dead. At least her situation wasn't quite so perilous. Still, she identified with David as she read the prayers that lifted up pleas for God's salvation from his foes. A shiver pricked her spine as she sent up an urgent petition for her own life.

She'd never thought she'd be running from an enemy. An enemy she couldn't even identify, for that matter. The risks of living in the RD were something she took seriously by implementing as many security measures as she could. Never driving alone at night ... Avoiding certain areas of town ... Ensuring she was always aware of her surroundings ... Arming the security system on her house at night

... Yet this faceless foe had pushed her into a war in which she didn't know the rules of engagement.

She read Psalm 91. "He will save you from the fowler's snare and from the deadly pestilence. He will cover you with his feathers, and under his wings you will find refuge; his faithfulness will be your shield and rampart."

A shield and rampart ... a refuge from trouble.

That's what I need, Lord. Your covering and protection. Your wisdom to figure out what is going on. She fingered the edge of the page. *I can't do this by myself.*

But what *was* going on? A village cleared out by a dozen rogue soldiers ... A UN-monitored presidential election ... Hints of a rigged election ... A modern-day slave trade ... They all had to be connected. Even without knowing all the details, she couldn't ignore the deadly consequences they were facing. Or the helplessness she felt.

Her shallow breathing left her feeling as if a pile of bricks sat on her chest, a feeling overshadowed only by the sense of urgency that gnawed at her.

What do we do, God? Joseph's father will die if we don't find him quickly—

A knock on the door drew her from her thoughts. "Are you ready to go?"

Wishing she had a few more minutes to spend in prayer, Natalie opened the door to Chad. An open line of communication throughout the day with her heavenly Father was going to have to do. "Yeah, I just need to grab my backpack."

"Joseph found a boat that will take us up the river to the capital. Are you sure you're up for it?"

"You bet." Natalie slung the strap across her shoulder and stepped out into the morning light. They were already a day late, and there was little time to waste. "Let's go."

NINETEEN

After thirty minutes aboard the massive boat, Chad was ready to disembark and take his chances with the relative quiet of the jungle. The relentless *chug-chug-chug* of the giant riverboat's diesel engine competed with the chatter of a thousand passengers. Pigs, goats, and chickens ambled around him. Women cooked breakfast. Men traded their goods and slaughtered animals while drinking bottled beer. The jazzy rhythms of Africa rang out over several battery-operated radios, none of which played the same station.

A fly buzzed in his ear and he slapped it away. Both the lack of a good night's sleep and the constant jarring of the other passengers added to the assault on his senses. Obviously the craft Joseph had managed to secure their passage on wasn't simply transportation in a country whose road system left much to be desired. The three huge barges chained together had become a floating marketplace.

They'd left Joseph to chat with one of his friends from school. Chad glanced at Natalie, who worked to keep up with him as they pressed through the heavy crowd. Her face was pale, emphasized further by the bruise on her forehead. They were going to have to battle to find a shady place along the edge of the boat among the sellers and their goods. He wiped beads of moisture from his forehead. A warm, humid breeze skirted off the water, a sign that in a few short hours the metal deck would be blisteringly hot from the afternoon sun.

He grasped Natalie's elbow and maneuvered her past a heaping pile of fish swarming with flies. "Are you all right?"

"Yeah." She pressed her hand against her nose and skirted another pile of unidentifiable carcasses. "A dead lizard seems like nothing compared to this."

He chuckled in agreement. "Any headache left?"

"A slight one, but who wouldn't have one in this place." She pointed to insects and lizards piled on tables ready for tonight's supper and rolled her eyes. "The variety doesn't end, does it?"

A man walked by carrying a smoked porcupine under his arm. Natalie was right. There was no limit to what might be sold between those from the villages and those on board. Villagers came to trade their fish and dwarf crocodiles for salt, batteries, shampoo, and cigarettes. Bush meat was another viable trade despite environmentalists' attempts to stop the practice. Already he'd noticed a number of endangered species getting tagged and packed into the massive onboard freezers. In the capital, elephant steaks had become a gourmet food for urbanites willing to pay the high prices.

An *oof* resonated behind him. Natalie jumped sideways, knocking into him.

Chad steadied himself, then turned around. "It's a baby chimpanzee."

Its owner, dressed in shorts and a bushman's hat, hushed the chimp clinging to him like an infant.

The anxiety on Natalie's face dissolved. "He's adorable."

Chad didn't agree. "Adorable until it escapes from its rope and bites someone. Wild chimps can be both strong and vicious."

Natalie took a step backward.

With a grin on his lips, he maneuvered them toward an empty spot at the starboard railing. "Come on. There's a shady space up ahead."

The warm breeze from the river helped to erase the pungent smells drifting off the boat. Making his way past a covered flatbed truck filled with layers of tin sheeting, Chad grabbed onto the rusty rail. The boat rounded a bend in the river. Ahead women washed clothes along the shoreline, the colorful patterns of the material standing out against the white sand of the river. Within minutes of sighting the village, a jumble of overloaded boats raced toward the larger vessel, their passengers ready to trade with those on board.

"The river's beautiful, isn't it?" Natalie shoved a piece of wind-blown hair behind her ear before handing him a bottle of water from her bag.

He nodded his thanks. Nightmarish memories from his family's escape down the Congo had faded enough that, for the moment, all he saw were fishermen standing in dugout canoes, waiting for another catch. Children played on the green banks along the edges of the water. A pelican resting among the dense trees shook the long feathered plumes on the back of its head.

It was beauty that vied for prominence against the atrocities done to the country's people.

Natalie loosened the lid on her water bottle. "You're not regretting coming, are you? At this pace, Nick will beat us to the capital."

Chad took a sip from his water bottle and watched a pirogue ripple through the river beside them, its pilot's even strokes propelling it toward their own heavy boat. "Considering how we slow down at every village, I'd say you're right."

The noise escalated behind them, and Natalie lowered her water bottle from her lips, turning toward the source of the commotion. "What are they yelling about?"

Chad studied the two men and their animated gestures. "Sounds like a heated bartering session over a piece of slaughtered meat."

"Sounds more like an inquisition."

Chad laughed. Instead of abating, the shouting only increased as another man joined the discussion. How much deliberating did it take to buy a few kilos of meat? "You have noticed the camaraderie hidden in people's expressions, haven't you, despite their fiery words?"

He smiled at the determined set of her chin as she regarded the situation with obvious concern. He liked her. Her sensitivity. Fortitude. Intelligence. Passion. A rare combination in the women he typically encountered. Either he needed to get out more, or he'd found someone worth getting to know.

He turned away from her and shook his head. He had to keep his focus on why they were here and not on how her smile managed to make him wish he had time to get to know her better. Truth was he had little time to put into a relationship. Something he'd best not forget. Once they returned to Kasili, life would resume its unending cycle of twelve-hour shifts and late-night emergency calls.

Natalie's arm brushed against him, interrupting his thoughts. "Raw meat is something I can't handle here. Seems like I can't get away from the whole animal issue. I was flipping through my Bible this morning and opened up to Leviticus." She shuddered. "It never seemed to have much relevance to my own life — the Levitical laws and the need for a blood sacrifice."

"I'm sure you're not the only one who's ever confessed to skipping through those passages. I know I have."

Her soft laugher filtered through the breeze. "I'm glad to know that."

"But it does have some significance. Christ offered a one-time sacrifice for sin with his death."

"'One died for all, and therefore all died.'"

"It's a powerful thought," he admitted.

Someone screamed.

Beside them, a woman grabbed her child, knocking over a basket of oranges in the process. Chad stared across the crowd, trying to figure out what had happened. The meat barterers were gone. Then he saw the source of the commotion. A thin rope lay slack in front of them on the deck.

The chimpanzee was loose.

TWENTY

Natalie skittered backward, searching the crowded deck for the escaped monkey. Her ankle scraped against a wooden crate, but she ignored the sharp sting. The boat had dozens of places the animal could hide, from bags of maize to racks of smoked fish to wooden stalls piled high with goods for sale. And if it bit someone —

The monkey let out another shrill *oof* from atop one of the stalls and the crowd scattered.

Chad grabbed her hand, and they darted toward the railing to avoid being trampled. A child screamed. Someone slammed into Natalie's shoulder. She pressed against the railing as the monkey swung down onto the stall in front of them, toppling over a basket of fruit. Dozens of oranges spilled across the deck. Catching the edge of a blue tarp, the monkey scampered onto the deck and picked up a piece of fruit, its attention sidetracked for the moment. Or so she thought. Turning toward Natalie, it paused and then hurled the orange straight at her.

Natalie lunged sideways, but only managed to trip over a pile of rope. Chad grasped her elbow, stopping her fall.

"You all right?" he asked.

She wiped the perspiration from the back of her neck and forced a

116

smile, her gaze still fixed on the monkey. "Yeah, but this is definitely not my day."

Another orange flew across the deck, this time hitting a child in the head. Natalie's temper soared as she skimmed the crowd for the owner. As the child sobbed behind the crumpled skirt of his mother, the monkey's owner appeared from the middle of the crowd, holding out his hat and trying to entice the beast with a piece of fruit. Miraculously, it complied, climbing into the man's lap. Natalie blew out a sharp breath of relief as he tied the rope around the monkey's waist before disappearing back into the crowd.

"Why in the world would that man consider bringing a wild monkey on board this boat in the first place? Wait a minute." She pitched Chad an orange and groaned. "What am I saying? The place is filled with crocodiles, parrots, turtles, and all sorts of smoked animals. What's one loose monkey terrorizing a group of children?"

Chad tossed the orange into the air, then caught it again. "You've given me an idea."

Natalie watched as Chad picked up three oranges and started juggling. Many of the children, who minutes ago had whimpered in fear, now squealed with excitement at the one-man show. She couldn't help but grin at the children's smiles. Just moments ago, the deck had been filled with panic. Now a little boy with tattered clothes and a protruding belly smiled up at Chad, laughing, while one remaining tear rolled down his chubby brown cheek.

Chad reached for a fourth orange and several of the parents gasped as he kept them spinning through the air. Like father like son; the man had a knack for making people smile, easing the children's fears while at the same time easing hers. The applause grew when Chad, without losing a beat, threw one of the oranges to a young boy.

Natalie scanned the lively crowd, stopping at two men standing at the back of the boat, dressed in army fatigues, their gazes fixed on her. A scar edged the forehead of the tallest man, white against his dark skin as he squinted into the sun.

Nudging the man beside him, they moved on to one of the stalls. Natalie shook her head and turned back toward Chad. No. It was only her imagination chasing ghosts in her mind. No one could know they were here.

Finishing with a flourish, Chad took a bow, reached into his front pocket, and tossed a coin at the fruit vendor. He began giving out oranges to the children, who screamed with delight over the gift.

Natalie laughed when he finally managed to push his way through the crowd and join her at the railing. "I think you've got your own fan club. You really are full of surprises."

"Come on. I've got another surprise for you." He took her hand and started across the deck. "Besides, I'm out of oranges and have to get away from here before I get mobbed."

They pushed their way through the busy throng and its continual movement. Vendors bartered with customers. Men drank beer while playing a traditional game of kari, with its pebbles and pitted game board, to pass the time. A pig let out a bloodcurdling scream beside them. No one even seemed to notice.

"Where'd you learn to juggle?" she asked him.

"When I worked a few months in the children's ward back in Portland, I decided that I should add a few tricks to my bedside manner."

"I'm sure the kids loved it."

"I like to think it took their minds off their situation for a while."

He stopped in front of one of the stalls where an old, toothless woman sat over piles of food wrapped neatly in green forest leaves.

Natalie frowned. "What is that?"

He adjusted the strap of the backpack he carried for her across his shoulder. "You're telling me that you've lived here eighteen months and never tried *mandazis*?"

"Let me put it this way." She looked up at him. "When you work in my field and are trying to stop a cholera epidemic, you tend to avoid food bought on the side of the road or off crowded boats with absolutely no sanitation rules."

"I don't know how you've survived living here." He shook his head. "Come on. It's time you lived it up a bit. I used to eat these all the time as a child, and I'm still around and kicking."

Natalie laughed. "So what are they, exactly?"

He opened up the corner of one. "Balls of dough fried in hot oil. Add a dollop of peanut butter and voilà — you've got a bit of heaven."

Heaven? Natalie squinted down her nose at the bucket of peanut butter. Looked more like a great glob of brown goo in a dirty plastic container to her.

"Come on."

"Okay." She hesitated at the offered snack, then took a bite. Her taste buds watered. "Mmm. This is good."

"So you concede?"

She grabbed a second one and shot him a grin. "You could say that."

Something clattered above the persistent roar on the boat. Natalie glanced at the guilty party, a squawking chicken that'd escaped from its cage and knocked over a row of pots. She was about to turn back to Chad when she saw them again. The same two men she'd noticed earlier. They stood a dozen yards away in the shadows of the river-boat's two-story wheelhouse, watching her and Chad.

Natalie licked her lips. "Tell me I'm just paranoid after all that's happened?"

"Paranoid about what?" Chad popped another bite of fried donut into his mouth as the boat shuddered beneath them.

"I think those men are following us."

He shrugged a shoulder. "Okay, you're being paranoid. While I'd assume the government and military use radios that work even when the cell phone towers are out, we're talking third-world here. They don't exactly have the resources of the CIA, so I'd think it's highly unlikely."

"I suppose." She wanted to think she was wrong. That fear had taken over her instincts, making two ordinary passengers into the enemy. But she shivered as one of the men flicked his cigarette into the water, his gaze never leaving her face. Something wasn't right.

She shot a glance behind her, and Joseph waved as he wove his way toward them across the deck. If the men had been told to look for two Americans, she and Chad stood out like snowcapped mountains in the middle of the Sahara. How hard would it be for whoever was behind this to turn them into wanted fugitives?

Chad gripped her elbow as she turned around and looked again at the soldiers. "What's wrong, Natalie?"

She jutted her chin at the two men just as the taller man pulled back his shirt, exposing the butt of a gun. She swallowed hard. Now she had Chad's attention.

There was no time to react as the men surrounded them and raised their weapons.

TWENTY-ONE

"Natalie?" The boat shuddered again, causing both Chad and Natalie to momentarily lose their balance. Natalie slammed into a wooden crate. And then Chad was pulling her behind a stack of barrels, widening the barrier between them and the thugs and the weapons they now held in plain sight.

Blood seeped from a nasty gash down her left arm.

"What happened?"

Natalie glanced at her shoulder. "I gouged it on a something, but I'm okay. We've got to get out of here."

Chad took her right hand and pulled her through the crowd. Dodging goats and chickens through the overcrowded vessel suddenly seemed trivial compared to the possibility of dodging bullets. Surely only a complete idiot would fire shots with hundreds of people milling around.

He groaned, knowing their options were few. And the two men were closing in behind them. He surveyed their surroundings. He hadn't noticed it before, but the boat had edged its way to the shore and was in the process of docking. This must be Dzakan, the one major village between Kasili and Bogama. Already a crowd waited to board the boat at the bottom of the ramp, while others stood poised to disembark. The sight of weapons had added a layer of confusion to the chaotic scene, but that and the surge of passengers could work to their advantage.

They'd just been given their one way out.

Chad shouted to Joseph, who was maneuvering though the thick wall of people ahead of them. If they could get off, they might have a chance to lose the thugs. Pushing their way around a 4x4 jeep being transported down the river, Chad tightened his grip on Natalie's hand. He glanced back as they pressed their way down the wooden ramp. One of the men was trapped somewhere in a sea of people, but the second had managed to jump the railing and now scurried down the edge of the ramp less than twenty feet behind them.

Chad quickened his pace, praying Natalie could keep up. He heard her labored breathing beside him as Joseph's head bobbed ahead of them. A busy marketplace spread out fifty feet from the shore. The boy had the right idea — the market would be the best place to hide. While not as big as either Kasili or Bogama, it was crowded with dozens of small wooden stalls and packed with people.

Chad and Natalie followed Joseph as the boy wound his way down narrow dirt paths deep into the heart of the market, past fish vendors, vegetable sellers, and piles of used car parts. The stench from the trash pit along the edge of the market filled his nostrils, but his only concern was for Natalie.

They finally stopped to catch their breath behind a merchant selling shoes, hopeful they'd lost their pursuers. Natalie let go of his hand and grasped her shoulder below the wound. Blood smeared down her arm and across her left hand.

He had her sit on a stump, then examined the wound. For now he needed to concentrate on stopping the bleeding. He'd clean it properly once they found somewhere safe to stop. He glanced at the six-inch ruffle at the bottom of her skirt. He was going to have to make do with what they had. "Do you mind? We've got to stop the bleeding."

She shook her head, and he bent down to rip off the piece along the seam.

Natalie eyed the backpack he'd set behind him. "Do you think those guys are after the photos?"

"That and a guarantee we don't leak anything before the election." He ripped the center of the strip with his teeth, then tore it into a thinner band, saving the other piece in his back pocket in case he needed it later. It should be enough to stop the bleeding. "They're not getting us or the photos."

Natalie flinched as he wrapped the wound. "But this isn't just about Stephen and Patrick anymore. If they can find us in the middle of nowhere so quickly, that means their communications are beyond normal civilian communication of this country."

Chad tied off the ends, not liking the obvious conclusion. "Which points to some kind of government involvement."

"And which also means we've got to find another way to the capital before they find us again."

Joseph stood hunched over, the palms of his hands resting against his thighs. "We could hire a small boat and try to outrun them."

Chad nodded. "That's a good option."

And from the looks of things at the moment, their only option.

The boat Joseph hired was nothing more than a hollowed-out log, barely three feet wide. With the imposing walls of the jungle on either side of the rapidly moving water, their two pilots paddled the pirogue in unison down the Congo. Gurgles and yowls echoed from the massive trees looming along the banks of the river. Chad glanced back. As far as he could tell, they hadn't been followed.

For the first time, he was able to focus his attention on Natalie. The bruise on her head had turned a bright blue, and the purple makeshift bandage on her arm was caked with dried blood. "How are you feeling?"

"Happy to be alive." She shot him a weak smile. "I'm sorry I dragged you into this. I had no idea—"

He pressed his finger against her lips. "If you remember correctly, I volunteered."

"Then you obviously didn't know what you were getting into."

"Neither of us did." He shrugged. "Look at it this way. We're all alive."

"True."

"And we have the photos."

She nodded.

"Then let's just count our blessings." He eyed the covered wound again. "Do you have a first-aid kit in your bag?"

She grabbed the bag from the floor of the boat, unzipped it, then pulled out a smaller, clear bag. Perfect. It contained latex gloves, disinfectant, bandages, and a few other miscellaneous supplies he could use.

Gingerly, he tugged off the bandage, then poured on some antiseptic. "We could almost set up our own roving clinic between this and the pirogue."

She winced at his touch. "Sorry, but I've had enough of boats for a long time."

"Does it hurt bad?"

"Burns like it's on fire."

He tossed her a packet of painkillers from the bag. "Why don't you take these as well? It will at least help to ease the pain."

She swallowed the pills with a swig of water and turned back to him. "What if Patrick has something to do with this. He's the only person I know of that has both the connections and the resources."

"From what you've said, I guess I thought of him as more of a nuisance than a viable threat." He put on a layer of antibiotic cream. "Of course, maybe I'm wrong. Someone obviously doesn't want us getting to the capital with these photos."

Natalie shook her head. "But even if he is involved, I can't see him trying to kidnap us."

Chad ripped off a piece of adhesive to secure the gauze in place. "People aren't always what they appear to be on the outside."

He looked up at the clouds. The sky roiled in the distance, darkening by the minute. Great. The last thing they needed now was to get caught in a storm. Boat accidents along the Congo were frequent, particularly when the vessels were overloaded with passengers on the swollen river.

He closed his eyes for a moment and listened to the rhythmic sounds of the water lapping against the side of the pirogue, thankful that for now, they were safe.

TWENTY-TWO

Nick loosened the cowling with a screwdriver, praying that he'd finally found the problem. If it was the fuel line, though, his life had just gotten a lot more complicated — as if that were even possible. He didn't have time to be stuck in the middle of the jungle with nowhere to go for parts and no radio access on the eve of a presidential election that, according to Chad and Natalie, had a good chance of ending in disaster.

He glanced back at the plane. Not that he couldn't fix the problem. Three years flying bush planes through the jungle had prepared him for just about anything, but clogged fuel lines always meant more complications, something he wasn't in the mood for. It had already taken one miracle to land the plane. It was going to take a second to get it out of here.

With the cowling off, he cut the safety wire and shot up a prayer as he checked to see if the fuel was still getting to the filter.

Bingo. He'd been right.

Forty-five minutes later the plane was good to go. He grabbed his logbook from the cockpit and scribbled a few notes in the margin for the mechanic back in Kasili. As he wrote, an envelope slid out from the back of the logbook and landed on the floor.

Nick picked up the letter, staring at the return address, then shoved the envelope back into the logbook. At twenty-one, his reaction had been to run away. Some days it seemed as if he was still running.

Still looking for a way to buy your redemption, Nicholas Gilbert?

Shoving away the thought, he jumped down from the cockpit, focusing instead on a swarm of luminous butterflies hovering over the tail of the plane. Beyond them the trees, in a stunning array of greens and browns, were covered with orchids and creeping vines. The jungle never ceased to amaze him.

He took a swig of the small water bottle Natalie had left him. It was here, among the familiar noises of the jungle, that he'd made his peace with God. For the most part. Amy's letter managed to dredge up those doubts and drag him back to a time he wasn't sure he was ready to revisit.

The roar of a vehicle yanked him from his thoughts. He certainly wasn't expecting company, and whoever it was probably meant more trouble than a blocked fuel line ever would be. He moved away from the plane.

He was right. A jeep pulled up with three men carrying rifles.

Nick frowned. Apparently there was one thing he wasn't prepared for: a vehicle full of government soldiers and automatic weapons.

Setting the water bottle on the tail flap, he decided to take the friendly approach, a diplomatic tactic that had saved him more than a time or two when dealing with the authorities. "Morning, fellows. Hope you're not looking for a ride, because I've been having a bit of engine trouble."

The three men, wearing military garb, jumped from the vehicle, quickly bridging the distance between them in long, booted strides.

The tallest took an extra step toward him. "Where are they?"

Nick held up his hand. "Now wait a minute, fellows. No hellos, or how are you—"

He was cut off with a sharp blow to the jaw. He hit the ground with a hard thud, air whooshing from his lungs. Okay. So they didn't appreciate his sense of humor.

Struggling to catch his breath, he rubbed his jaw and forced himself to stand back up. He hadn't survived four years as an Air Force pilot to be taken out by a bunch of bullies in some godforsaken jungle. And while three rifles might put him at a disadvantage, he wasn't ready to surrender.

"I'll ask you one more time: where are they?"

Nick folded his arms across his chest and tried to look confused. "I don't know what you're talking about."

"The two Americans traveling from Kasili to Bogama on a private plane that never made it to Bogama."

"I don't — "

The soldier hit him again. This time on the left temple. Stars exploded in his head, and he blinked his eyes and tried to refocus. He decided to play it straight. "I was with a couple who left from here for the capital a few hours ago, but I haven't heard from them since. My radio's down, and I don't have any way to contact them."

Nick ducked as the man swung the butt of his rifle. He felt the deafening crack against his temple ... then nothing.

TWENTY-THREE

Nick opened his eyes, then squeezed them shut again. The blaring sunlight shot a stabbing pain through his temple. His skull — his entire body, for that matter — felt as if it had been run over by a tank. He struggled to clear the fog that enveloped his head. His plane had gone down ... Crashed ... No ... A mechanical problem. The fuel filter was clogged. He'd fixed the plane. Three men with weapons showed up —

"Mr. Gilbert?"

Nick jerked his head up at the sound of his name, wincing at the sudden movement. His head pounded. He reached up to find the source of the pain and found a rising lump on his forehead.

A familiar face hovered over him. Brown skin, yellow T-shirt, tan shorts. Bell ... Mel? Mbella. That was his name. One of Joseph's friends who had helped him this morning before Chad and Natalie headed for the river.

"Are you all right, Mr. Gilbert?"

"I don't know."

Nick looked around from where he sat on the ground, his vision still blurry. He rubbed his eyes, then tried to assess any other physical damage the soldiers had done. His limbs tingled, and his head and jaw were killing him, but he'd live. At least he hoped so.

An ant crawled up his pant leg and he swatted at it, knocking it onto the dusty red earth. Above him, vines twisted around a tree until the trunk disappeared into the thick vegetation. The three rough-necks must have dragged him away from the plane after knocking him out. He glanced at his watch. He didn't think he'd been out for more than a couple minutes, but if the lump on his forehead was any indication of the force they'd used, he'd be lucky if he didn't have a concussion.

His stomach roiled as he glanced at the plane. At least it was still there, but if they'd done any damage he was sunk. No tools, no radio, few resources ... Walking to the capital on foot was an additional nightmare he hoped to avoid.

Mbella squatted in front of him. "Don't worry. They're gone now."

Nick tried to swallow, but his mouth was too dry. Where had he put his water bottle? He managed to stand. "Did you see the soldiers who attacked me?"

"Yes, sir." Mbella shrugged. "I heard them talking. There is a reward for your friends."

"A reward?" Nick stopped at the open door of the plane and spun around. Surely the boy had heard wrong.

"Everyone will be looking for your friends. The army, police, maybe even the taxi drivers in the city."

Great. If what Mbella said was true, he was stuck in the middle of the jungle with no way to warn Chad and Natalie. He turned back toward the plane. This news didn't put any of them in a good situation. And it proved Chad's theory that something big was about to happen. Why else would someone care about a handful of photos taken in the middle of nowhere?

A wave of dizziness passed over him. "How long was I out?"

"Five, ten minutes, maybe." Mbella's gaze lowered. "I would offer to take you back to my village, except ..."

Nick frowned at the pause. There was fear in the boy's eyes.

"What happened, Mbella?"

"Other men, not with the army, they ... they came to our village looking for you too," he finally continued.

Other men ... Ghost Soldiers?

Nick grabbed his water bottle and took a swig, not sure he wanted to hear what was coming next. "And ..."

The boy pressed his lips together. "They burned down three of our huts and beat my father."

"So this has become personal." Nick wiped his mouth with the back of his hand.

Mbella just shrugged. "Will the plane still fly?"

"I hope so."

Nick glanced around him. The rebels had far less scruples than any government soldier and wouldn't hesitate to kill him. And this was the kind of jungle where it wouldn't be hard to disappear and never be found.

The distant rumbling of an engine reached them. Mbella scrambled toward the plane. "They're coming. We've got to go."

Nick shook his head. Before he could take off, there were things he had to check. Procedures to follow. He glanced down the narrow strip he'd planned to use as a runway. While the airplane didn't require a long runway, taking off still wouldn't be easy. One mistake and he'd end up clipping a tree and bringing the plane down.

And there were other issues to consider. He'd changed the fuel filter, but there were no guarantees that the plane was ready to fly. No way to check weather patterns or ensure there were no other mechanical issues —

Mbella tugged at his sleeve. "Come on, Mr. Gilbert. If the men who were at our village find you, they will do more than hit you on the head with their guns. You've got to hurry."

The boy was right. Money was always a huge motivator. Forcing himself to ignore his pounding temple, Nick made sure the path in front of the plane was clear before climbing into the cockpit and throwing on his seat belt. He pressed on the brake pedals to check the pressure and made sure all the electrical switches were off. So far, so good.

"I can see them, Mr. Gilbert. They're coming!"

"I want you to run home."

"No — "

"Now!"

Nick drew in a sharp breath as Mbella tore off into the jungle. He forced himself not to turn around and watch the boy. He'd be fine. It was him they were after.

Taking off without letting things warm up to operating temperature might not be good for the engine, but at the moment, that was the least of his worries. He turned the battery switch on. The fans began to whirl. Pumping the throttle, he turned the key and listened to the propeller start to turn.

He glanced back. They couldn't be much more than fifty meters behind him.

I need a miracle, God . . .

The plane shook beneath him as Nick eased the plane forward. The interior panels rattled, blocking out the sound of the pursuing jeep. Nick pushed the throttle further. A bullet pinged off the side of the plane.

Twenty more seconds. That's all he needed.

Another bullet skimmed the side of the plane. If any damage had been done, it was too late now.

Ten seconds.

Nick eased up on the throttle. Trees whizzed by. The jungle closed in around him.

He was out of runway.

TWENTY-FOUR

Stephen slammed down the phone. The line was dead. He glanced at the clock on his computer screen and tried to shake the uneasy feeling that wouldn't leave him. It was after eleven, and Natalie hadn't shown up for work. Combing his fingers through his hair, he tried to make sense of the photos she'd brought him. Tried to find another explanation for what had happened.

He rubbed the beads of moisture from his forehead with his handkerchief and eyed the stalled ceiling fan. No power meant no fans to relieve the heat. He might have lived beneath the Dhambizao sun for over four decades, but today was blistering hot.

He undid the top button of his shirt and walked to the open window to catch the breeze. The uncut grass along the edge of the property stood motionless in the heat. The only thing moving was the uniformed security guard walking along the inside of the front gate.

He pushed open the window farther and waited for a stray breeze to find him. Power outages, limited supplies, and the lack of progress, as the West called it, had always been a part of his life, rarely questioned along with the corruption, disease, and death that surrounded him.

Rarely questioned, perhaps, but ever present. And with it, the underlying current of frustration and restlessness. The photos reminded him of that. Natalie's claims that the photos were tied to a slave trade and rumors of a rigged election was something he didn't want to believe. Among the dozens of candidates, Bernard Okella was the only real contender running against President Tau. The fifty-five-year-old from a rival tribe had risen through the ranks and managed to find a few friends in parliament — supporters who dared to openly oppose President Tau. No one expected Okella to win, but Stephen was afraid of what might happen if he did. He wanted to believe the UN's promises of a fair election, but even President Tau's additional assurances that this time things would be different rang hollow.

Stephen moved to sit back down at his desk, still trying to erase the lingering horror of that fatal election seventeen years ago. That day, like today, had been stiflingly hot. Shops lining the streets had closed and been cleared of pedestrians by the police. The only vehicles out were driven by military officials ensuring people stayed in their houses. No formal meetings were allowed. No schools attended. No power ...

No power.

His fingernails bit into the palm of his hand. The former president had given orders to cut the power in the city as added insurance people couldn't communicate with each other or the outside world. He wanted complete control over the situation to guarantee his reign of supremacy continued.

Stephen shook his head. Today was different. The power outage had nothing to do with the election. It was simply a technical issue. The power plants were too old and weren't able to keep up with the demand. The same problem that had plagued the city for years.

But if the power outage was connected through the elections ... If there was a plan to rig the election to gain power over the country's resources, including hundreds of slaves ...

He fished his car keys from the top drawer of his desk, then stepped outside and into his one luxury. Most Dhambizans didn't even dream about one day owning a car. The odds were simply too remote. Unfortunately, he feared it wasn't nearly as remote anymore as the odds of the wrong person gaining the presidency. Maybe there was one thing he could do to dismiss the connection of the lack of power and the upcoming election.

He drove to the power station, hurried inside the one-story building, then flashed his government badge at the receptionist, demanding to see Mr. Diagne. Amadzi Diagne had been in his graduating class at the University of Bogama. They'd lost track of each other until they both found jobs in Kasili. Since then, they'd met for drinks every few months, rehashing their naïve days when they'd foolishly thought they could save the world — or at least their small part of it.

The receptionist told him to take a seat and went back to drinking her morning tea. He complied and sat down on a cracked leather chair beside a man who was either looking for a job or a handout. More than likely, he'd get neither.

Thirty minutes later, a second woman wearing a navy-blue uniform led Stephen down a long hall with chipped blue walls.

"Stephen." Amadzi stood as Stephen entered the office, reached out to shake his hand. "It's been too long. I think I owe you a drink."

"It has been a long time." Stephen shook his friend's hand, then took the offered chair across the desk, wondering where the past twenty years had gone since they'd graduated together. Wondering even more so how many of those years he'd wasted. "Dema seems to be treating you well."

Amadzi patted his round stomach. "My wife complains that I work too many hours, but she still feeds me well so I can't complain."

Stephen laughed. "And your children?"

"They are fine. Neema graduates from university this year."

This time Stephen's smile was forced as he remembered what he was missing with his own two girls. "You must be proud."

"I am. And what about your wife? I haven't seen Anna in two, maybe three, years."

Stephen squirmed in his chair, hoping Amadzi didn't sense his sadness. One day he'd learn to hide his grief. "She is well. She's visiting her mother in Bogama with the twins." He'd never admit she'd been there for the past seven months, or that she had no plans to return to their sparsely furnished apartment he'd bought for her five years ago. There were certain aspects of his life he had no intention of sharing with anyone.

Stephen glanced around Amadzi's office, trying to find some value in his own career. He couldn't. Unlike the walls in the hallway, this room had been recently painted and lined with a half dozen file cabinets. Several calendars hung on the wall alongside diplomas and framed photos of family. The newness, though, stopped there. An archaic computer sat on the desk.

Bernard Okella promised to change technology throughout the country with upgrades in electricity and phone lines if elected president. Stephen didn't trust a word. Ten years from now they'd still be using out-of-date equipment and struggling to feed their children. That was the spoiled pot of goza they'd been handed.

"I heard they promoted you." Stephen swallowed any signs of jealousy. Stroke the giver and he just might receive the information he wanted.

Amadzi held up his hand and shrugged. "They pay me half of what I'm worth, but even that bought me a second home outside Bogama."

"At least they have a good man in line to revamp our decrepit power system."

"Trying to flatter or insult me, Stephen? Why don't you just admit yours is a dead-end job?"

Stephen flinched. When he was half drunk the comment would have rolled off. Today it felt like a poisoned arrow to his heart, but he couldn't afford to return the insult.

"What I want is the truth," he said instead. "The election is in two days and the city's without power. A plot by President Tau or perhaps Bernard Okella, who wants to make a point to the voters of how rundown our city is?"

"This has nothing to do with the election." Amadzi's gaze flickered, his lips pressed tightly together. "There was a fire."

Stephen read his eyes. "I don't believe you. I need to know the truth. You remember as well as I do what happened seventeen years ago. Thousands were butchered in the streets and even more left homeless — "

"You've never been one to push for answers, Stephen." Amadzi stood and rested his hands against the top of his desk. "I wouldn't start now if I were you."

"Why not?" Stephen stayed seated. He wasn't ready to walk out. Not yet.

"Like I said, there was a fire. One of the conduits overheated and will have to be replaced. I've been told that part of what is needed for the repairs won't arrive until Saturday. Until then ... well, I'm afraid we will all have to wait."

Stephen glanced out the open window that overlooked the power plant. A repair truck sat vacant. No workers. No sign that anything was being done to resolve the issue. A sick feeling knotted his stomach. With the phones down and the power out, they were like a zebra surrounded by a pride of lions: helpless.

No. Stephen tugged on the collar of his shirt. Amadzi had given him a reasonable explanation. He should just walk away and accept the answer as truth. What did it matter? Nothing he could say or do would make a difference.

Amadzi smiled as if they'd been chatting about the next World Cup. "Let's go out for drinks next Friday night. The election will be over and life will go back to being normal again."

It was a dismissal. Stephen shook his old friend's hand, said his good-byes. Amadzi was right. Why start asking questions now?

Stephen walked down the sidewalk toward his car, jingling his keys in one hand. Patrick was there, leaning against the hood of Stephen's car.

Stephen stopped a few meters away. "What are you doing here, Patrick?"

"I could ask you the same question." Patrick slid a pair of sunglasses from his front pocket and put them on. "Let's just say that Amadzi owed me a favor."

Stephen decided to ignore the clear implication that Patrick was having him shadowed. For now, anyway. "The power's out. Phones are out. I thought — "

"You thought what? That you could sweep in and save the day. You're simply a liaison for the government aid programs, Stephen." Patrick folded his arms across his chest. "There was a fire."

"That's what I was told."

"And you don't believe it?"

"With the elections in two days, I'm not sure what I believe."

"That's your problem, Stephen. You're like the president, running with both sides so you can please everyone. Eventually, you're going to have to make a choice."

Stephen tried to ignore the hidden insult. "Natalie is missing."

If he'd hoped for a reaction, he didn't get one. "She took a plane to Bogama yesterday afternoon with one of the doctors from here and the boy who took those photos."

"How do you know?"

"It's my job to know these things." Patrick took a step closer to him. "Remember the proverb: 'If you try and run after two warthogs, you'll never catch either of them.'"

Stephen's jaw tensed. "Meaning?"

"It's time you decide which side you're on."

TWENTY-FIVE

Nick lined up the nose of the airplane with the narrow runway on the outskirts of Bogama, then let out an audible sigh of relief as the plane touched down onto the tarmac. His unexpected trip to the capital had taken him almost eighteen hours since leaving Kasili *and* had left his plane looking like a wedge of Swiss cheese. He knew his boss wasn't going to be happy, but at least he'd made it here alive. Now he just needed to pray that Chad and Natalie had made it as well.

He wiped off the beads of sweat on his neck. If they'd found a boat quickly and hadn't run into any problems, there was a good chance they were already sitting in the air-conditioned lobby of the embassy. Which wasn't a bad place to be at the moment.

If nothing else, his recent brush with death had convinced him of two things. One, he was going to take out a bigger life-insurance policy. Second, he was going to call home as soon as he could find a comfortable bed for the night and a decent phone connection.

He parked the plane, finished up the final landing checklist, then climbed down onto the steamy tarmac. Strange. The entire airport seemed to have been taken over by the military. Instead of the typical workers scattered across the runway in their bright orange jackets, uniformed military personal, tanks, and jeeps were everywhere.

Two soldiers in full uniform hollered at him as he moved to assess the damage from the bullets that riddled the belly of the plane. The men approached the plane, stopping a couple of yards in front of him. Nick rubbed his jaw, which was still sore from his last encounter with the military. He wasn't looking forward to another unscheduled meeting.

Nick forced a smile. "I wasn't expecting a welcome party, gentlemen."

"Captain Gilbert?"

"Yes."

"We're looking for two Americans we believe were on this flight."

Nick pulled a piece of gum from his pocket, took off the wrapper, and shoved the cinnamon stick into his mouth. What was it with these military-type guys? Apparently none of them were up for chit-chat. "Which two Americans are you looking for?"

The tallest eyed the interior of the plane. "According to the flight plan, Chad Talcott and Natalie Sinclair were due late yesterday afternoon. Where are they now?"

Nick hesitated, unsure if it was even possible to get around the request. With one man holding a machine gun in his hands and the other with his fingers resting on the trigger of his holstered handgun, it wasn't likely. "As you can see, I didn't have any passengers on this flight. I'm here to pick up some relief workers from Australia later."

From their grim expressions, neither seemed impressed with his answer. "Where are Talcott and Sinclair?"

"I had to make an emergency landing in the jungle last night. Ended up being a blockage in the filter." Nick thrust his logbook, with all his notes, into the man's hands. "It's all right there. We spent the night at a nearby village."

"That still doesn't answer my question. Where are your passengers?"

Nick bit his tongue to stop himself from saying something he'd regret. "As I already told your pals who paid me a visit in the jungle, they needed to get to the capital in a hurry. And since I wasn't sure how long it was going to take me to get the plane ready to fly, they decided to take a boat."

"So they left on their own?"

"Yes."

"How many hours ago?"

A knot formed in Nick's stomach as he glanced at his watch. "About four, I guess."

"And do you know where they are now?"

"No, I don't." Nick frowned at a second pair of uniformed men approaching. "What's with all the extra security?"

The man handed him back the logbook. "The army has mobilized for the upcoming election."

Mobilized? They'd all but taken over.

"We need to search the plane."

Nick waved at the open door. "Then it's all yours, boys."

They hesitated for a moment. He knew the way things worked here. They wanted him to be the one who sorted through the luggage holds, seat pockets, storage areas. Well, tough. He had nothing to hide. He'd be respectful, but they could do their own dirty work.

Ten minutes later, they exited the plane. Nick folded his arms across his chest, irritated. Time was passing. If something had happened, and Chad and Natalie were still out there on the river somewhere, he couldn't even call to let them know to be careful.

"Did you find what you were looking for?" Not that he knew for sure what they'd hoped to find. It wasn't as if he could have stashed two Americans beneath the floorboards.

"We're going to need you to come with us."

The knot in Nick's stomach tightened. "I'm not sure that's possible — "

"Oh, it's very possible. A reward has been issued to bring them in, and you're going to help us."

TWENTY-SIX

Chad looked at his watch, surprised at how much time had passed. While Joseph dozed behind them in the afternoon sun, he had tried not to stare at Natalie as she answered his questions about her life in Africa and shared snippets about nights preparing dinner by candlelight and listening to the BBC over a shortwave radio.

Water lapped against the sides of the boat, rocking it gently. The sky had cleared, alleviating any chances of a storm. The last thing he'd expected during his six-month stint in the RD — besides his current position of floating down the Congo River — was meeting someone who made him want to stick around and find out more about her.

Chad cocked his head and caught her gaze. "How are you feeling?"

"Okay." She laughed.

"What's so funny?"

"I've never had a day quite so ... I don't know." Natalie took off her sandals and stretched out her toes. "*Scary* doesn't seem quite strong enough an adjective."

"*Terrifying*?"

"You're getting closer."

"At least you're smiling." Now it was his turn to chuckle. "Plus, we're alive, and we have the photos."

"So far, though I'm beginning to wonder if we'll ever make it to the capital at this pace." She looked up at him again. "What if we were wrong, Chad? What if the incident on the boat was some isolated attack that doesn't have anything to do with the photos? You know the statistics as well as I do. Terrorist attacks against foreigners are rising. There are dozens of unidentified militants and rebels on the loose, magnified even greater by the upcoming election."

Part of him longed to believe her theory that they had simply blown the entire situation out of proportion. She was searching for the same alternate answers he was. Trying to find that one inkling of truth in a situation that didn't make sense. One excuse to abandon the precarious quest they'd begun was all he needed.

"I suppose there is that off chance that all this is nothing more than a coincidence. A couple of misdirected thugs who happen to have a deep-seated vendetta against foreigners."

He wanted to accept her reasoning, but from the look on her face, they both knew it wasn't true. Someone was determined to make sure no one else saw those photos.

"I knew there were risks to living here, but I guess I thought I was immune." She pulled her legs up against her chest, facing him. "These past couple days have changed everything. It didn't even matter that I'm here to try to help."

He read the fear and vulnerability in her expression. It hadn't taken much to shatter any remaining traces of safety. "It's easy to think that because we're trying to do this noble act for mankind, we have some sort of shield surrounding us."

"Which means there is no assurance that something like that won't happen again." She pressed her lips together and blinked back tears.

"Chances are it won't."

"Maybe not, but what about Joseph's family? When is someone going to put a stop to their horror?" This time she didn't try to stop the flow of tears from streaming down her face as her voice continued to rise. "After hundreds of more villagers are ripped from their homes, their women raped, children left starving, and their dead rotting beneath the African sun? Or maybe when another civil war erupts and thousands are butchered in the bloody coup? Do you think the rest of the world will take notice then?"

"I don't know, Natalie."

She wiped her cheeks with the backs of her hands and stared out across the churning river. A crocodile splashed into the water, its head bobbing along the surface as it swam away from them. "I don't know either." She followed the crocodile's trail through the water, then turned back to Chad. "We talked yesterday about coming here to make a difference, but I'm starting to wonder if I can do this anymore. It's like when you hear about some horrid tragedy and you can't fully grasp the reality of what has happened. This time, though, I saw the results with my own eyes, and I still can't comprehend what happened."

"I'm struggling with the same questions."

She glanced up at him and caught his gaze. "Then tell me, where is God now?"

Chad struggled for answers — answers to the very same questions he was grappling with. "All I know is that man's greed and wickedness can't diminish God's goodness or His plan for us. His death ransomed us along with every tribe and people group. That's the reality I have to hold on to right now."

She grabbed a handful of tissues from her bag and blew her nose. "I know my faith falls short in all of this, but then I think about how one of us — or maybe all three of us — might not make it out of here alive. Joseph's family is suffering right now; his father might be dead ..."

"It's not a lack of faith, Natalie. And it's okay to be scared."

"So what do we do now?"

"Try and find some answers." He knew from experience that action was one of the best strategies against fear. And at the moment, besides some fervent praying, it was the only answer he had.

"How?"

"Tell me about Patrick."

Natalie wadded her tissues in her hand and took in a deep breath. "I think I told you that he used to be the former head of security to the president. He now leads a specialized task force that is apparently involved in investigating rumors of the Ghost Soldiers."

"Could he be involved with the opposition?"

Her eyes widened. "I suppose. If Okella or someone in his party were willing to pay more, I'd say Patrick could be a willing candidate."

"What about his fiancée?"

"Rachel and I used to work together in Kasili, where we became good friends. About six months ago, Patrick helped her get a job with the minister of health in the capital, which is why I want to talk to her first. She has access to information, including a compilation of demographic research for the country that might help us narrow down where Joseph's family is."

"And you trust her not to tell Patrick?"

"I think any information she might have is worth any risk."

Chad paused, wondering if they were even on the right track. Without telephone access, finding out who was behind this wasn't going to be easy. "Okay, what about Stephen?"

"For starters, he's not nearly as compulsive as Patrick. He's organized, educated, of course, and seems to be well respected in the community."

"What about his weaknesses?"

"Weaknesses." Natalie shook her head. "It's hard to say. Stephen tends to try to pacify everyone. Even with the photos, he acted as if he didn't want to get involved."

Chad clasped his hands together, mulling over her answers. "I don't know. Maybe that figures in somehow. Let's look at another angle, then, not related to the election. Have you ever noticed any irregularities in the books, or skimming of funds?"

"Stephen runs a very tight ship and has always struck me as

honest, though indecisive." She shrugged, wincing at the movement. "I'm sorry I don't have more answers."

He eyed her dressed wound. "Has the pain eased any?"

"For the most part, and I think the bleeding's stopped."

He leaned forward to push back a strand of her hair that had fallen out of its clip. "You're getting a sunburn."

Her smile, reflecting across her brown eyes, caused his heart to lurch. She was close enough that he could see the dark color that encircled her irises. He brushed his thumb across a sprinkling of freckles on her cheek and wiped away a stray tear. He wasn't sure exactly when he'd first realized it, but Natalie was exactly the kind of woman he'd spent his life looking for. And all he could manage to think about at the moment was how badly he wanted to kiss her.

"Natalie, I …" He stopped midsentence and leaned back. What was he supposed to tell her? That he wanted to kiss her? That he'd like to be sitting together with her at his favorite restaurant back in Portland right now discussing their dreams for the future and not racing toward the capital on some sort of James Bond-like mission?

"You okay?" she asked.

He dropped his gaze to the frothy water lapping against the side of the pirogue and nodded. Maybe when all of this was over …

He looked up at her again, wishing she wasn't quite so beautiful and her lips not quite so kissable. "Do you happen to have any sunscreen in that bag of yours?"

"I think so." Her brow lowered. "I should have thought about it hours ago."

She dug around for a minute, then pulled out a small tube. Before he could stop her, she'd dabbed some on his nose.

"Hey!" He caught her wrist and laughed.

"I'm not the only one turning into a lobster." She continued spreading it across his nose and cheeks while he tried to keep his thoughts in line. "Now could you get the back of my neck?"

He complied and spread the sunscreen across her neck and shoulders. Sometimes life could be so unfair.

She dug in her bag again and pulled out a package of licorice.

"Hey, forget the sunscreen." He snatched the candy from her hand and held it up above his head.

"Now you wait just a minute. I told you I have a sweet tooth."

He quirked a brow. "And I thought your stash was for emergencies only?"

She shot him an exasperated look. "This is an emergency. And any woman who's been chased then left to fend for her life on a perilous escape down the Congo River at the very least deserves a gallon or two of double-fudge ice cream."

"Possibly."

She grasped for the candy and missed. "Unfortunately, in this situation, one small package of licorice will have to do."

"Touché." He tossed the candy her direction, but he wasn't through yet. "Will half a package do?"

She glanced behind her at Joseph, who was still sleeping, then ripped open the package. "How about a third?"

Chad took his share with a grin before gazing across the churning waters of the river. The thick tangle of jungle had faded into green, rolling hills as they approached the chaotic harbor now framing the bottom of the capital's skyline. In the distance, blocks of apartment buildings rose alongside governmental buildings and a couple of hotels built for the occasional tourists and businessmen.

Ahead of them, a ferry lowered its plank along the shore, allowing laborers to drop heavy bags of rice onto the dock below. Hordes of passengers charged up the loading dock past several wheelchair-bound polio victims struggling to make a living selling goods along the river.

Chad turned away from the confusion and looked further abroad. All they needed now was a taxi into the city . . . and a miracle.

TWENTY-SEVEN

Natalie grasped the edge of the seat with her fingertips as the taxi driver raced down the two-lane dirt road heading away from the harbor, making her wonder if it had been worth waiting over an hour for the ride. Not like they had any options. The city's taxis were the only transportation available between the harbor and the capital.

The driver swerved to avoid a herd of cows on the edge of the road. Natalie's shoulder smashed against the window, shooting pain down her arm. Obviously, the brand-new cabs with their new coat of paint and drivers wearing ties and name badges didn't guarantee safe passage. She glanced out at the shoreline, now tinged orange from the setting sun. The silhouettes of a dozen pirogues skimmed across the golden waters alongside an overcrowded barge.

The view vanished behind the crest of a hill, leaving instead the dozens of sprawling slum rows before them. Women wearing tattered dresses and carrying loads of wood on their heads lined the edge of the dusty road. Half of them had infants tied to their back. For the thousands of Dhambizans living here, none of the makeshift shacks had running water or electricity. Sanitation facilities were inadequate, and access to health care was virtually unobtainable. The goal for living here simply meant survival.

She tried turning on her cell to call Stephen, then groaned at the dead battery. Great. Finding a taxi at the busy harbor might have been difficult, but communication had become a nightmare. She dropped the phone back into her bag. Maybe it was a good thing she couldn't reach him after all. If Stephen was involved, it was better he didn't know where she was. Her gut feeling, though, told her he had nothing to do with the shooting on the barge. Or, for that matter, the Ghost Soldiers.

Chad snapped his phone shut, yanking her away from her thoughts.

"No luck?" she asked.

He shoved his cell into his pocket and shrugged. "Dead battery."

"Me too. What about the driver's phone?" Natalie asked.

"All my numbers are on my phone."

Natalie groaned again at the realization. So were hers. And there was no calling information in Bogama.

Joseph tapped Innocent, their driver, on the shoulder and spoke a few words. Innocent pulled over, flipped on the overhead light, then picked up his cell phone as Joseph climbed out to use the restroom.

Natalie lay her head back against the headrest and closed her eyes to block out light from the bare bulb overhead. The chatter of the driver intensified her pounding head. All she wanted was a decent place to sleep for the next eight hours. Bogama boasted a couple of adequate hotels, but she'd prefer a mat on Rachel's apartment floor. Not only was staying with someone she knew more appealing than a hotel room, but if Rachel could give them answers, they'd be that much closer to locating Joseph's family.

The chattering in the front seat increased. Chad squeezed her hand.

"Ouch." She pulled her hand away and opened her eyes. "What's wrong?"

He shook his head, motioning for her to be quiet. "We've got a problem. Do you have a piece of paper?"

Natalie grabbed the backpack off the floor and rummaged through the front pocket where she remembered putting a pad of sticky notes and a couple of pens. She found both at the bottom. At least no one could accuse her of being unprepared.

Chad grabbed the pen from her and started scribbling on the paper. *Driver arguing over price of reward for two Americans. Taking us to a military compound.*

Natalie's mouth went dry. She blinked her eyes and looked up at him. "You're kidding —"

Chad held his finger to his mouth. She clenched her jaw shut as slivers of panic sliced through her. She had to relax. Panicking wouldn't help. She glanced out the open door. They could run now, but then what? They were still miles from the city. They needed a vehicle to get to safety. But where in the world could they get one?

Joseph slid back into the car, slamming the door shut behind him. Innocent flipped the light off, gunned the accelerator, and merged into the light traffic.

Natalie tried to think. She'd been certain that she'd exaggerated any ideas of a conspiracy theory. Apparently that assumption was wrong. And radioing the police, military, and taxi drivers to be on the lookout for two Americans would be fairly simple in a city where less than one percent of the population was foreigners.

Chad brushed against her arm. "How much time will it take to get there?"

The only military base she knew of lay in the northern outskirts of the city. "Fifteen minutes. Twenty, tops."

Chad leaned over and whispered to Joseph, who hesitated, then tapped the driver's shoulder again. This time the man was obviously irritated. He shouted something in Dha, but pulled over. Joseph scurried halfway up the short embankment that ran along the side of the road.

Moving quickly, Chad pressed against the front seat, then wrapped his right arm around the driver's neck. Innocent flung his arms toward Chad's face, hollered, then stopped in mid-sentence. His cell phone clattered against the console. Three seconds later, he slumped against the back of the seat.

"Chad!" Natalie sucked in a breath.

Chad released pressure, but kept his arm around the man's neck. "I promise you, this is the safest way to take someone out if it's done right, and considering our circumstances, I think we're pretty much out of options."

Her mind spun with the implications of what he'd just done. They already had the entire RD army after them. Now if he'd killed the man ...

"And you know how to do it safely?"

"It's a martial-arts move." Chad rushed around to the driver's door and swung it open.

Natalie leaned across the seat to check the driver's pulse. At least he was still alive. "You told me you dabbled in martial arts."

"I guess I forgot to mention that I have a black belt in karate." Chad undid the man's seat belt.

"You said 'dabbled.' I dabble with painting and playing the piano in my spare time, and you ... you just knocked a man out."

She needed to stop babbling, but all she could see at the moment was an unconscious man. She swallowed hard. "How much time till he wakes up?"

"Anywhere from a few seconds to a couple minutes. There's no way to know, but we've got to get him out of here." Chad hollered at Joseph to help him.

Natalie jumped out of the cab. "We can't just leave him — "

"He'll be fine, Natalie." They dragged him from the front seat and laid him on the side of the road. "This road has people walking on it all night. Someone will find him."

She glanced at the shadowy image of the unconscious man, then squeezed her eyes shut.

Chad slid into the driver's seat. "Can you get us to Rachel's with the address you have?"

"In the taxi?"

"Have you got a better idea?"

She shook her head. We can call her on a public phone to get directions. The photo of Joseph's sister emerged in her mind. It was enough to make her scramble around the car into the passenger seat. Joseph jumped into the back.

Chad slammed his foot against the accelerator. "Then let's get out of here."

TWENTY-EIGHT

Chad breathed in the smell of exhaust and grilled meat through the open window of the taxi. A car sped past them, its headlights briefly illuminating the cab. His stomach soured as he drove down one of the main streets of the capital. A pair of soldiers patrolling the streets walked in front of a colorful barbershop sign, their guns held high across their shoulders. He sucked in a lungful of air, then glanced briefly in the rearview mirror as they drove past a row of shops made from wood slats and sheets of tin. The soldiers seemed unaware that two Americans had just driven by in a stolen taxi.

He blew out a sharp breath of relief. Perhaps in the darkness that now settled over the city their chances were better. Tomorrow the street corners would be filled with the noisy clamor of vendors and pedestrians. Staying undetected would be impossible.

Natalie turned on the radio, scanning for stations until she found one broadcasting the news. Tonight's report was no different from most nights. Political, educational, health, and tribal issues ruled the headlines, with the added assurances of a peaceful election on Friday despite some random outbursts of violence in the city. And there was, to quote the president, nothing to fear.

Nothing to fear.

Chad frowned. If that were true, then why had the RD army been sent after him and the photos? If nothing else, today's events proved that Joseph's photos threatened someone's rise to power. But whose?

A broken streetlight dangled above a group of street children huddled on the sidewalk. Their haunted expressions reminded him how fragile life was. Earning a few cents every day by sweeping stalls in the market, shining shoes, or selling fruit on street corners gave them barely enough to survive on. Going a day without food wasn't uncommon. Education was a luxury not even dreamed about by most. Joseph had been one of the lucky ones.

He turned and looked at the young man. "Where does your uncle live, Joseph? It's too dangerous for you to be traveling with us."

Joseph shook his head. "I must find my family... How can I do that at my uncle's house."

Chad stopped at a signal light, then glanced at Joseph in the rear-view mirror. "If you're not with us you'll be safer. And we promise to do everything we can to find your family."

Joseph's jaw clenched. "I know this city ... the streets ... the people ... and the language. You need me."

Natalie's frown deepened. "Maybe that's true, but if anything happened to you, I could never forgive myself — "

"Don't worry." Joseph shook his head. "This is my choice."

Chad caught the reflection of a pair of lanterns alongside the road ahead and let out a low whistle. "Maybe not. There's a police roadblock ahead, which means that none of us may have a choice as to where we're going tonight." He eased off the accelerator. "We've got less than thirty seconds to decide whether or not we storm through the roadblock."

"You've got to be kidding." Natalie flipped shut the map she'd been looking at. "We can't just drive through."

"If we stop, they'll arrest us," Chad countered. "And I don't know about you, but I've heard the RD prisons don't exactly compare to Holiday Inn."

Natalie shook her head. "In other words, doomed if we do, doomed if we don't."

"Wait." Joseph leaned forward and rested his arms on the back of the front seat. "Slow down, then at the last minute, speed up."

"And break through their barrier?" Natalie asked.

Joseph nodded.

"You sound like you've done this before," Chad said.

"They won't expect it, and because they are on foot, they won't come after us." He pointed up ahead to the left. "There is a road ahead where you can turn."

"Everyone get down." Chad gripped the steering wheel. "And start praying."

Chad continued slowing as if he were preparing to stop. One of the guards searched the back of another taxi. A second one waved them down. Two large barrels were the only things blocking the road. Chad waited until the last minute, then jammed on the gas. A sick feeling washed over him as the taxi clipped the edge of one of the barrels. The front of the car shimmied as gunfire erupted behind them.

TWENTY-NINE

Gabby stepped off the Boeing 767 onto the people mover and felt a cold gush of air fill her lungs. The pungent smell of diesel fuel mingled with the musty scent of travelers who'd flown from Paris to DC the past eight hours with little more space than a sardine can. Readjusting the strap of her backpack, she grabbed onto the nearest metal pole while trying to fight the fatigue.

She took a swig of water from her plastic bottle and forced it down as the mobile lounge crossed the tarmac toward the terminal. All she needed now was enough oomph to make it through Immigration and Customs. She turned her mind to plans she had to make for her upcoming trip to Aspen with her family over Christmas. A far cry from the blistering heat and mining camps she'd just spent the past couple of weeks investigating. And the horrors of her last night in the RD.

A man wearing a green baseball cap with a red dragon glanced back through the crowded people mover and caught her gaze. European, mid-forties, balding ... and vaguely familiar. Her stomach roiled, but she shoved aside the wave of panic Tuesday night's attack had spawned. She'd found out that their driver had survived the attack, but they'd all been lucky.

The man stared out the window. More than likely he was simply another businessman who made his living traveling seventy-five percent of the year to make money for a family he rarely saw.

She'd known the risks of her investigation when she'd agreed to the assignment, and that just because she was on American soil again didn't guarantee she was safe. She tightened her grip as the mobile lounge docked at the terminal, believing the risk had been worth it. Once published, she hoped the information would explode across the front pages of dozens of newspapers around the world.

Forty-five minutes later, she breathed in a sigh of relief as she hurried toward the Arrival escalators in the main terminal, thankful she'd opted out of checking any bags — a choice that could easily have added another hour to her wait.

Sabrina, her best friend and roommate, stood at the front of the crowd wearing blue jeans and a Washington Redskins sweatshirt. "Hey! You made it back."

"Finally. It's good to see you." Gabby forced as smile, then looked past her friend, searching the sea of faces, not sure what she was looking for. "I had my doubts once or twice."

Someone collided into her, knocking her bag from her shoulders.

"Sorry about that." An older man nodded his apologies and walked away.

Gabby stiffened at the innocent assault.

Sabrina handed her the bag. "You look like you just saw a ghost."

Gabby automatically felt for her neck pouch with its wire-reinforced strap. Adam might have tried to assure her that Tuesday night's attack involved nothing more than being in the wrong place at the wrong time, but she wasn't willing to take any chances — even this far away from the Dark Continent.

"I'm fine, really." She followed Sabrina outside the main terminal. "Just tired. You know how grueling a couple of days on a plane is, then add someone who can't stop talking beside you."

"Yes, actually, I do. Remember that flight I took last year from Singapore. That woman talked all the way to LA nonstop."

A message came through on her cell phone. She sneezed, then clicked it open to check. She'd already checked them upon arrival, but if Adam had found Yasin, there was a chance she might still be able to add a quote before today's deadline.

Sabrina was still talking. "Michael took me to this fantastic little Indian restaurant while you were gone that you're going to love. If you're hungry, they make the most incredible spring rolls, and you wouldn't believe their ... Gabby?"

Gabby stopped at the edge of the curb. "I'm sorry, Sabrina ... I ..."

She replayed the message. Surely she hadn't heard it right: *"Last night wasn't a mistake."*

"Gabby?" Sabrina grabbed her arm as a car zipped around them. *"Last night wasn't a mistake."*

A chill swept through her. She took a deep breath, exhaling on the overwhelming odor of exhaust from a passing car, and shoved her phone back into her front pocket. She might have been targeted last night, but what about the hundreds who couldn't simply walk away from the terror like she could. How could she let a threat stop her from doing what she knew she had to do?

THIRTY

Camille's face haunted Stephen. Memories he'd buried years ago now refused to lie dormant. He dug through the bottom drawer of his desk until he finally found the worn photo. Seventeen years had passed. He'd since married, fathered two children, and made a new life for himself. And still he'd never forgotten. He knew his wife, Anna, would never understand the hold Camille held over him, and she would be right. He'd let ghosts from the past turn him into someone he hardly knew anymore, and in the process he'd lost both Anna and his girls.

Camille stared back at him from the picture, reminding him of how beautiful she'd been. He wasn't sure why he'd kept the snapshot. Perhaps as a reminder of what he'd lost — and of what he could never have.

He frowned. He knew what Camille would tell him right now if she was still alive. But while he'd always admired her zeal for life, she'd failed to understand one thing: sometimes standing up for what one believed in not only managed to hurt oneself, but also those one loved.

He'd escorted Camille home from work the day of the election, alongside houses with corrugated tin roofs and swept front yards. The roads were filled with potholes and bordered by dozens of kiosks where people sold everything from dried fish to shoelaces simply to make enough to eat one meal a day.

Bogama had become a city on the brink of war whose citizens were used to hiding behind high walls topped with razor wire. Despite the concentrated military presence, he'd never trust Camille's safety to the dozens guarding the streets. They patrolled in uniformed groups beside tanks and other signs of the upcoming election. Huge banners blew in the wind claiming victory by both sides. Stephen was afraid no one would win. Promises from their leaders were rarely fulfilled.

He'd tried to convince Camille to leave the chaos along with the thousands of others who had already fled the capital. Anyone who could was leaving. The current president had given them little choice. At eighty-four-years old, his health had deteriorated to the point where he could no longer make rational decisions, but even that hadn't loosened his tight grip on the country. Samuel Tau had stepped up with promises to lead the country into an era of peace and development despite those who insisted the president's son was to take the next term of power. The resulting tribal clashes had already left two hundred dead from fights in the streets between the army and the police.

Those who could afford it fled the city. Those who couldn't leave hid in their homes, praying that God would save them and bring an end to the conflict. God chose to do neither, and Camille had ignored the warnings and insisted on staying. The children at the mission where she worked needed her, she told him. Her mother needed her. It didn't matter that he needed her too. That he wanted to get her out and protect her.

Then what he'd feared most happened. A group of solders stopped them halfway to her house. One spun a pistol around his finger, laughing at the game of Russian roulette he played. They were drunk, loud, and focused on displaying their power. They proved it by forcing him to stand helpless as they raped and killed her in front of him.

There was nothing Stephen could have done to save her — or so he'd convinced himself as the scenario played over and over in his mind during the months after her death and the bloody election that followed. President Tau might have managed to eventually squelch the uprisings when he took power, but even his lengthy rule couldn't erase the mistrust Stephen had toward authority.

He'd heard the promises that this current election would take place without any of the horrors his country remembered. Natalie's discovery had managed to shatter any illusions that this time would be different — that this time his country might escape another mass bloodshed. Natalie was too much like Camille. Too stubborn to leave. Too naïve to realize the consequences.

Stephen lit a match and watched the yellow flame eat at the corner of Camille's picture. Its faded colors blended together before spilling black chunks of ash across his desk. He shook the match and tossed it beside the ashes. With his pointed accusations Patrick had been right about one thing: he'd spent his life pleasing both sides, while at the same time making no claims to either. He'd thought he'd be able to survive unscathed, but in the end it had cost him his career, and now his wife and children.

He blew out the flickering flame, then tossed the damaged photo into the metal trash can beneath his desk. He had one card left to play, and this time he knew what he had to do.

THIRTY-ONE

Joseph had been right. Except for a few warning shots, the police hadn't tried to stop them. But that hadn't stopped Natalie's heart from racing the following fifteen minutes as they'd made their way toward Rachel's building in the cover of darkness. Now the three of them sat exhausted and dirty, needing to convince Rachel that the Ghost Soldiers weren't a myth and that they might be the only ones who could stop them.

Natalie studied Rachel's expression as one by one her friend flipped through the pictures on the coffee table in her apartment. These images were the only thing they had to convince Rachel to help them. The three of them had been greeted cautiously at the door. Whether this was because of their presence or simply a reflection of the tension in the city before a major election, Natalie didn't know, but with the photos of Aina and the other villagers in front of her, Rachel's normally warm smile had vanished completely.

Natalie shoved aside a loose strand of hair, then felt it fall across her forehead again. Twenty-four hours of running had left her needing a shower and a good night's sleep, but sleep would have to wait. For now, they had to ensure Rachel was on their side. Showing her the photos had seemed the best place to start.

A minute later, Rachel dropped the last picture onto the small coffee table in front of her. "I've worked in hospitals for over four years now, and in that time I've seen things I'll never forget. Accident victims, rape victims, women beaten by their husbands ... But these photos tell a story I don't want to hear. The Ghost Soldiers are supposed to be rumors, nothing more."

"The photos prove otherwise," Natalie told her. "They're real, Rachel, which means the slave trade is real. That's why we're here. We need your help."

"Is there anyone you recognize?" Chad asked.

"I don't know. Most don't have clear shots of the soldiers' faces." She picked up the photo Joseph had captured of the two men talking about the assassination. "This man ... the man on the left is Daniel Biyoya. He's one of the county's senior military officers."

Chad let out a low whistle. "What do you know about him?"

"Nothing, really. I've just seen his face on the news."

"It's a start." Chad tapped his finger on the other man in the photo. "What about the man he's talking to?"

"I don't know." Rachel shook her head and pressed her lips together. "And even if the Ghost Soldiers are real, I don't understand what this has to do with me."

"You have access to demographics of the country that might help us pinpoint where they are taking people. If we could compare them, look for discrepancies ..."

"I've studied the research, and I've never seen anything that hints of the existence of slave camps."

"There's more. Someone is trying to cover up what's happening," Natalie continued. "When Joseph took the photos, he overheard one man assuring another that the election was set."

"A rigged election?" Rachel stood and crossed the worn carpet, stopping beside the closed window that overlooked the city, and turned to face them. "That's a strong accusation for such little proof."

"What's happened the past twenty-four hours is enough proof

for me, and if whoever wins is behind the slave trade, then it will continue." Natalie caught Rachel's gaze. "Patrick is high up in the government — "

Rachel's chin shot up. "You think Patrick has something to do with this?"

Natalie held up her hand. "I'm not saying that."

"Then what are you saying?" Rachel asked.

Chad cleared his throat. "Patrick was leading an investigation. An investigation that claims there isn't any proof of the Ghost Soldiers or a slave trade — "

"No." Rachel's voice rose a notch. "You'll never convince me Patrick is involved in some cover-up conspiracy."

She stormed from the room, slamming the kitchen door closed behind her.

Chad drummed his fingers against his legs. "I guess that didn't go so well."

"She's scared," Natalie said. "And I think there's more. When I brought up Patrick, she had to defend him. Like she already knew he might be involved in something." Natalie knew Rachel had a generous heart and a deep love for her people, but that didn't mean she was immune from avoiding the truth. "I'll try to talk to her."

Natalie opened the door into the small kitchen, praying she could convince Rachel to help them. Her friend stood in front of the sink, her hands resting on the edge of the counter. She looked up as Natalie entered, then pulled a bag of cornmeal from the small cupboard.

"I'm sure you all are hungry. I don't keep a lot of food in the house, but I can make some goza and sauce. Patrick recently bought me a gas stove. It's a lot quicker than cooking over charcoal."

"We didn't mean to upset you. Maybe we shouldn't have come."

"No." Rachel grabbed a large pot from the cupboard. "It's okay. I've always told you that you were welcome here, and I meant it. It's just that ..."

"That what, Rachel?"

Without answering Rachel turned on the tap, filled the pot with water, and set it on the stove to boil.

"You saw the faces of those people, Rachel," Natalie began. "Many of them died on that mountain. And if we don't find out the truth, more will die, including Joseph's father. I don't want that to happen, and I know you don't either."

"Stop!" Rachel began chopping another onion, narrowing her eyes as the strong smell made her eyes water. "Patrick never spoke to me about the Ghost Soldiers or a slave trade."

"We just want answers, and I believe the place to start is with the demographic reports. But in the meantime they've put out a reward on us."

"I can't believe Patrick's involved in something like this, but those photos ... Has Patrick seen the photos?"

Natalie nodded.

"Then he knows the truth, and he's still trying to cover it up." Rachel spoke like it was a fact rather than a question.

"What else do you know?"

Rachel shrugged. "I've heard the stories about the Ghost Soldiers. Everyone has. People disappearing into the night and being worked as slaves in the mines. Anyone who tries to escape or is too weak to work is brutally murdered in front of their family. I never wanted to believe it. Patrick always assured me that they weren't anything more than rumors spread by the opposition to discredit the president — "

There was a bang on the front door. Natalie jumped. Surely the police hadn't found them. They'd been careful they weren't followed and had even left the car a mile down the road. There was no way anyone could know they were here. Unless ...

"I'm sorry." Rachel pressed her hand against her mouth.

"Please say you didn't call the authorities."

Tears welled in Rachel's eyes. "I promised Patrick I'd let them know if you showed up. When you called me to get directions, I thought ... I believed Patrick."

"And you called the police."

"I'll get rid of them. I promise."

Natalie froze, still not sure if she should trust her. But what choice did she have?

"Quickly." Rachel swept into the living room ahead of Natalie and motioned at the door at the end of the hall. "Hide in my room for now. I don't have anywhere safe to hide you if they search the house, but I'll try and convince them you left."

Natalie grabbed the photos from the coffee table and followed Chad and Joseph down the short hallway and into Rachel's bedroom. She slid onto the floor behind the double bed. Rachel was either putting her own life at risk, or setting a trap that would land them all in prison.

THIRTY-TWO

Gabby took a sip of water and eyed the lunch Sabrina had picked up for her on the way home. She'd tried to eat, but the now cold French fries and ham sandwich sitting on the edge of her computer desk turned her stomach. She flipped her cell phone over and over between her fingers. On the drive home from the airport, she'd reviewed everyone on the list she'd interviewed. But unless someone stepped forward and claimed responsibility for the threat she'd received on her phone, narrowing down whom she'd angered enough to seek revenge wasn't going to be easy.

She quickly scanned her social networks, Twitter, Facebook, and her blog comments, but decided to forgo any updates for the moment. No need announcing to the world where she was. Not until she knew how seriously she should take the phone threat.

Instead she scrolled through her e-mails, erasing the junk mail, marking the upcoming singles' party at church on her calendar, and setting a reminder for next week's dentist appointment. She stopped at a message from Natalie Sinclair.

Thought you might be interested in this. I went to a village that one of my translators claimed was attacked by a group of Ghost Soldiers.

I'm attaching several photos he took. Call me when you get home
and we can talk.
— Natalie Sinclair

Gabby clicked on the attached photos. Her empty stomach roiled
at the graphic images and the terror on the victims' faces. No matter how many times she saw evidence of abuse, it always struck her
afresh. She clicked through the photos again. Natalie had mentioned
she was aware of the dangerous working conditions of some of the
mine workers and then had brought up the Ghost Soldiers.

*What if there's more involved than just the exploitation of
workers . . .*

Gabby rubbed her temple. What had Natalie meant? Was there
a connection between her research and the Ghost Soldiers? Patrick
Seko's explanation had made sense, but what if the missing villagers
had nothing to do with nomadic practices and were instead victims
of violent mercenaries? Like the photos suggested.

Picking up her cell phone, she punched in the fifteen digits of
Natalie's number. The phone rang a half dozen times, then switched
to voice mail. She clicked open the next e-mail while waiting to leave
a message.

Her heart froze.

"Drop the story. It's not worth your life."

Gabby clicked the phone shut and reread the message. No subject
line. No sender information. Tracing the author would be impossible
due to remailers who stripped e-mail messages of all electronic ties.
She pressed her hands against the desk and tried to breathe, wondering what exactly it was that she'd stumbled on to.

THIRTY-THREE

Chad's heart beat in his throat as he crouched in the corner of Rachel's bedroom. He'd seen the photos and heard Joseph's account of what happened in the village. He knew what these men were capable of doing.

An arrow of guilt shot through him. If they were found, they could all be charged with treason, including Rachel. His father had once had a friend who'd been arrested on political charges. The man had vanished without a trace.

Voices rose in the other room. Footsteps shuffled. Chad held his breath and started praying. Someone shouted. A sick feeling rose in Chad's gut. If Rachel was playing for the other side ...

Natalie sat beside him staring at the floor. He wanted to pull her into his arms and tell her that everything was going to be all right, except he couldn't promise that. He couldn't promise anything. Instead he took her hand and squeezed it gently. She glanced up at him, some of the determination back in her eyes.

Joseph sat on the other side of her, a young boy who'd seen far more in his fifteen years than anyone should see in a lifetime. Even if they did manage to make it out of here alive, the emotional scars were going to take time to heal.

A minute later a door slammed. He heard a bolt slide into place ... light footsteps down the hallway ... The bedroom door creaked open.

Rachel stood in the doorway. "They're gone."

Beside him, Natalie trembled. He pulled her tight against his shoulder, careful not to touch her wound. "Thank you, Rachel."

Rachel sat down on the edge of the bed and rested her face in her hands. "He'll kill me if he finds out what I've just done."

"He won't find out. For all they know, you told him the truth." Chad helped Natalie to her feet. "Which means we've got to get out of here now."

"Wait a minute." Rachel looked up at him. "I don't think it's safe for you to leave."

Natalie coughed. "It's certainly not safe here."

Rachel started back down the hall in front of them. In the living room she drew the curtains closed. "They'll be out there watching my apartment. If they see you leave, they'll arrest you."

"She's probably right, Chad." Natalie perched on the couch, her face still pale from their close encounter. "We probably should stay, at least for a little while."

Rachel closed the second set of curtains. "They'll give up waiting before morning, but by then we'll have another thing to worry about. Patrick's due to fly in tomorrow."

"So what do we do now?" Natalie asked.

Rachel smiled for the first time all night. "How does dinner and a hot shower sound?"

"What about tomorrow?" Joseph asked.

"I don't know." Chad sat down beside Natalie. "I guess Jesus put it best: all we can do is let tomorrow worry about itself. I'd say we've already had enough trouble for one day."

THIRTY-FOUR

Natalie pulled the cotton sundress Rachel had loaned her over her head, careful not to scrape the hem of the sleeve across the gash on her shoulder. The coffee-colored skirt was a couple of inches too short, but at least it was clean and in far better condition than the wrinkled outfit she'd worn the past two days.

She glanced into the small mirror above the sink and pressed her fingertips against her cheekbones. There were shadows under her eyes. Despite the decent bed she'd slept in, she still felt exhausted. The humid air, buzz of mosquitoes, and occasional gunshots hadn't helped. Neither had the troubled dreams that had kept her tossing and turning half the night. She'd woken up in a cold sweat a dozen times, thinking they'd been found, each time someone banged on a door down the hallway or shouted from outside. She was getting tired of the bouts of panic, fear, and darkness surrounding her.

God, I simply don't have any energy left.

Pulling her brush from her backpack, she tried to ignore the sting of pain that shot through her arm. Bringing any semblance of order to her hair was an impossibility. Instead she gritted her teeth and managed to stick it up in a ponytail.

Stepping out of the tiny bathroom into the living room, she pasted on a smile. "Good morning."

Joseph nodded his greeting, then took his turn in the bathroom.

She glanced at Chad, who sat on the couch, and wished she looked half as perky. Even in his wrinkled T-shirt and shorts he looked more awake than she did.

"How do you feel this morning?" he asked.

She stifled a yawn. "Besides needing another eight hours of sleep, I suppose I'm okay."

He chuckled. "Then I'm guessing you slept about as well as I did."

She sat down beside him and handed him the first-aid kit. "Do you mind?"

"Of course not." He started removing the old bandage. One side of the adhesive stuck as he pulled on it.

"Ouch!" She glanced at the reddened wound. "It's not getting infected, is it?"

"No, but I need you to hold still."

She wiggled as he ripped the bandage off the rest of the way.

"Natalie."

"Sorry, but it hurts."

Chad shook his head. "You know, you're not a very good patient."

She stuck out her lip, pretending to pout. "And you have terrible bedside manners."

"I wouldn't go there if I were you." He unscrewed the lid to the antibiotic cream. "You're lucky I'm on call this morning. I haven't had my coffee yet."

Natalie forced herself to sit still. "Have you talked to the embassy yet?"

"Changing the subject?"

She shot him a wry grin. "Yes."

He chuckled as he dabbed on the ointment before putting the clean bandage in place. "Rachel let me use her phone. Someone can meet with us at nine."

"It's about time." Natalie glanced at the window. Rachel had kept the curtains closed as an extra precaution, but Natalie knew none of them would relax until they got to the embassy. "Rachel said she'll meet us there with the relevant files from her office later this morning, but do you think it's safe for us to leave?"

Chad's smile faded. "No, but it's not safe to stay here, either."

Natalie shoved the ointment and extra bandages into the bag. "I've been thinking about something. We need to split up."

"Not a chance. I'm not going to let anything happen to you."

She blinked at his refusal. The two of them on the streets together would be a bigger target than a pair of elephants walking down Main Street. "We'd be crazy to go out there together."

He grabbed his tennis shoes off the floor. "Maybe it is crazy, but I didn't come this far with you to leave you to fend for yourself now."

She yanked her phone from the cord where she'd plugged it into Rachel's charger the night before, thankful she'd at least have a way to communicate. Chad would have to buy a charger that fit his phone off the street. "I've been fending for myself for the past eighteen months—"

"You're not going alone, Natalie."

"You know, there is more to this than you playing the hero." Forty-eight hours of stress, frustration, and anger seeped into her words, but she didn't care anymore.

Chad frowned.

"I know this is none of my business, but she's right, Chad." Rachel shook her head. "They're looking for two Americans. Your chances of getting to the embassy are far greater if you go separately."

"Forget it." Chad slid on his shoes as if the conversation were over. It wasn't.

Natalie glanced at where the sleeve of her dress grazed the bottom of the bandage, and her resolve strengthened. "Stop thinking with your heart, Chad."

She strode into the kitchen, shaking. He hadn't deserved her harsh words, but neither did she want her opinions dismissed like a bad idea. No way out of here was without risk, but surely he could see the foolishness in them leaving together.

"You know, Natalie, I've made a lot of mistakes in my life."

Natalie glanced up at Rachel, glad it was her and not Chad who'd slipped into the room behind her. "Like I just did?"

"Right now it looks as if Patrick might be one of my biggest mistakes, but Chad's different. You need to hold on to him."

Natalie's gaze dropped to the beige-colored tile. "He's not mine to hold on to."

"Not yet, maybe, but if you let pride get in the way, I can promise you'll end up regretting it."

Natalie bit her lip. There were simply too many variables in an equation that had become impossible to solve. "Have you ever felt like you were drowning in some hopeless situation and there was nowhere to come up for air?"

"Yeah, I have." Rachel twisted her engagement ring.

"I'm sorry." In all that had transpired, she'd ignored Rachel's heartache. And the heavy risk she'd taken in hiding them. "I've been completely insensitive."

Rachel grabbed a rag and started wiping down the counter. "No. It's okay. If I'm honest, there have been plenty of signs I shouldn't have ignored, but it was always easier just to look the other way."

Natalie reached for the slight ray of hope that still lingered. "There's still a chance Patrick isn't involved in all of this."

"Part of me would like to believe that, because despite everything I can't help but love him." Rachel leaned against the counter and caught Natalie's gaze. "Patrick offered me the life I'd always dreamed about. I love the way people treat me when I'm with him. I like the apartment, the presents, and the trips he's taken me on ..."

"So what are you going to do?"

Rachel squeezed out the excess water into the sink and shrugged. "If Patrick is involved, I don't think I have a choice but to play along for now. Then after the election — after all this mess is over — I'll have to find a legitimate reason to break things off."

Natalie hated the fact that they'd both been presumably wrong about Patrick. "I am sorry."

"Better now than later, I suppose." Rachel looked up at Natalie. "I know he loves me in his own way, but maybe he simply isn't capable of loving the way I've always dreamed of."

"Then you deserve more."

"Maybe." Rachel laid the rag across the dish rack and leaned against the counter. "Somehow I thought I could keep my faith and have Patrick, too, but the past twelve hours have shown me just how far I've gone the wrong way. Makes me wish my mom was still alive to tell me what to do."

Natalie caught the deep heartache in her friend's voice. "About Patrick?"

"About Patrick ... and the fact that the Ghost Soldiers aren't just some crazy myth. If Patrick's involved, I don't know how I'll ever be able to forgive him. Or how God will forgive me for all the compromises I've already made."

"All you have to do is ask, Rachel. God loves you, and He wants you back."

"I know." Rachel wiped her cheek, then nodded in the direction of the living room. "Go talk to him."

Sensing Rachel needed a few moments alone, Natalie gave her a hug, then headed back into the living room. Forgiveness might not be easy, but the first thing she had to do was ask Chad for his. He was sitting on the couch, going through the photos again.

"I shouldn't have snapped at you," she started.

"I deserved it." He looked up at her. "I was being unreasonable. We're all under a lot of stress."

"That's no excuse."

"For either of us. I guess it's impossible to erase the influence of the past. It's given me this determination. If anything was to happen to you ..."

She shook her head. "You don't have to be my hero."

"Maybe I want to."

He stood and bridged the gap between them, his gaze holding hers.

Natalie's defenses fell. "I suppose it is kind of nice having a knight in shining armor come to my rescue."

She drew in a deep breath and held it for a moment. All the stress of the past few days vanished for an instant until all she could see was Chad's face hovering in front of hers. He was close enough for her to feel his warm breath against her face. Close enough to let him kiss her.

And suddenly she wished he would.

Joseph stepped into the room, slamming the bathroom door shut behind him.

Chad cleared his throat and took a step back. "We need to go."

Natalie's gaze dropped. "Yeah."

"When this is all over ..."

She shook her head. She wasn't ready for any promises or expectations. For now all she could handle was getting through the next hour and making it to the embassy in one piece.

She turned to Joseph. "Are you ready to go?"

"Yes."

Natalie gnawed on the corner of her lip. She didn't want another fight, but she hadn't changed her stance on leaving. "I still don't think we'll make it out of here together without getting caught."

"I know. I just wish things were different." Chad combed his fingers through his hair. She'd obviously struck a chord. "I'll go first, and then you leave with Joseph in fifteen minutes. Walk half a mile as inconspicuously as possible, and then get a taxi to take you to the embassy."

"You're sure about this?"

"Yeah. You're right. It's the only thing that makes sense."

He held her gaze, and her breath caught in her throat. She wished they had time to explore what was happening between them, but that would have to be saved for another day.

"I'll buy a charger on my way there." He dropped his phone into his back pocket, then reached for her bag. "And I'll take the photos."

"Chad—"

Pressing his finger against her lips, he shook his head.

"Okay," she conceded.

He shoved the photos into the side pocket of his cargo shorts, then looked up at Rachel, who'd just entered the room. "I think we should pray before we leave. Do you mind?"

She shook her head and joined them. They stood side by side with different cultures, different levels of faith, and started praying.

Natalie looked up as Chad said amen and smiled. A sense of peace washed over her for the first time in days. In the presence of her Creator was where she should have started this morning. She'd needed to be reminded that God was her protector, and that somehow He could use even this situation for His glory.

Chad reached out and grasped her hand. "Be careful."

"I will. I promise."

He leaned forward, brushed his lips gently against hers, and walked out the door.

THIRTY-FIVE

Natalie glanced at the clock above the couch in Rachel's living room. Three minutes had passed. It seemed like thirty. She finished packing her backpack, checked the clock again, and joined Rachel in the kitchen.

Rachel looked up from the coffee mug she was washing. "Do you need anything else?"

Natalie shook her head. "Thank you so much for everything. You risked your life for us when you didn't have to."

Rachel set the mug on the rack. "I did it for Aina ... For Joseph's father ... For all of them. They didn't deserve what happened to them."

"We're going to find them."

"I know you will."

Natalie leaned against the counter, reminding herself again that God was her protector. Words easily spoken when things were going right. Why was it a completely different matter when the whole world seemed to be falling apart? Rachel's mom had been right: God was still bigger than all of this. Even that, though, couldn't take away all her worry. If Patrick found out what Rachel had done, and if he really was one of those behind the raids, there was no telling what he would do.

Natalie grabbed a towel and began drying the dishes. "Are you going to be all right?"

"I'll be fine." Rachel sucked in a deep breath. "No matter what Patrick's done, he'd never do anything to hurt me."

Natalie wasn't convinced. "Even if he finds out what you did?"

"It doesn't really matter. I'd do it all over again." Rachel reached out to squeeze Natalie's hand. "Don't worry about me. I'm going to believe that God has something good to bring out of all of this."

Natalie hoped so, but she knew how difficult it could be to find that good. She'd seen too much pain and suffering the past year and a half to completely dismiss the possibility of a bad ending to their situation. Yes, God was there. She knew that. But so was the evil side of man.

"You haven't eaten anything." Rachel held out a plate of bread.

The thought of eating turned Natalie's stomach. "I can't."

"You need to."

Knowing Rachel was right, Natalie complied and took a piece of the bread.

"I meant what I said earlier," Rachel began. "I don't think you should let go of Chad. He's different, and he cares about you."

Natalie felt a blush creep up her cheeks as she remembered his kiss. Ten years ago she would have done anything for Chad to notice her. Funny how everything seemed so much simpler back then. She just hadn't realized it at the time. Today it was a different story entirely. "Chad and I ... Well, it's complicated."

Rachel shook her head. "Tell me what's complicated about two people being attracted to each other?"

Natalie frowned. "How can I think about love and attraction right now?"

"Why not? Love is simple. People are the ones who try to make it complicated."

Natalie tore off a piece of bread, wondering how much truth there was to Rachel's statement. Compared to saving the world, maybe love really wasn't all that complicated.

Rachel glanced at her watch. "It's time. Chad's going to worry if he has to wait very long for you."

Two minutes later, Natalie was hurrying down the alley behind the apartment with Joseph right behind her. Trash littered the narrow pathway leading toward the street. An unfinished cement wall, its mortar crumbling onto the ground, rose beside them. Tin roofs lined the top of the wall, with no backyards, sunny patches of grass, or flower gardens.

On the street, Joseph took the lead, weaving them in and out between narrow, muddy passageways and piles of garbage. Living in Kasili, she'd visited some of the worst parts of the city, but seeing a man sleeping beneath a pile of cardboard added a depth of desperation that ran chills down her spine.

They hurried past lines of shops with peeling paint and traders standing on the street corner. At the first busy corner, she glanced behind her, looking for signs that they were being followed. Women wearing traditional dresses and colorful head wraps chattered on the sidewalk. A young girl walked by carrying a plastic tub filled with fresh loaves of bread on her head. Another woman sat on the ground beside a pile of pineapples, waiting for a customer. But beyond a few casual glances, no one seemed to care she was there.

They rounded a corner and Natalie stopped short. Her breathing quickened. Two soldiers stood buying roasted corn from a woman. Joseph grabbed her arm and pulled her into another side street, where they hurried past a wooden stall where a woman cooked rice and fish.

Natalie pulled her cell phone from her pocket to check the time. If Chad had been able to catch a taxi right away, he should be at the embassy by now. In another fifteen minutes, they'd be there.

A street child approached them for money. Natalie felt a tug of guilt but hurried past. As much as she longed to give the girl something, she'd learned firsthand that giving to one would quickly escalate into more requests. And a small mob surrounding her was the last thing she needed at the moment.

A taxi came toward them, bouncing over the potholes that filled the street. Natalie's heart pounded. She wished there were another way to get to the embassy, but the only alternative was an hour-long walk across town. Definitely not the way to be inconspicuous. Out of options, she waved the vehicle down.

The driver slowed, splashing mud from a puddle across the bottom of her dress. So much for clean clothes. Joseph opened the door, but as she stepped off the curb to get in, a fight broke out in front of the store behind them. She paused to see the commotion — a woman with a broom chasing away a couple of kids.

Just as Natalie turned back to the taxi, someone grabbed her from behind and gripped her forearm. Twisting her body, she lunged for the backseat of the vehicle, but the man was too strong. Panic swept through her gut. A hand covered her mouth. Joseph shouted and tried to pull her free, but he was knocked onto the sidewalk.

A second man grabbed her backpack as they dragged her down the street and pushed her into a waiting car.

THIRTY-SIX

Chad checked the time on his watch as he continued pacing outside the high electric fence that surrounded the embassy compound. Over an hour had already passed since he'd left Rachel's, giving Natalie and Joseph plenty of time to get here. The combination of coffee and acid from stress burned his stomach.

Something had gone wrong.

He wiped the beaded perspiration from the back of his neck. Even at nine-thirty the sun had already raised the temperature substantially. By noon it would reach the mid-nineties. Ignoring both the humidity and the questioning stares of the armed guard protecting the entrance to the embassy, Chad turned at the busy street corner and searched the narrow thoroughfare. A taxi approached then zoomed by. He let out a sharp puff of air. Where were they?

He stepped out of the way of a group of uniform-clad kids who chattered their way past him to school. He couldn't panic. Not yet anyway. There had to be a number of legitimate reasons why they were late. He'd seen a couple of rallies being set up in the streets. Traffic had crawled by as supporters waving banners and hanging posters crowded the streets. But from what he'd seen, it was nothing more than a last-minute push for their candidate in tomorrow's vote. It was the aftermath of the election that could bring the surge of chaos into the streets. He could only pray it would stay peaceful.

Another five minutes passed, and there was still no sign of Natalie and Joseph. With his cell phone dead, he crossed the street and dialed her number again from the public phone on the corner. The phone rang, but she didn't answer. Something was wrong.

He returned to the front of the embassy as a taxi pulled up alongside the curb. Joseph jumped out. The backseat of the cab was empty.

"Where's Natalie?"

"They took her."

A wave of nausea washed over him. "What do you mean, they took her?"

Joseph's rapid explanation in Dha was lost on Chad.

He grasped the young boy's arm. "Slow down and tell me what happened. Where is Natalie?"

"They took her!"

"Who?"

"I don't know." Joseph gasped for air.

Chad rested a hand on each shoulder. "I want you to breathe slowly."

"I ... can't."

Chad tossed the taxi driver enough coins to cover the ride and pulled Joseph away from the curb. "I want you to hold your breath, count to three, then take a slow breath."

Joseph closed his eyes while Chad counted. The teen's breathing slowly returned to normal, but Chad was afraid to hear what he had to say. Whatever it was, the bottom line was that Natalie was gone.

"Tell me what happened."

"We were getting into the taxi ... Two men grabbed her ... shoved her into another car." Joseph took another deep breath. "I tried to follow, but people were burning tires. The police started throwing tear gas ... I lost her ..."

Chad felt his heartbeat accelerate. He had to think. Now wasn't the time to let his emotions run away. This was no different than an emergency in the ER. Staying calm was vital; he'd deal with his emotions later. "I've got to talk with someone inside the embassy."

Joseph glanced at the guard. "I can't go in."

"No, but there's a small café a block away." Chad dug some money out of his pocket and handed it to Joseph. "Go order something to eat and stay out of sight, then meet me back here in one hour."

Joseph nodded.

Chad pulled out his passport and shoved it toward the guard. "I need to report a kidnapping of an American citizen."

The man looked stunned. "You'll have to speak to someone inside."

Chad was ushered into a small room, where he was told to take everything out of his pockets, including his cell phone.

He threw his phone, along with a handful of change, onto the counter. "I don't have time for this. Take me to whoever's in charge, now!"

"Please, sir." The Dhambizan guard shoved a plastic tray in front of him. "Place everything in here first. Then we will see about your friend."

Chad dropped the photos along with his passport into the tray, then added the phone charger he'd just bought along the side of the road.

The guard glanced briefly at the photos then snatched up his passport. "Chad Talcott?"

"Yes. I—"

The guard picked up the phone and started conversing in mumbled tones. *Passport ... Photos ....Security ...* Chad felt his stomach knotting; he was unsure if it had been the photos or his passport that had caught the guard's attention. What he did know from the one-sided conversation was that something wasn't right.

The man set down the receiver. "I need you to come with me."

"Wait a minute ... Why?"

"Please, just follow me."

Chad wasn't ready to admit defeat. "You don't understand. An American citizen, Natalie Sinclair, has been kidnapped. Her life is in danger because of those photos. I need to talk to someone who can help — immediately."

The man turned around. "You're the one who doesn't understand. With the upcoming election, we've been told to stay on high alert, and your name just kicked up a red flag."

Chad blinked twice. "Wait a minute — someone's been kidnapped…"

The guard threw open a door and shoved Chad through the narrow hallway. He opened another door to a small room that held nothing more than a table and two chairs. "Sit down. Someone will be in to talk with you in a few minutes."

Before Chad could say another word, the guard slammed the door behind him and was gone.

THIRTY-SEVEN

Natalie opened her eyes to semidarkness. Lying on her side, she watched a lone stream of sunlight filter down from a hole in the ceiling and scatter across the dirt floor. In the amber flecks of light, she could see her backpack sitting a couple of feet in front of her with some of its contents strewn across the floor. Beyond that, a thin mattress on the ground, a small table with two wooden chairs ... and shadows.

A thick rope ate at her wrists where they'd tied her hands together behind her back. Pulling against the taut binding only made it rub against the raw skin, adding to the pain from the wound on her shoulder and the lingering headache she'd had the past three days.

She glanced at the closed door and tried to orient herself. Pulling her right knee toward her chest, she pushed against the ground, then managed to sit up. Four wooden walls, a packed dirt floor, and a tin roof. The shack could be located in any corner of the city. Any squatter camp or compound. Faint smells of a latrine and a cooking fire filled the air, turning her stomach. A radio played in the background. Screaming was an option, but more than likely that would only alert her captors. The tightness in her chest increased.

There had to be a way out.

She blinked her eyes against the darkness. Maybe Chad had been right and they should have stayed together. Or maybe it had been absurd to think she could simply show up at the capital with no opposition. For all she knew, they had captured Chad and Joseph as well and were holding them somewhere nearby — making their entire expedition a quest in foolishness.

She kicked at her backpack with her toe, refusing to believe that the odds were completely against her this time. If she could get to the bag, there might be something in it that could help her out of here.

The door swung open, temporarily blinding her with the light from outside. A man's silhouette framed the doorway, shooting slivers of fear through her. She took in his uniform and heavy, black boots. She'd be no match against him physically. She'd have to find a way to convince him to let her go.

He grabbed her arm, catching her off guard. "Where are the photos?"

So Patrick — or whoever was behind this — must have concluded that her escape to the capital meant she had her own set of the photos. "I don't have them."

He slapped her across the face. She reeled at the impact as he picked up her bag and dumped the rest of the contents onto the floor. "Where are they?"

Her mouth went dry. "They're not in there."

"I know." He picked up her flashlight and squatted in front of her, his expression hard. "Then who has them?"

Natalie gritted her teeth, knowing she couldn't succumb to the pain or the fear enveloping her. But did she admit the truth and throw away the only bargaining chip she might have or try to convince him that she could get the photos for him?

"Here's the deal, lady. There's a reward out for you, but it's not worth anything without the photos."

His response cinched her decision. Without the photos, it was clear he didn't need her. "I can get them for you."

"Are they with your American friend? Or with the boy?"

She hid the relief she felt at his question. Chad and Joseph, at least, appeared to be safe. If they'd made it to the embassy, then maybe the authorities could find a way to track her down.

"They're with my American friend." If she could convince him she could help find Chad, she'd at least buy herself some time. "We knew someone was after us so we split up."

The man dragged one of the chairs across the dirt floor, then sat down before pulling out a cell phone from his pocket. Her cell phone. "Then you will call him."

She eyed the phone, hoping Chad had found a way to charge his phone by now. "You're going to have to untie me."

He hesitated for a moment, pulled a knife from his back pocket. "Don't try anything. Trust me. Outside these four walls there are plenty of others who won't be near as amenable as I am."

Once the rope had fallen to the ground, Natalie flexed her wrists, then grabbed the phone from his open hand. "What do you want me to tell him?"

"Tell him to be outside the Oasis Hotel with the photos in an hour. And that if he talks to anyone about them ... I'll kill you."

She tried to swallow her fear. So much for being amenable.

Natalie punched in Chad's number. The phone switched automatically to voice mail. If he had made it to the embassy, his phone would be turned off and left at the front desk. She waited for the beep to leave a message.

"Chad this is Natalie. I'm being held for ransom. They want the photos — "

Her captor grabbed the phone from her hands and flipped it shut.

She eyed the phone. "Let me try back in another five or ten minutes. You know how unreliable the cell phone towers can be sometimes. It's probably just a glitch in the system. He's got to be worried and waiting for me to call."

He shoved the phone into his pocket and tied her hands again.

"By then it might be too late. If those photos get into the hands of someone else ..."

"How much are they paying you to turn me in?"

He paused, seemingly taken aback by her candid question. "My share is two thousand American dollars if I can get the photos."

For a man who probably made thirty dollars a month plus a couple hundred in bribes, two thousand dollars was a fortune.

He retied the rope around her wrists. "I'll be back in a few minutes with the phone. You'd better pray he answers this time."

Striding out of the shack, he slammed the rickety door behind him.

THIRTY-EIGHT

Patrick shoved a stack of files into his briefcase and snapped the top shut. In forty-eight hours this would all be over. He'd be in the capital by one, giving him just enough time to complete the rest of his plans. His only loose end at the moment was Natalie and her doctor friend. Even if he had to search the streets of Bogama and the surrounding countryside himself in order to find her, he would. Besides, how long could she realistically stay hidden? By the end of the weekend he'd be enjoying himself at the Oasis, the capital's best hotel, where he'd booked a deluxe suite for him and Rachel — a small reward for all his hard work.

Patrick's satellite phone rang. He dropped the briefcase onto the desk and picked up the receiver.

"Where have you been?"

Patrick reined in his frustration at his boss's brisk question. He might not be the one in charge, but he was the one taking the biggest risk. Which meant he deserved a measure of respect.

"I'm getting ready to fly to the capital to finalize our plans."

"Well, we've got another loose end. Gabby Mackenzie, a reporter in the States, is getting ready to run an article that could tip off the authorities."

Patrick dropped into his chair. Gabby Mackenzie?

Had Natalie managed to send copies of the photos to the reporter, or had he simply convinced himself that he'd covered all his bases and Gabby wasn't a threat? He'd searched Natalie's computer and had found no trace of her sending out copies of the photos to that reporter ... or anyone for that matter. There were other ways of checking—

"Do you realize what will happen to you if this plot fails?"

The other man's menacing tone snapped him back to the present. "I know the importance—"

"And I need to know that you can handle things."

"Everything's under control." This wasn't the time to mention Natalie's involvement. He'd handle that himself. Instead he threw it back into his boss's court. "What about the reporter you mentioned?"

"She's being taken care of as we speak. We're not taking any chances of a connection being publicized."

He hung up the phone a minute later, ignoring the wave of anxiety that swept through him, then checked the top of his desk to ensure he hadn't forgotten anything. No matter what the outcome of the next forty-eight hours, he had no plans of returning to Kasili anytime soon.

The door to his office creaked open. Stephen stood in the doorway, looking like a typical businessman in his tie and suit jacket.

Patrick let out a sigh of irritation. "Stephen. I wasn't expecting you."

Stephen cleared his throat. "Looks like you're on your way out."

"Yes, I am, actually." Patrick pushed in his desk chair and picked up his briefcase. He didn't have time for—nor was he in the mood for—another conversation with the man. "I'm flying to the capital in an hour."

Patrick watched the muscles of Stephen's jaw tense as his gaze dropped. Another sign of weakness? He moved toward the door, but Stephen blocked his way.

"Please." Stephen held up his hand. "I've been thinking a lot about what you said in the parking lot earlier."

"Feeling guilty?" Patrick raised his brow, still skeptical. "Or are you still trying to save the world?"

His encounter with Stephen in the parking lot had been a calculated attempt to find out just where the man stood. Patrick was either about to find out, or this was a last-minute attempt to convert him back to the virtuous side.

"I ... You were right," Stephen began.

"Really?" Patrick stopped and leaned against the edge of desk. He'd expected a timid argument on the evils of their corrupt government, not a confession. He didn't have a lot of time, but this might actually prove interesting. Maybe he could spare a few minutes.

Stephen's chin rose until he was looking Patrick straight in the eyes. "I want to come with you to the capital."

Patrick shook his head and laughed at the implications. "You don't know what you're saying."

"I know that the Ghost Soldiers are real, and that you're a part of a plan to rig the election."

Now Patrick was the one to squirm uncomfortably. "What else do you know?"

"That I can help you."

"Even if you could, why would you want to?"

Stephen jingled his car keys between his fingers. "I've spent the past eighteen hours thinking about my life and realizing that I don't have a whole lot left. My wife's gone. My children are gone. My job's become nothing more than pacifying big donors in the West who want to ease their conscience by throwing money at impoverished African countries. I'm tired of ending up with nothing in my pocket for what I do other than a paltry salary and an empty house."

"How do you propose to help me?"

Stephen shoved the keys back into his pocket. "In the past ten years or so, I've made connections with numerous people who are, let's say, sympathetic to our cause. These contacts have continued to increase now that the president has decided to go along with the UN. A trend I expect to continue."

Patrick wasn't convinced. "I have my own friends and connections."

"Who pay you well for what you do. I know that. But from my experience, it never hurts to have another source of income. I have something else, Patrick. A bank account in the Cayman Islands."

"You're telling me you've been skimming funds?"

"The last time I looked, a few million spread out still goes a long way, and no one seems to notice the few thousand taken off here and there. It's easier than you think, Patrick."

Patrick began to smile. "And you're smarter than I thought."

Stephen was right. Another source of revenue never hurt anyone.

"But this amount is only a fraction of what is available. Tracking money is not only painstaking but time consuming to the authorities. They don't have the time to sift through aid funds earmarked for some obscure Central African country."

Patrick still had his questions. "Why come to me now? Why not keep it all for yourself?"

"I could, of course. Now that our government is playing with the United Nations, they might be gaining more aid, but the strings are also getting tighter. I started to realize that if there were a turnover in power, I needed to make sure that the new government won't cause me any problems. And I can't see you walking away from an additional hundred thousand dollars or more a year."

Patrick tamed his enthusiasm. There was no need to make Stephen think he had the upper hand. "An interesting proposition, but there's another problem — Natalie."

Stephen's smile faded. "What about her?"

"I've done what I can to prevent those photos getting into the wrong hands, but if they are released, everything I've worked for could vanish in an instant."

"She'll do what I say. I'll convince her that it's in the best interest of the people. That exposing the photos would only up the chances of another election turning bloody."

"What if it's too late?"

"You've got a reward out on Natalie and the doctor?"

Patrick nodded, again refusing to let the worry gain control.

"How long do you think they can stay hidden while the entire city of Bogama is looking for them? They'll never make it to the embassy without getting caught."

"It's been almost eighteen hours, and I'm still waiting."

Patrick's satellite phone rang, and he picked it up. "Patrick here."

"It's me."

Patrick felt his heartbeat surge. "Did you find them?"

"We've got her."

"Good." Maybe his problems were almost over after all. "What about the doctor and the boy?"

"That's one of the reasons I'm calling. They split up and those two disappeared — with the photos."

"That's why I said I wanted all three of them." Patrick clenched his fist. "Where are they?"

"We don't know, sir. We have every available officer on the lookout for them, both police and army, as well as the taxi drivers in the city."

"And you still let them get away." It was a good thing the man wasn't in the room. Heads were going to roll when he got to the capital. "What about the embassy?"

"We're still waiting to hear from our contact inside." There was a pause on the line. "There's one other thing you need to know about. Your fiancée ..."

"What about her?"

"She lied to our men and kept them there overnight."

Patrick slammed his fist against the desk as a wave of nausea coursed through him. Rachel had always gone along with what he said. It was something he'd impressed upon her because of his high-profile role. And now she'd gone and betrayed him?

Panic began to take root. First Natalie, now Rachel. The loose ends were starting to multiply. And this was something he couldn't afford. Especially when losing this game meant losing everything he'd worked for.

He closed his eyes. He could see Rachel's face. She'd been the perfect woman for him. Charming, beautiful, with just enough innocence to please him as well as impress others at official gatherings. He'd even gone as far as getting her a job with the minister of health because a woman who served her country helped him look good.

But none of that mattered. Not anymore.

"Sir?"

"Yeah, I'm here." He rubbed his fingers against the back of his neck. "You know what has to be done. I can't have a liability."

Even if it was someone he loved.

"Consider it done."

"And find the doctor. I don't care how you do it. Just get it done."

Patrick slammed down the phone and glanced up at Stephen. Whether he liked it or not, he could use the man. If things went bad, he had no plans of taking the fall. "You're not planning to back out on me now, are you?"

Stephen shook his head.

"Good, because I've got a job for you. Go pack your things. We're leaving in less than an hour."

THIRTY-NINE

Chad jiggled the handle of the door to the holding room and resisted the urge to try to break it down with his shoulder. He still had no idea why his name had produced a red flag worthy of detaining him, but he did know that every minute of delay put Natalie's life in more danger.

The nine-by-nine holding room closed in on him. He had no way to communicate with the outside world and no way to leave. Crossing to the other side of the room, he stopped beneath the small window six feet above the floor. Even if he could open the window, the bars made escape impossible ...

He pressed his fingers against his pulsating temples. He must be going crazy, coming up with scenarios to escape from his own country's embassy.

The door opened behind him, and Chad spun around. A well-dressed officer entered the room and tossed a file folder and a pad of paper onto the wooden table. Tall, burly, and obviously American, the guy meant business.

"You're Dr. Chad Talcott?"

"Yes."

The door slammed shut behind him. "Sit down."

Chad hesitated, then complied. There was something unnerving about being treated as a suspect on American soil. The United States Embassy was supposed to be his one place of refuge.

"I want to know what's going on." Chad leaned forward. "My friend, Natalie Sinclair, has been kidnapped."

The man sat down across from him. "I've been made aware of your concerns for Miss Sinclair, but we have another problem to deal with first."

"I don't think you understand. Her life is in danger."

"My name is Paul Hayes." He opened the red file folder and leaned back, folding his arms across his chest. "Security is high across the city with the upcoming elections, and your name just came up with a red flag on our computers."

"So I heard." Chad shook his head. "What does that mean?"

"It means that the government here has placed you on their wanted list."

Chad reached out to grab the stack of photos from the open file, but Mr. Hayes was too quick. He flipped the file shut. "Not yet. We'll get to the photos, but first I want you to tell me why you're living in this country."

Chad combed his fingers through his hair. "I'm a doctor working with Volunteers for Hope International. You have my passport and work visa. You can check it out."

"I already have."

"Then why the twenty questions?"

"How long have you known Natalie Sinclair?"

Apparently the game wasn't over. "I met her three days ago. She came by the clinic with a boy who had a head injury."

Mr. Hayes glanced at the file. "And yet this says you arrived in the country September thirteenth of this year?"

"Yes." Chad's head began to throb as he searched for an explanation to this round of questioning.

"And you're telling me that in all this time you didn't run into her?" Mr. Hayes continued.

"Why would I?"

"In my experience people of the same nationality and language tend to run in the same social circles."

Chad let out a long, slow breath. "It's a big country. Besides, between twelve-hour shifts and emergency cases, I don't exactly have time for afternoon tea."

Mr. Hayes frowned but let the comment slide. "When you met her at the clinic, was this the first time the two of you had met?"

"We went to the same high school back in Oregon, but that was ten years ago. She was younger than I was, so we weren't exactly friends. In fact, I didn't even recognize her at first."

Mr. Hayes thumped his notepad with his pen. "Is it true that Natalie has access to government aid funds?"

"I don't know." Chad fought the urge to knock the table over and give the guy a piece of his mind. If the other man didn't have the advantage of six inches and fifty pounds and the authority to arrest him, he would do it. "What does that have to do with anything?"

"Dr. Talcott. For now, I'm the one asking the questions."

"Listen." Chad stood, walked to the window, then turned to face his accuser. "I understand that you have some sort of procedure to follow, and that you have to follow that procedure to help ensure the safety of this country, but — "

"Dr. Talcott." The man held up his hand. "I don't believe you are grasping the seriousness of this situation."

"I think I am. Are you aware that not only has Natalie been kidnapped, but we believe that the election has been rigged? Those photos, in the right hands, could help stop it and save the potentially hundreds of people being held in slave camps."

Mr. Hayes flipped the folder back open. "What are you talking about?"

Chad grabbed the stack of photos and spread them out across the table. "These photos were taken in a village outside the city of Kasili by a fifteen-year-old boy named Joseph Komboli. He came to Natalie after watching his family being taken from their home by Ghost Soldiers. He also overheard two men talking about a fixed election." Chad rested his palms on the table and gripped the edge. "With the phone lines down in Kasili, we've spent the past forty-eight hours trying to get here in order to alert *somebody* who will do something about it."

"So despite the fact that you've only known the woman for three days, you left your job at the hospital and set off on some wild trek across the RD because of a handful of photos some boy claims he took?"

"If you'd look at the photos, I think you would understand why I'm here." He took in a quick breath. "And if I'm right about the election, how do you think that will look in the midst of your peaceful UN election process?"

Paul picked up one of the photos and studied the image. "Who are these two men?"

"One is a senior military officer, and there's obviously a lot more going on behind this than a simple rendezvous in the jungle."

"Who knows you have these photos?"

For the first time, Chad felt as if he had the man's attention. "Patrick Seko, who runs a security task force for the president. Stephen Moyo, who works as a liaison between the RD government and non-profit organizations working in the country. And Patrick's fiancée, Rachel. Maybe more by now."

Mr. Hayes rubbed his graying goatee and frowned. "I'll be honest with you, Dr. Talcott. I'm having a hard time believing all of this."

"Someone with a whole lot of clout wants these photos. Our plane went down, we were chased down the Congo River, and now Natalie's missing. We also found out they have a reward out for our capture." Chad's head pounded, but he wasn't done yet. "Look at those photos and you'll see a village being ransacked. People were murdered, and the rest dragged away. You can't just dismiss all this as coincidence."

Mr. Hayes' frown deepened. "I know about the reward to bring you both in, but the problem is that it doesn't have anything to do with this stack of photos."

"Then I don't understand." Chad sat back down in his chair. "I think it's time you told me exactly what I'm being accused of."

"It's all right here. I have evidence of wire transfers to an undisclosed off-shore account with signatures on the bottom." Mr. Hayes shoved a stack of documents across the table and cleared his throat. "You're being accused of embezzling two and a half million dollars of aid money earmarked for the Republic of Dhambizao."

FORTY

Nick eyed the bullet-riddled belly of his plane from the tarmac run-way, then shook his head. So much for doing a simple favor for a friend. His plans to fly to the capital and return home the next day had turned into a night in the jungle followed by a harrowing takeoff and another twenty-four hours detained in a shabby back room of the airport.

Landing in Bogama was supposed to have been his ticket to freedom — or at least his chance to get away from the goons who'd knocked him out and shot up his plane. It would have been, he sup-posed, if the airport hadn't been recently overrun by army personnel. And if they weren't all looking for insurgents on the eve of a presi-dential election.

Like he fit the description of a mercenary.

Except he apparently did, because as soon as he'd landed, three men had escorted him into a back room of the airport for a barrage of questioning with no intentions of allowing him to call the embassy. Nick assumed that the crackdown was under orders of President Tau, but knowing what he did about the photos, he wasn't sure who was in charge anymore. Managing to escape down a makeshift runway in the dense jungle had been a piece of cake compared to convincing authorities that he had no idea where Chad and Natalie were.

Not wanting to lose any more time, he started for the edge of the hangar. He'd tried to get ahold of the embassy, but their line was busy. Finding Chad and Natalie was now his number one priority. The fact that he had no idea where they were had him worried.

He punched Chad's phone number into his cell phone, thankful his temporary captors had returned his phone and other personal items and that his battery wasn't dead.

It rang. No one answered.

He called Natalie next. Again, nothing.

He clicked his phone off and studied the chaotic scene outside the airport. Passengers milled among security officers, law enforcement agents, and army personnel, making him wonder again exactly who was in charge.

But who held control of the country was immaterial at the moment. After little to eat for twenty-four hours and a sleepless night, there were certain priorities. He was starving. Natalie had scribbled her friend's address and telephone number on a piece of paper for him before she'd left. He'd quickly find something to eat, and then pay Rachel a visit. If nothing else, she should know where they were.

Forgetting the taxi route, Nick opted for a shuttle run by one of the local hotels, hoping it would be a safer way into the city. Forty-five minutes later he was sitting not far from Rachel's apartment, inside a cheap café that sold strong coffee and ham-and-cheese baguettes. It wasn't much, but it would be enough to keep him going the next few hours.

Nick took another bite of his sandwich, then grabbed a folded copy of the day's paper off the table beside him and started reading the top stories.

While President Tau and the UN promise a peaceful turnout for tomorrow's election, security has been heightened on all levels, including the airport and all border crossings. Roadblocks have been set up throughout the capital as well as on all major roads. With over two dozen foreign diplomats arriving within the next twelve hours, anyone raising the suspicions of the government is being detained for further questioning to ensure tomorrow's election proceeds without any problems.

While it is believed that there are only two real contenders for the vote, current President Samuel Tau and Bernard Okella, there are officially thirty-two candidates vying for the position of president, with President Tau clearly expected to win.

About one hundred and fifty United Nations election observers have spent the past month handing out electoral kits to the country's seven provinces. But with a population of just over ten million people, there are continued concerns because of the lack of infrastructure, current power failures in some key cities, and a substantial percentage of the population located in remote villages in the mountains.

Nevertheless, flights from South Africa continue to arrive daily in Bogama carrying ballot papers, ballot boxes, and privacy shields. These are being dispersed to villages and cities throughout the country. After months of international pressure, President Tau has assured the United Nations that this election will be fair, and that he will not contest the decision if defeated. But considering this country's past, many wonder if the chance of a fair election is even a possibility.

Nick frowned. His thoughts exactly. He flipped over the paper and felt his breath catch. At the bottom of the page was a blurred photo of Natalie and Chad.

He skimmed the short article. Natalie Sinclair and Chad Talcott were being called enemies of the state, currently wanted for embezzling funds given as aid to the people of the Republic of Dhambizao. Nick blinked his eyes. Surely this was some kind of joke. But there it was in black and white. Charges of wire fraud and embezzlement were being brought against the couple. Sources confirmed that they were currently on their way to the capital in an attempt to escape the country.

Nick shoved the paper into a trash can beside him. He had to find them. Now.

Forgetting about the rest of his breakfast, Nick managed to find Rachel's upscale apartment building three blocks away. While the outside was a bit run down, he was certain the price tag wasn't.

Nick glanced at the address Natalie had scribbled on a piece of paper as he approached the third-floor apartment. He knocked on the closed door. A shot of fear ran through him when no one answered. When Chad and Natalie had left for the river yesterday morning, they'd had no idea how far things were going to get out of hand.

He knocked harder this time, glanced down the empty hallway, and then tried the handle. It was unlocked.

"Rachel?"

A door slammed from somewhere inside the building. Nick hesitated — the last thing he needed to do was give the police a reason to arrest him. He stepped inside, then paused. Red splotches stained the carpet in the center of the room.

He glanced up. A woman was lying on the couch, her blouse discolored with blood.

FORTY-ONE

Natalie pushed against the wooden door of the shack with her shoulder. She'd managed to shimmy her legs through her arms so her hands were in front of her, but she couldn't loosen the rope. She blew out a sharp sigh and banged again on the door. The tin roof rumbled, but the structure was sturdier than it appeared.

She moved to the middle of the darkened room and turned slowly in a full circle. There had to be a way out. Growing up, she'd watched enough episodes of *MacGyver* to know all she needed was a Swiss army knife and duct tape to escape from any situation. Thanks to her captor, she didn't have either. Her Bible lay beside a can of tuna fish, a couple of PowerBars, two candles, and a roll of toilet paper. None of them exactly suitable items for an escape. And anything that might help — like her pocketknife and cell phone — had been confiscated.

She picked up her backpack and shook it upside down. A box of matches tumbled to the ground. She picked it up and fingered the box. With her hands tied together, lighting a match would be awkward at best. She shoved them into the front pocket of her dress and continued studying the room. Beyond a few pots and pans piled up in the corner and some bags of cornmeal to make goza, the room was empty.

205

She rolled her head from side to side, trying to work out the kinks in her neck, then moved past the rickety table to study the walls. Sunlight pierced through narrow cracks. If she could find a loose board or a crack big enough to see through, she might be able to signal someone.

Halfway around the room she found a hole at eye level. Squinting into the morning sun, she waited for her eyes to adjust to the change of light.

From her limited view, the walled compound appeared empty. A rusty car sat next to the cement wall surrounding the premises. A dog slept in the shade of a mango tree, his tail swatting at the flies buzzing around him. Nothing else indicated where she was or gave her a sign of another way out.

At the far end of the compound she spied her guard. He sat on a tree stump with a gun in his hand.

Her shoulders dropped in frustration. When she'd asked Chad why he'd chosen to come to the RD, she never imagined that their choices might end up costing them their lives. She had no desire to play the role of a martyr. The risks of living in this country had always been evident, but she'd expected a bit of common sense and a lot of prayer to keep her alive.

Maneuvering around a large bag of cornmeal, she pressed against the wall with her hands. A splinter dug into her finger, drawing a drop of blood. Beneath a narrow beam of light from a crack in the wall, she managed to pull it out. She sucked her finger, then continued her search.

Christ's love was a compelling factor that had brought her here. A chance to make a difference in the lives of the people here. Comprehending God's love for those who were behind all this wasn't easy. She glanced back at her Bible. Why had Jesus come to a messed-up world full of pain and suffering? In moments like this, nothing made sense.

Natalie continued moving around the square room, pushing on

the boards one at a time. She'd talked to Rachel about forgiveness, but before today, she'd never had to forgive anyone for anything except a few careless drivers and a teacher in eighth grade who publicly accused her of cheating on her midterm. What about now, though? She'd been chased down the Congo and was being held for ransom. Forgiveness wasn't going to be easy.

The dog barked. The door hinges creaked. Natalie spun around as light flooded the room.

Her captor held up the phone. "You'd better pray your friend answers."

"What if he doesn't?"

The man ignored her question.

"You said they were going to pay you two thousand dollars. I can get you ten thousand." The words were out before she had a chance to weigh the consequences. "You let me go and I promise I will get the money to you."

The man hesitated. She knew she'd managed to get his attention, but she didn't miss the suspicion in his eyes.

She took the phone from him. "All you have to do is let me walk out. No one will know what happened and no one will blame you."

He shook his head. "If I let you go, they'll kill me."

"You don't know that."

Natalie eyed the door but knew that any attempts of escape at this point would only get her hurt ... or worse. The only way out at the moment was for him to choose to let her walk out.

"Ten thousand dollars wired to whatever account you want." She pressed her lips together. She had five thousand in savings and knew her parents wouldn't hesitate paying the other half to save her life. "Ten thousand dollars."

"You expect me to trust you?" He took a step back. "Call your friend. I want those photos."

Her fingers trembled as she searched the menu for Chad's number, then punched Call. Her captor stood over her, waiting for the call to connect. "Why are you doing this?" she asked.

"What do you mean?"

"Why are you guarding me? Why this place?"

"I didn't choose you or this place. I should be back at the camp where the army is mobilizing for action, not babysitting some spoiled American who obviously stuck her nose into someone else's business."

The call switched to voice mail, but she wasn't ready to give up yet. "I've got another number I can try."

He reached for the phone, but she pulled her arm back. "I want to find those photos as much as you do. Let me try."

God, you've got to let this work.

She called the second number.

He answered on the first ring. Natalie blew out a sharp breath of relief. "Chad?"

There was a momentary pause on the line. "This is Nick Gilbert. Who is this? Natalie?"

"Chad." Natalie forced a smile. "Where are you?"

There was a second pause. *Come on, come on ...* He had to go along with her. It was her only chance.

"I was on my way to find you."

"I need the photos," she told him.

"I can try. Are you in trouble?"

"Yes. I need you to bring them ..." She turned back to her captor. "Where do you want them?"

He glanced at his watch. "Twelve o'clock, same place."

Natalie nodded. "Bring the photos to the Hotel Oasis by noon."

He grabbed the phone from her. "Those photos had better stay with you ... or the girl is dead."

FORTY-TWO

Chad had thirty minutes in the holding room to let the reality of Paul Hayes' words sink in. Which also meant thirty minutes of worrying about Natalie. He slid back into the hard plastic chair and rested his head against the table while he waited for someone to return with answers. Fatigue washed over his body. Lack of sleep and stress had become a lethal mixture, leaving his senses dulled.

He still couldn't comprehend the accusation. Two and a half million dollars wasn't pocket change. Patrick obviously wanted them out of the way and had gone to a lot of trouble to try to remove them from the equation.

Hayes had assured him that he'd already been in contact with several people from Washington and that they would try and do everything they could to both find Natalie and get the charges dropped. But there were limits to what they could do quickly. And even with possible evidence of a rigged election, there was only so much they could do in an understaffed, underdeveloped Central African country.

Which meant Chad needed to get out of there and help find Natalie. Once he did, his first line of business was going to be arranging a confrontation with Patrick Seko.

209

Chad sat up as the door squeaked open. Paul walked into the room, stopping at the edge of the table. "You found Natalie?" Chad asked.

"No. We're still doing everything we can. So far there have been no reports of any American citizens being brought to a local hospital or prison. We're keeping our eyes open."

"And what about me?" He looked up at Paul, fighting the heavy wall of discouragement. "So do you believe me?"

"I'm not looking forward to dealing with the existence of the Ghost Soldiers, but yes, I believe you. I don't think anyone could look at those photos and think otherwise. As for the possibility of a rigged election, that's what we need to find out next. I'm going to need to talk to Joseph, but I've already talked to some people in Washington and warned the UN's election observers of possible complications with the election."

Chad glanced at his watch. "Joseph was supposed to meet me outside the embassy five minutes ago."

"Good. I'll have the guard send him in. You can come with me."

Chad followed him down the hall and into a large administrative center divided by partitions. Paul's office was separate and simply decorated with traditional masks and a few photos of the Rocky Mountains. One silver frame held a photo of twin girls about seven or eight years old.

"Does your family live here?" Chad asked.

"My wife and daughters. But they've gone home for the holidays. I was planning to meet them in Denver for Christmas. "

Chad understood the older man's deep frown. If a crisis swept the country, everyone's plans for Christmas would be cancelled.

He glanced at the door leading out to a courtyard outside. He had to do something. Sitting here was getting them nowhere. "I want to be out there looking."

Paul shook his head. "I'm sorry, but for now my advice would be for you to stay here at the embassy. With a reward out on your head, you'd only be asking for trouble until the current tensions resolve." Paul reached into his pocket and slid Chad's phone and charger across the table. "We can give you back your phone privileges. You can plug it in behind you."

Chad picked up the phone and plugged it in. Natalie had her cell phone. If it was turned on, there was always the possibility he could get through to her. If nothing else it was worth a try.

His phone found the server then beeped. There was a message. His heart hammered. It was from Natalie. Chad switched to speakerphone and played the message.

"Chad, this is Natalie. I'm being held for ransom. They want the photos—"

He dropped the phone onto the table. A sick feeling spread over him. "Joseph was right. They're holding her."

Paul frowned. "Looks like we can now officially call this a kidnapping."

Chad hit Redial and tried to put a call through to Natalie. It rang half a dozen times then cut off, not even allowing him to leave a message. He shoved the phone into his pocket and tried to find a scenario other than the one he feared was true. She'd been kidnapped by thugs who hadn't thought twice about killing innocent people in the mountainous village. Why would they do any differently with Natalie once they didn't need her anymore? Or if they found out he was sitting at the embassy with the photos.

"I'll contact the FBI's legal attaché in Nairobi and have them send a negotiator to the capital."

Chad let out a sigh of relief. They might finally make some progress. "What can they do?"

"They're trained to secure the release of American hostages overseas."

"Even if we don't know who we're dealing with yet?"

"We'll find her."

Chad squeezed his eyes shut, praying the man was right. "How soon until they can get here?"

"I'm not sure. I'd hope by tomorrow morning, but this isn't the same as catching a commuter flight from New York to DC."

Chad's mind flickered to Joseph's father and then to Natalie. Tomorrow morning might be too late.

FORTY-THREE

Nick hung up the phone with Natalie. He had one hour to get to the hotel with the photos. Despite the humid weather, a chill ran down his spine as he stared at Rachel's body. He glanced out the window from Rachel's apartment and onto the street below. Their jaunt across the country had just taken another horrible twist.

The green curtains covering Rachel's open window waved in the morning breeze. Gone was the hope that this excursion involved nothing more than a quick delivery of goods to the capital. Now he was simply determined to make sure the death toll didn't rise any more.

Two policemen stood outside the building talking to a shopkeeper and blocking his escape. The last thing he needed was to be accused of being involved in Rachel's death. The TV and DVD player still sat on the cabinet. He was no expert, but he was quite certain this was no random burglary.

It wasn't hard for him to draw his own conclusions. If Rachel had taken in Chad and Natalie, it was more than likely against the wishes of her fiancé. And now she was dead. From what he'd heard from Natalie, this put Patrick Seko in the middle of everything.

For the moment, though, he couldn't worry about Patrick or

213

Rachel. With Natalie's life in danger, he needed to find Chad and the photos. He flipped open his phone and called Chad again. His friend answered on the second ring.

"Chad? It's Nick."

"Where are you?"

"At your friend Rachel's apartment."

"So you made it out of the jungle?" The normally upbeat tenor of Chad's voice was gone.

"I'll save that saga for another day."

"At least you're all right. I'm at the embassy right now. And Natalie ... she's been kidnapped."

"I know. I just spoke to her."

"What?"

Nick glanced out the window. The two uniformed policemen were still there. "When Natalie couldn't get ahold of you, she called me instead."

"What did she say?"

"Her captors think she was talking to you, and they want you to meet them in an hour at the Oasis Hotel with the photos."

"So they'll make an exchange?"

"That's what I'm hoping, but there's something else." Nick stared at Rachel's still form on the couch. "Natalie's friend Rachel ... she's dead. I can't see a weapon, but it doesn't look like a robbery either."

There was a pause on the other end of the line. "We stayed there last night. We knew they were after us, but ..." Chad's voice cracked. "I'll let the embassy know what's going on and arrange for them to take me to the hotel. But whoever these guys are, they mean business. Nick, if they find out that I'm here and have the photos, they'll kill Natalie too."

"Then we need to start praying that doesn't happen." Nick looked outside once more. The police were gone. "I'm heading to the embassy now, but if for whatever reason she doesn't return with you, we'll figure something out, Chad. We're going to find her."

FORTY-FOUR

Chad glanced at his watch again. It was already after twelve, and
Natalie was nowhere to be seen. The RD didn't have any five-star
hotels, at least by American standards, but the Oasis was the closest
thing they had to luxury accommodations. For two hundred dollars
a night, a guest could forget he was in a third-world country and
enjoy the swimming pool, gift shops, restaurants, and travel agen-
cies. Forget, that was, until they stepped outside onto the rush of the
main boulevard.

The lobby was quiet and filled with modern furniture, palm trees,
and touches of the local decor. He crossed the tiled floor, stopping
near the entrance where a security guard stood to ensure prostitutes
and other unwanted individuals didn't enter. Paul's car sat parked
across the street, barely within view of the front of the hotel.

His phone vibrated and he answered it immediately.

"Chad, it's Paul."

Chad could see the silhouette of the embassy worker in the backseat of his chauffer-driven car. "There's no sign of her yet."

"Then I'm taking you back to the embassy now —"

"No." Chad stepped away from the window. "She could still be
coming."

"If they arrest you, you'll be shoved in some prison cell, and you won't be able to do anything for her."

Chad turned around and searched the lobby. He wasn't ready to give up yet. "What about Nick? Has he arrived at the embassy yet?"

"I called five minutes ago, and he'd just shown up. Someone's doing interviews with both Nick and Joseph now."

"Give me fifteen more minutes."

A woman walked across the lobby, her back to Chad. His pulse skipped. Sundress, ponytail, sandals ... She turned and waved at someone sitting on the other side of the lobby. He let out the breath he'd been holding. It wasn't her.

"Chad —"

"Fifteen minutes."

FORTY-FIVE

Chad slid into the backseat of Paul's car, convinced he'd made a mistake in leaving the hotel. But thirty more minutes had passed and there was still no sign of Natalie. Which meant something had gone wrong.

As soon as he shut the car door, Paul signaled for his driver to leave. "They're not coming, Chad."

He rubbed the back of his neck. "There are a dozen demonstrations going on around the city. They could be caught in traffic, or detained at a police roadblock — "

"If that were the case, don't you think they'd call and let you know they'd run into some kind of problem, but were still coming?"

"I don't know."

"I'm just making a logical observation," Paul countered.

"Nothing's logical about any of this."

Chad checked to make sure his phone was still on — which, of course, it was. Paul was right. They simply hadn't called.

The images playing out in his mind didn't help, but he couldn't deny that the captors' silence probably meant that, for whatever reason, they didn't need Natalie as insurance anymore. The scenario churned his stomach.

He tapped his fingers against the armrest. "Tell me what's logical about kidnapping someone over a handful of photos, murdering your fiancée, and then —"

"We don't know for sure that Patrick is involved."

Chad ignored Paul's frown. "I might not be able to connect him directly to the Ghost Soldiers and the election, but he's involved. Since Stephan saw the photos Natalie was robbed, her house trashed, we were both chased through the middle of the jungle, and now he's put out a reward for our capture, Natalie's been kidnapped, his fiancée killed ... Sounds pretty involved to me."

Slivers of guilt sliced through him. What he did know was that he should have insisted they all stay together when they left Rachel's house. Of course, there was always the possibility they all would have been taken hostage, but at least he'd be with her and able to do something to help her. What he hated was not being able to do anything. Like now.

"We do have another lead on him."

"On Patrick?" Their car hit a pothole, and Chad smacked his head against the window. "What is it?"

"My secretary called a few minutes ago and told me that one of our embassy workers talked to Rachel this morning. Apparently they were friends and Rachel gave her something she wants us to see. We'll meet her at her apartment, which is only a few minutes from here."

The crowds were beginning to swell along the sidewalks. Banners for the election blew in the breeze. "I thought you said it was too risky for me to be out in public."

"It probably is, but it's quicker to meet her at her house than if we wait for her to return to the embassy on public transport. If we're going to get answers, we need them quickly."

"Fine." Chad prayed this wasn't going to be a wild-goose chase, but the truth was they didn't have any other leads at the moment.

Ten minutes later, Mercy greeted them at the door of a small apartment on the fifth floor of her building and ushered them into the tiny living room. It was decorated simply with locally made teak furniture, handmade doilies, and family photos. Chad sat down on the worn leather couch, thanked Mercy's mother for the drink and cookies she offered him, then proceeded — as tradition required — to ask the woman about her family. Even growing up in the RD couldn't erase the impatience of not being able to get to the point, but here time was relative. There was a process to follow and rushing through it would only leave him — and his hostess — frustrated. It was simply the way things were done.

Greetings took ten minutes. When her mother finally left the room, Mercy pulled an envelope from a drawer in the television cabinet, then sat down across from them on a plaid chair that had seen better days. "I'm sorry. I'm sure you are in a hurry."

Paul took a sip of his Coke. "It's fine. Your mother's a gracious hostess."

"Thank you." Mercy's pretty, dark face was etched with a deep frown. "She's really dead?"

"I'm sorry."

"I just talked to her this morning." Tears flooded the woman's eyes. "She came by my apartment right as I was on my way to work. She was upset. She was on her way to the embassy, but had forgotten something at her apartment."

She slid the envelope across the coffee table. "Rachel gave these to me and told me if anything happened to her ... I thought she was just being paranoid after a fight with Patrick. I never really thought anything serious was going to happen ... At least not this serious."

Paul picked up the envelope, broke open the seal, and pulled out a half dozen printed pages. "It's e-mail correspondence and photocopies of some kind of demographic government reports."

"Whose e-mail correspondence?" Chad asked.

"Patrick's." Paul flipped through the pages. "Rachel must have printed them from Patrick's computer."

"What exactly did Rachel say when she gave them to you?" Chad asked.

Mercy fidgeted in her chair. "She said she'd had company over last night and that there had been a problem, but she was in a hurry and didn't elaborate."

"I wonder if she told Natalie about the e-mails," Chad cut in. "She was obviously worried that something might happen to her."

Paul took another sip of his Coke. "Fear can be a powerful motivator. It can also be just as powerful a silencer."

Chad shook his head. "So she must have gone by Patrick's office and gotten onto his computer. Would they let her do that?"

Mercy nodded. "They know her there, so it wouldn't have seemed out of the ordinary for her to show up, even when Patrick wasn't there. She often went after work and helped him or waited in his office for him to return from a business meeting."

Paul tugged on the end of his tie. "How long have you known Rachel?"

"Four and a half, maybe five, years."

"So you know Patrick?" Chad asked.

"Of course. He's ... Well, I'll just say that I don't particularly like the man, but she seemed to love him, and he treated her well most of the time."

"Most of the time?" Paul handed her a tissue from the end table beside him.

She blew her nose with the tissue, then took a deep breath. "He can be a bit possessive and demanding, but that's Patrick."

"Is there anything else you can tell us about Rachel and Patrick?"

"Rachel never talked much about her personal life, especially when it came to romantic interests. But for the past few weeks, I believe she was starting to have reservations about marrying Patrick."

"What do you mean exactly?"

"When Patrick asked her to marry him, her family was ecstatic.

Rachel's father is a member of parliament, and they believed that marrying Patrick would help cement his post in the government."

"Did Rachel ever tell you specifically that she was having doubts?"

Mercy shook her head. "Not in so many words, though she did tell me once that she wasn't sure where Patrick's loyalties were."

"Meaning?"

"At the time it made me wonder if she was implying his loyalties no longer lay with the president, but instead with a higher bidder."

"Do you think the higher bidder in this case is Okella?" Chad asked.

Mercy shook her head again. "I don't know."

Paul handed Chad the stack of papers. He scanned through them and, while no names were mentioned, the intent was obvious. *Need to make the rest of my deposit ... I've taken care of it ... The problem has been neutralized ...*

If they were interpreting things right, Patrick had shifted his allegiance to the other side.

FORTY-SIX

Chad's footsteps echoed as he hurried down the metal staircase toward the ground floor of the apartment building. He moved out of the way of two girls who carried heavy bags of cornmeal on their heads and wondered how many people had escaped into the city only to find life as strenuous as it had been in the village.

Paul opened the outside door and they merged onto the crowded street, with Chad bringing up the rear behind Paul and Mercy. The light breeze felt good after the stuffiness of Mercy's apartment.

Chad stopped for a moment on the sidewalk. Strange. The clothes shop they'd passed coming in had rolled down its metal awning and closed for the day. The shop beside it was closed, as were several others on the block.

The crowds were getting heavier. Dozens of people milled through the streets. Children hung posters of President Tau on telephone poles while others waved banners for Barnard Okella. Chad groaned. Another rally was beginning.

He turned away at the sight of a police officer. He was tired of playing cat and mouse, and at this point wasn't sure which was the bigger threat — the authorities or a mob that could turn violent in an instant.

"Where's your driver?" he shouted at Paul above the roar of the crowd.

The embassy driver appeared from the alley behind them before Paul had a chance to respond. "I'm sorry. I had to move the car. The streets are too crowded and I was getting blocked in."

"What's going on out here?" Paul asked.

"Riots have broken out all over town," the driver told them, still trying to catch his breath. "I just heard on the radio that the army's moving in and every available police officer is required to report to work."

Street kids waved posters of President Tau and shouted his name in unison. Joseph had mentioned how it was common for the political parties to hire street children to help with the rallies. One of the flyers fluttered to the ground in front of Chad. He picked it up. President Tau looked back at him.

Chad glanced behind him. Antiriot police were moving in to block the street behind them. This was no pre-election rally. With the votes not even in to be calculated, how had things escalated into a riot?

"What do we do now?" Mercy's voice trembled in fear.

Chad searched for an escape. The way back to Mercy's apartment was blocked. The faint scent of tear gas filled the air. Black smoke from burning tires billowed in the distance. A gun fired and the crowd began to scatter.

"We've got to get out of here," Chad shouted above the chaos.

Their driver waved for them to follow him. "I'm parked a couple blocks north."

He ushered the three of them down one of the side streets past a row of closed shops. They reached the embassy car and had just managed to shut the doors when a ripple of gunfire broke out behind them.

Paul told the driver to floor it, then flipped on the radio. The local news channel was reporting how the current head of the military,

General Dumasi, was on his way to try to stop the unruly attacks that had taken place across the city during the past few hours with an unprecedented face-to-face meeting with the protestors.

Where were the president and vice president in all of this?

Chad gripped the armrest to keep his balance as they wove through the heavy traffic. Forty minutes later they pulled through the secure gates of the embassy. It should only have taken ten minutes, but at least he felt safe now. And guilty. Natalie should be here as well.

Paul led Chad into the building, barking orders to his staff. "Meeting in five minutes. I want to know what's going on out there." He turned to Chad. "You're with me."

Within five minutes, Paul's staff had assembled, and the guards were ordered not to allow anyone without an American passport inside the premises. With the city in turmoil, they were officially closed for the day.

"Political rallies across the city turned ugly this morning when a car exploded four blocks from here," the consular assistant, introduced to Chad as Brandon Carmichael, began. "Antiriot police arrived in key locations, but their presence only seemed to spark further demonstrations across the city."

Paul scribbled on his notepad. "What set them off to begin with?"

"From what we've been told," the assistant continued, "it began as nothing more than normal political rallies held to encourage voting. The parties hired a few dozen street kids to hang posters, wear T-shirts, and chant. It wasn't supposed to get ugly."

Paul looked up. "But it did."

"Fourteen are dead in the Umgani district, including two police officers and one minor. Another man was killed across town when a stray bullet hit him."

Chad scratched his ear. He felt as if he'd just stepped into a war-room discussion.

Paul scribbled something else on his pad. "What's the UN's involvement at this point?"

Another man, with wire glasses and a receding hairline, spoke up. "The plan at the moment is a continued military presence throughout the city with the addition of a curfew if things don't settle down immediately."

"We heard on our way here that General Dumasi is planning to meet with the protesters," Chad spoke up. "Is that true?"

Carmichael nodded. "I believe they are even planning to televise the exchange in an attempt to encourage the population to stay away from the rioting areas."

"Shouldn't that be the role of the president, or, at the least, the vice president?" Paul threw out.

"General Dumasi is still head of the military, and at this point, he's as good a man as any," Carmichael continued. "No one has forgotten the last coup that almost destroyed this country. Today's death toll is nothing compared to what happened back then, but it's got to stop now if we're going to avoid it happening again."

Chad noted the worried expression on Paul's face. They all knew what would happen if something went wrong in this election. The cord was already pulled too tight, despite the UN's attempts at a peaceful election. Protests, flares of violence, killing, and tribal conflict could set off another civil war that could last for months and destroy any strides the country had made in the past few years.

"I understand there's been no word yet from Natalie Sinclair," Paul continued.

The man with the glasses shook his head.

Chad swallowed his panic. It had been over six hours since he'd seen Natalie, and there was nothing he could do about it.

"We just received an official report from the police department regarding the death of Patrick Seko's fiancée," the consular assistant continued. "Her death, though, is believed to be completely unrelated with today's violence."

"And?" Paul prodded.

"From the initial investigation, we were told that her death is being called a suicide."

Chad spoke up for the first time. "That's impossible."

"Excuse me?"

Chad leaned forward in his chair to address the consular assistant, wondering if he'd just spoken out of turn. "When I talked to Nick Gilbert on the phone, he was at her apartment and distinctly told me that she'd been murdered. There was no sign of a burglary or a weapon."

"He told us the same story in his statement," Paul said.

"The bottom line is that if you start looking at all these pieces side by side," Chad continued, "I don't think there's any denying that someone's trying to cover up something. The photos, Natalie's disappearance, Rachel's death, and who knows? Maybe even the riots. There's no way I can be convinced that all of this is simply coincidence."

Joseph walked into the room and took an offered chair across from Chad. At least they'd managed to keep Joseph safe.

Paul passed the boy a Coke. "How are you doing, young man? Guess you've been through the wringer today."

"Yes, sir."

"Sorry we're late." Mercy entered the room behind Joseph. "We've gone over his story thoroughly and have a report ready to file."

"Anything new —"

An explosion rocked the room. Windows shattered. Chad felt the vibration of the blast as he dropped to the floor and covered his head.

FORTY-SEVEN

Gabby stared at the ringing cell phone that sat on the kitchen table beside her while the yellow center of her egg oozed across the plate onto a slice of half-burnt toast. Any appetite she'd managed to recover vanished.

"Gabby, what are you doing?" Sabrina entered the room from the kitchen with a cup of coffee and reached for the offending object. "Your phone's ringing."

"Don't answer it."

"You have to — "

Gabby knocked the phone from Sabrina's hands and watched it slam onto the tile floor. The persistent ringing stopped. "I said don't answer it."

"Hey." Sabrina pushed aside the pile of *Bride* magazines cluttering the table for her and Michael's Valentine's Day wedding in order to set her coffee mug down, then slid into the seat beside her. "What in the world's going on?"

"Nothing."

"Nothing? Look at yourself. You can't sleep, and you're not eating." She picked up her fork, then dropped it back onto the plate. "You've been a wreck ever since you returned from Africa."

Gabby pressed her fingertips against her face. She'd tried to sleep, but how could she sleep when her dreams were haunted with images she couldn't forget.

Sabrina took a sip of her coffee. "I thought we were best friends. Tell me what's going on."

Rising, Gabby stalked into the kitchen with her uneaten food and dumped the cold eggs down the garbage disposal. Sabrina would pester her until she told her, and she didn't have the energy to fight. "I've received some threatening phone calls and e-mails the past couple of days."

Just like her father.

Sabrina followed Gabby back into the dining room, where she sank back into the padded chair. "Why didn't you tell me any of this before?"

"Because you'd worry — like my mother worries — and try to convince me not to have my series printed."

"An article isn't worth your life."

Gabby waved the notion away. "You don't understand."

"What happened over there?"

Gabby flipped through the pages of one of the magazines, wondering how different her life would be today if she'd opted to cover wedding trends. "Apparently someone didn't like all the questions I was asking."

"Do you know who's behind the threats?"

Gabby shrugged, wishing the answer wasn't so elusive. "I talked to at least a dozen investors from Lusaka to Bogama to Dar es Salaam. There were some who seemed to legitimately want to help the people working for them, and others who were obviously exploiting their workers and pocketing all the profit. All it would take is one who didn't like what I wrote about them."

"Apparently you found that one."

"That's not all." She toyed with the rounded handle of her half-empty coffee cup. "The last night we were in Bogama, I was involved in an ... incident."

"An incident?"

Gabby sat back and folded her arms across her chest. She could still hear it all — the shouts, the glass, the gunshots ... "We stopped at a red light. A gunshot shattered the driver's window, and a half dozen men surrounded the car and dragged the driver out onto the street."

"Oh, Gabby ..."

"The men were scrambling to get into the car when another shot was fired," she continued. "Apparently our driver had a weapon they hadn't counted on. In the confusion, my translator, Adam, managed to scoot into the driver's seat and drive away. It all happened so fast ..."

"What happened to the driver?"

"We found out later he was taken to the hospital with several broken bones and a concussion, but he lived."

"He's lucky."

"We all were." Gabby shoved back a strand of hair that had fallen across her forehead. "But I can't live in fear. My father didn't."

"No, he didn't, but that doesn't mean you can take chances with your life."

Gabby glanced up and caught Sabrina's gaze. "So I live in fear and never go out until ... when? I can't even trace this guy."

"Isn't that what you're doing now? Living in fear?"

Gabby pressed her lips together. She'd spent the past twenty-four hours trying to figure out where to go with this. Holing up in her house wasn't the direction she wanted to take.

Sabrina reached out and squeezed her hand. "Maybe the truth in this case isn't worth your life."

This was the conversation she'd wanted to avoid. "I'm not the first journalist who's believed they're onto something that's worth the risk of exposing. Look at Don Bolles, Ivo Pukanic, Anna Politkovskaya — "

"And your father?"

Gabby slumped against the back of the chair and shut her eyes.

She could still read the headlines as if it were yesterday. *"Freelance journalist murdered for his hard-hitting commentary that angered corrupt officials ..."*

She opened her eyes and caught her friend's worried gaze. "This isn't about my father —"

"This has everything to do with your father. Everything to do with your trying to finish what he wasn't able to do."

Gabby slammed her fists against the table, rattling the remaining dishes. "Did you even read what I wrote? Businesses, foreign investors, and even governments are coming into these small, unknown countries promising schools and roads and hospitals, but in exchange they're stripping them of their natural resources and exploiting their people. Working conditions are deplorable, children are dying because of the lack of safety regulations —"

"I read your article and saw in it the compassion you have for those people, but it's not worth your life."

"But you didn't see what I saw." Gabby choked back the tears. "Children, some of them only three or four years old, caked in mud from riverbeds, were working in narrow tunnels mining coltan for cell phones. Others I found sifting through sand for gems inside homemade mineshafts. These children are dying from dynamite accidents and floods and ..." She pressed her fingers against her pounding temples. "I can't get them out of my head. I see them at night when I close my eyes, and they're still there in the morning when I wake up. They need a voice —"

"And you can't be their voice if you're dead."

Her cell phone started ringing again from beneath the kitchen table. Her hand trembled and knocked over the coffee mug in front of her. Lukewarm liquid ran off the edge of the table and splattered onto the floor. She grabbed for a napkin and stopped the thread of coffee snaking its way toward the stack of magazines.

"This has gone too far." Sabrina picked up the phone and answered the call. "I don't know who you are, but —"

She stopped mid-sentence.

"Excuse me?" Sabrina's face paled. She listened to the response, then handed Gabby the phone. "I think you ought to take this. It's someone from Interpol."

FORTY-EIGHT

Joseph stared across the room as if he were watching the nightly news on his uncle's color television. This couldn't be happening here. Blood dripped from his forehead and now stained his pants, but he couldn't feel anything. Nor did he care. All he noticed at the moment was the gaping hole on the other side of the room. From his vantage point, he could see the green lawn of the embassy. Sirens screamed in the background. People rushed by. Paramedics pushed a man on a stretcher.

"Joseph?"

He heard his name but couldn't stop staring at the hole. Bricks and debris filled the side of the room where Dr. Talcott had been sitting just moments earlier. Now he was gone. A wave of nausea struck. They'd killed him. Just like they'd killed his grandfather. And the way they'd kill his father.

Someone touched his shoulder. "I need to look at your head, Joseph."

The doctor's chair lay upside down beside the pile of bricks. "Where is he?"

The woman pulled out a sliver of glass, then pressed a cloth against his head. "Who?"

"Dr.... Dr. Talcott."

"Dr. Talcott —"

Someone shouted.

The woman hovering over him looked away. "Press this against your forehead. I'll be right back."

Joseph couldn't wait. He got up and walked toward the sunlight streaming in through the hole. Ducking down, he started scooting through the opening. A brick scraped against his back. Someone hollered at him to move. He stumbled backward at the order.

A portion of the wall crumbled in front of him.

Still pressing his hand against his head, he tried to escape the roar of voices pressing in around him. He left the room and ran down the hall, looking for a sign of the doctor. Paul Hayes, one of the men he'd met earlier, stood in the center of one of the offices shouting orders.

Joseph tried to slow down his breathing. Natalie had told him that prayer worked. Maybe it was time he started praying.

If you happen to be there, God ... we need a miracle. Several, to be exact.

"Joseph."

Joseph turned around at the sound of his name. Dr. Talcott stood in the doorway.

Joseph's jaw dropped open. "Dr. Talcott ... I thought ..."

"I heard you got cut on the forehead. Are you all right?"

"I think so."

"Can I take a look?"

Joseph nodded, noting the long scratch across Dr. Talcott's left arm. Other than that, he seemed fine. They'd both been lucky. He squirmed as the older man touched the wound.

"No stitches this time, but you're going to have matching scars."

Joseph smiled. Maybe Natalie was right and prayer really did work.

"Why don't you sit down over there and wait for me, Joseph? We've got a triage set up outside where we're treating the injured, though so far there don't seem to be any life-threatening wounds." Dr. Talcott turned back to Mr. Hayes. "I was told you had an extra first-aid kit in here?"

He watched as Mr. Hayes rummaged in the bottom drawer of a desk and tossed a kit to the doctor. "Boy, I'm glad you're here."

"So am I." Dr. Talcott shoved the kit under his arm and caught Joseph's gaze. "You'll be safe here. I'll see you in a little bit."

Joseph pressed his hand against the bandage, wondering if he really was safe. He hadn't felt that way for days. If only he could disappear into the walls like he didn't exist. Maybe there he wouldn't feel any more pain.

FORTY-NINE

Gabby stood gazing out the window that overlooked the front lawns of the office building, hoping that her tailored black slacks and white button-down shirt projected the image she wanted. Typically, she thrived on the unexpected, but Tuesday's attack still had her reeling. She licked her lips and turned to the door as it opened. No need for the law to see that.

A man walked into the room. Late forties, gray suit. "Miss Mackenzie. Thank you for coming. I'm Mickey Chandler." He set a file beside his can of Coke on the table and shook her hand. "Can I get you something to drink? Coffee, tea, or maybe a soda?"

"No, thank you. I'm fine." She drew in a deep breath, still curious about Interpol's interest in her articles.

"Good, then we can get started." He motioned for her to take the chair across from him, then sat down. "I appreciate your agreeing to meet with me on such short notice. I understand you just recently returned to the States?"

"Yesterday."

"Still a bit of jet lag, then, I'm sure."

"Some." She set her briefcase down beside her, then clasped her hands in front of her on the long conference table. "Mr. Chandler,

235

I'm still not sure I understand what this is all about. On the phone, you mentioned my recent article in the newspaper and the need to see my research."

He took another sip of his Coke, then flipped open the file. "I was flying back from New York yesterday and happened to read in yesterday's paper the first installment on your series on the surge of investors going into Africa. It was extremely well written and thought provoking."

Enough to catch Interpol's attention?

"I'm hoping that what I wrote will catch the public's eye, as well as that of the governments involved." Gabby spoke from passion as much as facts. "It's time we forced these businesses and investors to change the despicable working conditions thousands are forced to live under. Nothing will change if they aren't held accountable."

"I can see that you're quite the advocate."

"It's a heart-wrenching reality in our world, especially when one realizes human trafficking, child slavery, and a booming sex industry are all alive and well right here in the United States."

Mr. Chandler tapped the edge of his drink against the desk. "I assume you have proof backing up your claims of negligence for each of the investors you named?"

"I wouldn't be a good journalist if I didn't, now would I?" Was it possible for Interpol to help? "I have all the proof you need to start an official investigation. I'll admit, though, that I never imagined that Interpol might want to be involved — "

Mr. Chandler held up his hand. "While I admire greatly what you are doing, at this point I'm only interested in one person. Alexis Yasin."

"Yasin?" She shook her head. "I don't understand. Yasin is only one of a number of wealthy investors and corporations mentioned in my series."

"I realize that, but for now let's just talk about Yasin. Your article said that you weren't able to secure an interview with him, but that you had proof of his involvement in a number of the mines."

"I tried numerous times to contact him after a source informed me he was staying in the capital of the Republic of Dhambizao. I even stayed in the country an extra day in order to track him down, but I was never able to verify he was there, and any attempts on my part to get his side of the story were completely ignored. I can, though, verify his financial involvement with at least two questionable mining companies operating in Central Africa whose low standards of safety and—"

"I'm going to need everything you have on him."

Gabby's gaze narrowed as she fingered the leather briefcase beside her. "I don't understand. If this doesn't have to do with my article—"

"You understand that much of the evidence we have is classified, but we believe he is involved in money laundering throughout Africa and Western Europe."

Gabby's mind spun through the implications. "Which means he's using these mines along with other legitimate businesses as fronts?"

"That's what I intend to prove."

She opened her briefcase, flipped through the copied files, and pulled out everything she had on Yasin before sliding it all across table. The three photos she'd printed out from Natalie stared up at her from the back of the folder.

"Can I ask you a question?"

"Of course."

She pushed one of the photos toward Mr. Chandler and pointed to one of the men. "I've been trying to identify him."

"In connection to your series?"

She nodded.

"Off the record?" Mr. Chandler picked up the photo. "His name's Benjamin Ayres. He works directly under Yasin."

Which potentially put Yasin in the middle of whatever had

happened in the RD. Which meant he was probably the one after her. Gabby felt her lungs constrict.

"Where did you get these photos?"

"Off the record?" she asked.

Mr. Chandler shot her a half smile.

"Natalie Sinclair is an American working in the RD as a health care worker," she began, then quickly filled him in on what she knew of the situation. "Unfortunately, I haven't been able to get ahold of her since my arrival back in the States, so I still have a lot of unanswered questions."

From the look on the older man's face it was obvious they were thinking the same thing: Gabby might not be the only person on Yasin's bad side.

"I'll keep trying to get ahold of her."

"Keep me informed, then. And there is one other thing I wanted to mention to you." He stopped her before she left the room. "You know there's a chance that these people aren't going to stop at e-mail threats. I know about your father —"

"My father?"

"I read about his death in Sudan."

"I'll take my chances." Her frown deepened. "Just like my father did."

Mr. Chandler pulled out a card with his private number on it and handed it to her. "I'll be in touch, but if you find out anything else … or if you need something, call me. Anytime, twenty-four hours a day."

She took the card and slipped it into her front pocket. She had to find Natalie. It was time to connect the dots.

FIFTY

Natalie paced the room. Her calves ached from the repetitive movement of marching back and forth across the cement floor, but she
simply couldn't sit still. After seven-plus hours, she'd finally accepted
the reality that there was no way out. She'd memorized every crack
in the wall and followed every shifting shadow in a room that was
now growing darker by the second. In fifteen more minutes, she
estimated, the sun would drop below the horizon and leave her in
complete darkness.

Twelve o'clock had come and gone without any sign of her captor, a fact that had her worried. She'd seen the exchange as her one
chance of freedom. Instead, she'd been forced to spend her time trying to escape. The faint cracks in the wall had eventually revealed
more than the glaring African sun. A guard with a machine gun
stood half a dozen steps from the front door. She'd hollered at him
until her voice was hoarse. All he'd done was turn up his radio and
ignore her.

She walked to the other side of the room, following the now familiar path around bags of cornmeal and charcoal. The dog barked,
reminding her of its presence. She knew she could handle the dog.
The typical African mutt was little threat. It was the discovery of

another guard on the east side of the building that had discouraged her from using the can of tuna as a hammer in an attempt to remove the hinges from the door. When it came to an armed man, canned goods weren't much of a defense.

A cramp gripped her calf, and she sat down on the chair to rub the sore spot. Shifting to the left, she felt the box of matches she'd shoved into her dress pocket. Once the tight spot in her muscle dissolved, she pulled out the box of matches and took one out. She lit it, letting the flame burn until she could feel the heat against her fingers before she shook the match to extinguish its yellow glow. Burning down the place was always an option, except for the high odds of getting trapped inside.

The endlessness of not knowing what was happening was torture.

A key rattled in the lock. Fear left room for a smidgen of hope as the hinges squeaked and the door opened. If she could at least talk to someone, she might be able to do something to help with her escape.

She squinted to make out the burly figure in the doorway.

Patrick stood with a lantern and a plate of food.

The blackened match she'd held between her fingers dropped to the floor. "Patrick?"

Her stomach clenched. Gut instincts she'd tried to ignore surfaced. She hadn't wanted to believe Patrick was behind all this, but unless he was here with a rescue party, that's exactly what he'd done.

He set the plate of food on the table before pulling out a chair and sitting down.

She stayed standing as her heart sank. This was obviously no rescue. "What are you doing here?"

It had been hours since she'd last eaten, but the rich scent of the sauce turned her stomach.

"I could ask the same of you. I think I told you more than once not to get involved." Patrick pushed the plate toward her, then started to untie her bound wrists. "You've got five minutes. Eat."

"Not get involved with what?" Anger seared through her. "The demolition of a village? The disappearance of Joseph's family? The reality of a slave trade in these mountains? Don't tell me you actually expected me not to say anything."

"I warned you to leave things alone. No one was paying any attention to your little demographic reports, but you had to keep poking and asking questions."

So that was why he'd been interested in her statistics? To make sure she wasn't close to finding out the truth? Which, thanks to Joseph, was exactly what had happened. She'd discovered the truth: Ghost Soldiers weren't legends told around the dinner fires at night. They'd stolen hundreds, maybe thousands, of people from their homes and turned them into slaves.

Natalie eyed the door and weighed her options. She knew she should eat. As much as she had no appetite, losing strength because of not eating wasn't going to help. She needed to be ready to escape if given an opportunity.

Patrick gripped the rope between his fingers. "I wouldn't try anything. Trust me, you don't want to be out there at night in this part of town."

Despite the balmy breeze floating through the open door, Natalie shivered. She sat down and managed to swallow her first bite without gagging. If she couldn't escape, at least she could get some answers. "Did you get the photos from Chad?"

"Things have changed and I decided it wasn't worth the risk."

Natalie bit back her frustration, tired of the game. "Then what happens now, Patrick?"

"A good question, but you, unfortunately, have found yourself in the middle of something far bigger than a simple village raid."

She pointed to her wounded shoulder. "Is that why you sent the cavalry after me? Because of the photos?"

"The photos don't matter anymore."

Fear returned. Then why she was still here ... alive? Up until now, she'd believed the photos to be her one source of insurance.

"The other night at Stephen's party you told me that if something happened during the elections, you would simply blame it on the UN committee. What do the elections have to do with the Ghost Soldiers?"

"I've always believed that it pays to be on the right side."

She let her spoon clink against the edge of the metal plate. "And whose side is that? The one who pays the most?"

"You never were good at politics, Natalie. I'd suggest you stick to your health care projects."

She toyed with the edge of the plate. "You're the one who put out the reward for Chad and me, aren't you?"

Patrick's brow rose. "If you think this is my time for confessions, you're wrong."

"I can't believe you were behind all this."

"Then what do you want to believe? The truth is that this country will never be worth the diamonds hidden inside its mines unless someone stands up and takes advantage of what we already have. We could wait a thousand years and nothing would change."

She shoved her plate aside, her appetite gone. There were too many people who believed there was no chance for change, and she refused to be one of them. But this way would never help anyone. "I don't get it, Patrick."

Patrick retied the ropes around her wrists. "Get what?"

"You're throwing away everything you have for a chance at what? No, let me guess. A bigger paycheck? The thing is I thought you were too smart to bow to the highest bidder. Especially when you could lose it all in an instant."

"I don't bow to anyone."

"Maybe that's part of the problem. Your alliances don't run past the surface. They could change in an instant, and you would be left on the outside."

He tugged on the end of the rope, letting it bite into her flesh. "That's not the only way to look at things."

She ignored the pain. "Really."

"Have you ever stopped and thought that just maybe I actually want what's best for my people? So much, in fact, that I'm willing to risk everything to change this country for something better?"

"No, I don't believe you want what's best for your people. Not when hundreds are being held against their will and others are being killed because they're too old or ill. We all know that this election is a chance for the RD to finally prove they're willing to hold a fair election and listen to the voices of the people."

"Think about the discovery of oil reserves in Equatorial Guinea, for example," he countered. "Their per capita income isn't much lower than the United States."

"But how much of that income makes its way into the pocket of the average person?" Natalie replied. "I've seen the statistics. Thirty percent are unemployed, and their water isn't even drinkable. The money still stays at the top. Nothing really changed. Is that what you want for your country?"

"You put the right people in charge, and it doesn't have to be that way."

She didn't believe him. Prosperity for the people? Or for a lucky handful who managed to gain power? "And what about those who end up paying the price? What about Joseph's family?"

He shoved his chair back and stood. "There are casualties in every war."

"What does Rachel think about all of this? Or does she even know?"

"Rachel ..." His gaze shifted to the floor.

Alarm shot through Natalie. "Where is she, Patrick?"

"It doesn't matter anymore."

"It doesn't matter?" Natalie moved to stand in front of him. "What did you do to her?"

He pushed her back down onto the chair. "I didn't do anything."

Natalie's back struck against the chair, causing her to wince. "Then who did?"

Patrick stopped short in the doorway. "I loved her."

"You killed her, didn't you?"

Patrick wiped moisture from his forehead. "It was all supposed to be so simple. Then everywhere I turned, it seemed, things went wrong."

"I know that taking a life will never right a wrong." Natalie suppressed her growing anger. "So what happens now?"

"For the moment, I figure you're worth more to me alive. A sort of ... guarantee."

"A guarantee for what?"

"For the next twenty-four hours. That's all the time I need. After that, it won't really matter."

Natalie swallowed hard. Then he'd kill her. Just like he'd presumably done to Rachel. This had nothing to do with helping his people. "What's going to happen tomorrow, Patrick? How are you planning to sabotage the election?"

"I suggest you get a good night's sleep. Tomorrow's going to be a very busy day."

The door slammed behind him, leaving Natalie in darkness. She crossed the room, stopping at the small hole in the wall. Stars traversed the black carpet of sky, blinking like diamonds across the vast expanse of heavens.

Suddenly, she felt very small.

FIFTY-ONE

Gabby exited the crowded department store wondering when businesses had started playing Christmas music in November. Not that she didn't enjoy the season's hustle and bustle all wrapped in the nostalgic flutter of lights and decorations, but she hadn't even started thawing the Thanksgiving turkey yet.

She glanced behind her, an impulse that was quickly becoming a habit. While her meeting with Mickey Chandler had left her frustrated that the government wasn't interested in getting involved like she'd hoped, putting a plausible name to her target had only added to the realness of her fears. But even so, she had no intentions of living her life dictated by a string of threats, even if it was only a quick stop by the mall on her way home. Her father hadn't allowed fear to run his life. Neither would she.

She stopped at the edge of the wrought-iron railing that overlooked the bottom level of the mall and eyed her surroundings. Breathing in deeply, she let the canned music playing over the sound system and the smell of cinnamon soak in — which only managed to leave her craving cinnamon rolls from the vendor two stores down.

Tightening her hold on her black-velvet dress hanging neatly from a hanger and tucked inside plastic, she watched the shoppers and tried to relax. Sabrina had made her promise she'd do one thing for herself today, and there was nothing like a new outfit to lift her melancholy mood. While the black number hadn't been on her shopping list, discovering she could slip into a size smaller had cinched the deal and made the past six grueling months at the gym worth it.

Something gnawed on the edges of her mind and snapped her back to the present. Years of reporting and journalism had turned her into an observer of people, which meant ignoring instinct was no longer possible. A man stood in the shadows, talking on a cell phone … and watching her. Cropped hair, blue jeans, and nondescript T-shirt. Maybe she was only paranoid, but she knew she'd seen him before. At the food court an hour ago when she'd bought a cappuccino, and later when she'd left the gift shop with a small basket of soaps for her mother's birthday.

A familiar wave of panic gushed through her, but she shook it off. Her reaction was nothing more than plain old paranoia from all that had happened the last week. E-mail threats and phone calls were one thing. It didn't mean a sniper was aiming a bullet at her. And besides, what journalist hadn't received a threat or two in his or her lifetime?

Determined to enjoy the rest of her afternoon, she moved in front of a jewelry store to study a pair of black onyx drop earrings that caught her eye. The spendy pair was nestled in a bed of fake snow and was certainly more than she wanted to splurge on, but they would go perfectly with the dress. She weighed her options. The first article in her series had just been published, which gave her plenty of reasons to celebrate. She eyed the rest of the display case. A pair of purple tanzanite earrings sat in the top corner. Gabby felt her throat tighten. Six months ago, she wouldn't have thought twice about buying the stunning earrings on a whim.

But then she'd met Samuel.

Samuel was twelve, but barely looked eight or nine. He spent his days sifting through the sand for the sought-after gem in exchange for one meal a day. His mother sold vegetables at the nearby market, and when that wasn't enough to feed them, she subsidized her meager income through prostitution.

Gabby's fingertips touched the surface of the glass before she turned and hurried toward the nearest exit and the parking lot with her purchases, any joy in shopping lost. Outside, sounds of traffic from the busy street adjacent to the mall greeted her. Standing next to a donation bucket, a bundled-up volunteer rang his bell while the dreary skyline showed signs of the evening's forecasted storm.

She rummaged through her purse, dumped a handful of change into the red bucket, then pulled her coat tighter around her to block the icy wind. For a moment she wished for the clear blue skies of Africa. No matter what tragedies she'd witnessed, there would always be that mysterious pull to the continent where her father had been born and raised. The openness and friendliness of its people had dredged up longings for community that were hard to find in the hectic pace of this city. And with that same longing had come a measure of hope that things would one day be different.

Her fingertips were numb by the time she found her car. She clicked the fob on her keychain and popped open the trunk. Her father had to be right. One person could make a difference — one person at a time. It was enough to keep her going.

He attacked from behind.

Gabby felt the air rush from her lungs as her assailant tried to shove her into the trunk. She blocked her fall with her arms, then swung around and slammed her elbow into his throat, knocking him off balance. He wavered, but it wasn't enough to stop him. In an instant, he'd recovered and pinned her against the car. She swung her fists at the bulky figure, but he was too strong for her. She screamed, but he shoved something into her mouth.

Oh, God, not this way . . .

Gagging at the pungent scent of gasoline coming from the cloth, her mind fought to focus, because in order to survive she was going to have to fight to win. She caught the glimpse of his gun as he reached for it and countered by thrusting her fingers into his eyes. Her attacker let out a howl as he fell back and grabbed his face.

The gun slid beneath the truck beside her. Her attacker stumbled against the car behind him, one hand still on his face. She now had the few seconds she needed. She slid beneath the truck, skinning her knees in the process, but she didn't feel a thing. Nor did she have time to think through what she needed to do.

She picked up the gun as he lunged toward her, then aimed and fired. The smell of gunpowder filled her senses as the man dropped to the ground. She let the gun clatter beneath her, while a pool of red liquid formed beneath him on the cold, gray pavement.

She couldn't move. How many times had she reported on gunshot victims and murders in the past? She'd interviewed those very same victims' families and even the murderers themselves, but she'd never aimed a gun at a person. Never shot a man.

The insistent shrill of a car alarm brought her back to the scene. She pulled her cell phone from her purse and stared at the blurred numbers.

"Miss, are you all right?"

Gabby tried to answer the woman standing beside her, but she couldn't speak.

"You're bleeding."

"He ... he attacked me ..." She looked down at her hands. They were stained with blood.

"It looks as if you have a cut on your head. I think you'll be fine, but you need to go to the hospital." The woman led her away from the car ... and the body that lay there. "My husband's just called 911. Is there anyone else I can call for you? A boyfriend or husband?"

"I don't know ... I ..."

Gabby tried to concentrate, but she couldn't think. Her head felt as if it were about to explode. Hands trembling, she knew what she had to do.

She pulled out Mickey Chandler's business card from the side pocket and handed it to the woman. "I need you to call this man. Tell him it's an emergency."

FIFTY-TWO

Chad reread the first paragraph of the paperback for the fifth time, then flipped the front cover shut. If a suspense novel couldn't keep his attention, nothing would.

With half a dozen marines guarding the embassy property to ensure no further problems, Chad had spent the last six hours helping Paul deal with the current crisis of a bombed embassy and an election hanging in the balance. The problem was that with little personnel and even fewer resources, there was only so much that could be done.

Eventually Paul had suggested they grab dinner and get some much-needed rest. They'd taken Joseph to his uncle's, while Chad agreed to Paul's offer to use his guest room. Not that he was going to be able to sleep. He might be safe in the walled, government-issued house, complete with a guard in the front yard, but he had no idea where Natalie would sleep tonight. Or if she was even alive.

Paul entered the living room with two mugs full of decaf coffee and handed him one. "Need anything else?"

"No. I'm fine, thanks. I appreciate your letting me crash here." Chad grasped the offered mug and took a long sip. Hot and black, just like he drank it.

"Anytime. With my girls gone it's nice to have a bit of company."

"Not sure I'll be good company tonight." Chad shoved the book back into the bookshelf beside him and scanned the titles, but nothing interested him. He needed a distraction. Anything to escape the constant turmoil twisting inside his gut.

He turned back to Paul. Small talk seemed the easiest escape at the moment. "You've got quite a collection of books."

"My wife's determined we feel at home whether it's Colorado or Bogama. And of course, Bogama meant no decent library, so she decided to bring the library here." Paul sat down across from him and plopped his feet up on the edge of the coffee table. "You should see the kids' rooms."

"Normally I enjoy reading, but tonight — " Chad's cell phone vibrated on the coffee table in front of him. He paused for a brief moment, then snapped it up off the table. "Natalie?"

"Natalie ... no ... My name is Gabby. Gabby Mackenzie."

"Mackenzie?" Chad set his mug down. He knew that name. Where ...

"We met briefly Monday night at Natalie Sinclair's house. I was the journalist she invited."

"Of course. I'm sorry." Chad rubbed his temples. "I'm just ... surprised to hear from you."

"And I am sorry to bother you so late, but it's taken me a long time to track down your cell phone number. I'm trying to get ahold of Natalie."

"Natalie ..." Chad pressed his lips together, wishing this nightmare would end. "We don't know where Natalie is. She was ... she was kidnapped here in Bogama yesterday morning."

"Kidnapped?" There was a long pause on the line. "What happened?"

Guilt raised its ugly head. Chad swallowed hard. "She was headed for the embassy and someone forced her into their car. All we know is that she's being held for ransom and that her captors want some photos we have, but they didn't show up for the agreed-on rendezvous."

"So this does have something to do with the photos she sent me."

"Just a minute." Chad signaled for Paul to stay, then turned on the speaker. "I'm staying with Paul Hayes, who is from the U.S. Embassy here in Bogama, and I'd like him to listen in on our conversation if it's all right. He's aware of everything that's going on."

"That's fine." Thankfully, except for a slight delay, the connection was clear.

"She mentioned she'd sent you the photos," Chad continued. "What do you know about them?"

"Nothing much more than that they documented an incident that took place in the mountains of the RD where soldiers raided a village. You probably know far more than I do."

Chad spent the next ten minutes telling Gabby everything he knew about the raid of the village, ending with the threat against the president and the kidnapping of Natalie.

Gabby clicked her tongue. "So you believe the rumors of slave camps in the mountains are true?"

"Evidence certainly points that direction, though no camps have been located as of yet." Chad worked to put the pieces of the puzzle together. "How are you involved in all of this?"

"That's what I'm trying to figure out. Someone wasn't happy with certain questions I asked on my trip. I've been involved in two recent attacks, one the night I left the RD, and the second this morning here in DC. They don't want my series to run." There was another pause on the line. "At first I didn't think that the photos were involved, but I found out one of the men in the photos is Benjamin Ayres, who works for the man I've been trying to track down for an interview in regard to the series I'm writing. He works directly for Alexis Yasin."

"Who is this Yasin?" Paul asked.

"I found out today that Interpol is looking for him in connection with money laundering throughout Africa and Europe. I believe Yasin is using the RD as a hiding place for his money-laundering racket and using slaves to run his mines."

"It would make sense. The country has its share of natural re-sources and if tapped into by the wrong person ..." Chad's mind began to spin.

"I won't keep you any longer, but why don't you write down my number in case you need to get ahold of me," Gabby said.

Chad grabbed the piece of paper and pen Paul handed him and scribbled down the number she gave him.

"Let me know when you find Natalie," she continued, "and I'll keep you updated with what I find out on this side."

"I appreciate that." Chad let out a sharp breath. "And, Gabby ... be careful."

Chad flipped his phone shut and dropped it onto the table. What-ever they were dealing with had just exploded beyond the borders of this country.

FIFTY-THREE

"When's the last time you took a day off?"

Gabby looked up from her mug of hot chocolate to her editor Ty Guillory's heavyset stature and shrugged off the question. "Thanks for coming."

Guillory slid onto the empty red booth across from her, and for a moment neither of them spoke. A group of late-night patrons laughed over something on the other side of the café, but besides them, the elevator music playing in the background, and the sound of rain turning the early evening snow into a messy slush, the place was quiet.

"My flight from LA was delayed, or I would have been here sooner." Guillory took off his wool scarf and leaned back against the padded back of the booth. "Are you okay?"

Gabby touched the thin lesion running across her hairline. "That and a slightly sprained wrist, but I'll be fine."

"Then tell me what's going on."

"Two things. Alexis Yasin and the Republic of Dhambizao." Gabby smacked a red folder onto the table between them.

Guillory eyed the folder but didn't pick it up. "First, you need to know I'm considering pulling the second article in your series. I won't have you killed over this."

"You've got to trust me on this, Ty. You can't pull it." Gabby zipped up the top of her fleece jacket, trying to shake the late-night chill. "I've just spent the past ten hours calling in every favor I could finagle, and I'm in the process of uncovering a story far bigger than profits taken from mines and the exploitation of workers."

Guillory rubbed the back of his neck. "You've got your father's passion, and you're also just as stubborn."

She matched his hard stare. "I consider that a compliment."

He dropped his gaze. "Then tell me, what's the connection between a philanthropist and some third-world country nobody's ever heard of?"

"Millions of dollars a year in natural resources gained through illegal slave labor camps, for one."

His head snapped up. She had his attention now.

She slapped open the folder to the photos Natalie had sent her. "I was finally able to get ahold of someone in the RD who knew about these photos. They believe that this village was raided by a group of rogue mercenaries called Ghost Soldiers. I also found out that Natalie's been kidnapped in regard to the photos."

"Kidnapped?" Guillory waved off the waitress's offer for coffee. "I don't like any of this, Gabby. In the past forty-eight hours you've been carjacked, shot at, and threatened, and now you're talking about powerful men involved in an illegal slave trade? Your mother's not going to forgive me if you end up in a body bag like your father — "

"The story of those villagers deserves to be heard. And if that doesn't hit close enough to home, I can give you more."

"Like?"

"They took the man who tried to shoot me into custody today. His name's Kahil Naser, and it turns out the man's wanted in several countries. Without a deal, Naser knows he's potentially facing extradition, and in some of these countries that means the death sentence."

"What does he have to offer?"

"Alexis Yasin's head on a plate. There was a hole in my data on

Yasin from 1992 until 1993. Turns out, according to Naser, he was busy training in a terrorist training camp in northern Africa at the time." She paused for a moment to let what she'd said sink in. "Naser admitted that Yasin is involved in rigging the RD's presidential elections tomorrow. And trust me, no one needs a man like Yasin running a third-world country, even if it is behind the scenes."

"So you're implying that Yasin's trying to manipulate control of the RD for an even bigger piece of the profits?"

"Imagine the sizeable amounts of funding plus a protected base for his illegal dealings, and you've got a grasp on what he's planning to do."

Ty's expression hardened. "If you can give me credible evidence that this is true, I'll consider running the article, but realize that you'll be putting yourself and the paper at risk. More than likely Naser's just a pawn in Yasin's hand, which means he's got a dozen more to replace him."

"So we let fear stop us?"

"Never. I just want you alive to report the next big story." Guillory scuffed his foot against the floor and slid out of the booth to leave. "And find a way to get some rest. You'll be worthless if you don't."

She nodded, then gulped down the rest of her drink. He was right. Somehow, she had to find a way to save boys like Samuel — and her own life at the same time.

FIFTY-FOUR

Natalie glanced up at the ceiling and continued to formulate her plan. The trusses above her were the one escape route she hadn't yet tried. With the added rays of sunlight from the narrow cracks in the wall, she could see well enough to move the table against the wall and try out her idea. With a chair on top of the table, she should be able to reach high enough to loosen the tin sheeting. Maybe that would give her room to slip out over the wall.

She turned and felt the sting of her shoulder. The bandage from her wound needed to be changed, and more than likely she needed a strong round of antibiotics. But at least she was still alive. For now, anyway.

As good as her plan might be, though, there were still two major obstacles standing between her and freedom: the presence of a guard outside and the ropes around her wrists. She glanced down in frustration. She'd made progress loosening the bonds, but couldn't help but wonder if it would make a difference. Knowing Rachel was probably dead and Patrick was most likely planning the same fate for her was enough motivation for her to keep trying despite the risks.

Fatigue washed over her as she sat back down on the wooden chair and started on the ropes again. She'd woken up a dozen times throughout the long night with mosquitoes buzzing in her ear. Each time, as she stared up at the dark ceiling and remembered where she was, she'd worked to loosen the ropes, while praying for strength. The few times she slept, Chad had filled her dreams, working feverishly on the other side of the wall swinging an ax to get her out. But his efforts to save her had proved futile. She'd continued to pray until, somehow, in the middle of the night, a veil of peace had surrounded her and she'd finally drifted into a dreamless sleep.

Until daylight brought with it renewed fears.

If Patrick had killed Rachel, he wouldn't think twice about killing her. She had to find a way out. Stretching her tired muscles, she shuffled to the wall and peered through one of the thin cracks, pressing her forehead against the wall and waiting for her eyes to focus. The guard was gone. She skirted around the bag of cornmeal another four feet to the left to another crack. There was no sign of anyone. Making a complete circle around the room, she paused at the dozen tiny gaps in the boards that gave her a limited view of outside. For the first time in close to twenty-four hours, no one was in sight.

Natalie started working on the ropes with a renewed vigor, pausing every few minutes to check and see if the guard had returned. Twenty minutes later the ropes dropped to the floor. With no sign of the guard, she disregarded the pain in her shoulder, shoved the table against the wall, and set a chair on top. Now she was high enough to reach the roof. Balancing the wobbly chair, she glanced down at her backpack. She had the can of tuna in her hand that she planned to use as a hammer, but it seemed foolish to leave the rest of her things.

A minute later, she was back on the chair with the backpack slung across her good shoulder. A dozen precise blows with the tuna can were enough to loosen the nails so she could move one section of the roof. The nails screeched in protest as she pushed up the sheet of tin, then pulled out each nail until there was enough room for her to squeeze through. The pain in her shoulder intensified as she used the trusses to swing up onto the wall and through the gap. Tin scraped against her back.

Her heart pounded as she paused to catch her breath. From this vantage point, she could see over the cinderblock wall and into the maze of compounds that spread out beyond her. There was a door in the middle of the wall that led to a narrow alley ... and beyond that, a main street.

The alley would be her way out.

Something rustled behind her. Natalie glanced down at the ground and watched as a rat scurried by. She squeezed her eyes shut, thankful it wasn't the guard. If he caught her up here trying to escape ... No. She pushed the thought aside and prayed instead. She could do this.

Dropping her backpack onto the ground, she slid down the wall and landed beside it. She caught her balance, then brushed off her hands. A dog barked, but she couldn't tell where it was. As long as it kept its distance, she wasn't going to worry about it.

Cautiously, she picked up her backpack and tried to orient herself according to what she'd observed during her time in the shack. The guard had spent most of his time on the other side of the structure. A couple of banana trees grew against the wall a dozen feet or so from the broken-down car that sat to her left. Straight ahead of her was the way out.

Hurrying across the yard, Natalie shoved open the door and ran into the alley. Just as she thought she'd made her escape, she heard footsteps pounding on the hard dirt behind her. Her heart raced even faster than before. The guard had seen her. He would catch her.

Running as hard as she could between the high walls and its occasional wooden doorways leading into other compounds, she tore down the narrow alley toward the street. She didn't dare look back; that would slow her down. But it wasn't enough. As she neared the street, someone grabbed her arm. She opened her mouth to scream, and a hand covered her mouth.

No. It couldn't end this way.

As she struggled to free herself, someone else hollered behind them. The grip across her mouth loosened. Natalie gasped for air and struggled to catch her balance as she pushed as hard as she could against her captor. He stumbled. A second later, a shot rang out. The man, still clutching the edge of her dress, dropped to the ground. Natalie pulled loose from his grip and ran.

"Wait!"

Fear of being shot again stopped her in midstride. She turned around. In the yellow glow of the sun, Stephen stood at the back of the alley with a gun pointed at her. She felt a wave of nausea wash over her as anger replaced fear. While she'd felt betrayed by Patrick, a part of her had already accepted the fact that he'd deserted to the other side. But not Stephen. She'd trusted him, and he'd completely betrayed her.

The gun shook as he lowered it to his side and held up his hand. "Wait. You don't understand. Patrick told me where he was holding you. I've been waiting to find a way to get to you. I saw the guard leave and thought I had my chance."

She took a step back. Even the fear of the gun wasn't going to stop her from taking her only chance at escape. "You're in on this with Patrick."

He started to bridge the gap between them, but Natalie kept moving backward.

"Please," he begged. "There's so much you don't know, but there's no time right now. They'll be here any minute ... I made a mistake."

"By partnering with Patrick? I'd say that was a mistake. And I trusted you."

"You don't understand, Natalie. I saw your determination to do what was right no matter what the cost." He glanced behind him. "And it made me realize how I always take the easy way. I've spent the past twenty years looking the other way and in the process lost everything. Camille, my wife, my daughters ... I've lost it all."

"I don't understand." She glanced at the body at her feet. The man lay on his back, motionless, a red stain on his chest. Had Stephen really meant to shoot her, or had his aim reached his target?

"They're planning to assassinate the president tonight."

"Assassinate?" Natalie's chin jerked up, and her empty stomach heaved. "I thought ... we thought there was a plan to rig the election, but an assassination ..."

He shook his head. "Killing the president will throw the RD into a civil war, but the consequences go far beyond this country."

Natalie shook her head. "I don't understand."

"I don't have time to explain now." He bridged the gap between them and shoved a crumpled piece of paper and some money into her hands. "I want you to go to this address. She's a friend of mine you can trust."

"Why should I believe you? Besides, I need to go to the embassy —"

"I don't think it's safe there. I just heard on the radio that they bombed part of it last night. They'll be looking for you to go there once they find out you're missing. You can call from this place and tell them what I've told you. Let them decide where you should go."

"What about the assassination? What's the plan?"

"It's going to be during the president's gala." He glanced behind him.

Someone yelled Stephen's name.

"What else do you know?"

He squeezed her arm. "The main road is straight ahead. Find a taxi and go to the address I gave you. Now run."

Natalie ran without looking back. All she could do now was trust Stephen and pray she wasn't walking into a trap.

FIFTY-FIVE

Chad slid into the seat beside Paul at the embassy's large conference table and eyed his lunch. While he could have done without the head and its beady eyes staring up at him, the fish and fries still looked good after three days of eating little besides roadside fare.

He'd hoped for a decent night's sleep, but his dreams had been anything but restful. Now that he was awake, nothing had changed. Natalie continued to hover at the forefront of his mind. He had to find her.

Mercy set the last plate of food they'd ordered in front of Frank Anderson, a thin man with a mop of curly hair currently staying in the RD to educate the voters as well as facilitate the actual election process. For the past two and a half months he'd trained clerks, monitored the nomination of political party candidates, and ensured that all important election information reached the public.

"Anything else?" Mercy asked.

Paul looked up. "While we're meeting, I want you to keep me informed on anything newsworthy that happens outside these four walls."

"Yes, sir."

Frank stared at his plate for a few seconds, then cut off a piece of his fish. "Up until your phone call an hour ago, I had a peaceful pre-election process underway. Obviously you know something I don't."

"You didn't miss the riots yesterday and this morning, did you?" Paul asked. "Or the fact that my embassy was bombed?"

"I've been involved in the monitoring of a dozen other elections in third-world settings, and the last time I looked a few clashes and demonstrations are to be expected."

"Maybe, but most election riots take place after the election, not before."

"We both know that because of the continuing efforts of my staff—"

"And General Dumasi," Paul prompted.

"I'll admit he deserves some credit," Frank said. "His actions these past two days have managed to help get things under control."

"That's a bit of an understatement." Paul picked up a fry. "I understand that the general's well-chosen words not only managed to placate both sides, but put an end to the worst of the riots as well. The people are heralding the man a hero."

Frank took a sip of his water. "Considering the way he stepped in and pacified both sides, I suppose I have to agree."

Chad chomped on a fry and listened to the banter. While he preferred working the familiar setting of the hospital over a terse political exchange, the discussion did intrigue him. Frank hesitated to give too much credit to someone not on his team, yet General Dumasi had managed a miracle. Only time would tell, but for the moment the voting appeared to be going smoothly without any further reports of violence.

Frank wiped his mouth with his napkin. "So if everything's so hunky-dory now with the amazing intervention from the general, why am I here? I know you didn't invite me to talk about the weather—or the general's achievements in diplomacy, for that matter. And you know that with the election in full swing, I don't have time for chitchat."

Paul leaned forward. "While the people of this country are expecting a free and fair election, we have proof that something is going to happen to interfere with the results."

Frank's napkin dropped into his lap. "You're not one to mince words, are you?"

"Like you said. You don't have time for chitchat. Well, neither do I."

"But you can't be serious." Frank's face reddened. "I've had my hand on every stage of this election process and except for outbursts from a few constituents, it continues to move forward without a hitch."

His lunch forgotten for the moment, Paul pulled Joseph's photos from a folder beside him. He held up one. "Do you know this man?"

Frank scratched the back of his neck. "I believe his name is Daniel Biyoya. A senior military officer."

"I'm impressed."

"It's my job to know."

Paul slid the photo across the table in front of Frank. "His picture was taken five days ago on a suspected raid on a remote village. He was with this other man, Benjamin Ayres, who is currently tied to money laundering throughout Europe and Africa."

"I don't understand."

"You will. For starters, we recently found out that Mr. Biyoya is the cousin and close friend of none other than the opposition party's leading candidate, Bernard Okella."

"Which implies nothing."

"Or perhaps everything. Especially when you stop to consider why he was meeting in secret while a group of soldiers wiped out an entire village. A fifteen-year-old boy from the village took these photos and overheard a conversation between these two men that there was nothing to worry about because the election was 'set.' Someone, it seems, has a lot of confidence that the votes are going to go their way."

Frank blew out a sharp breath. "My staff has been all over this country setting up places for the people to vote, and I've never heard of anything like this."

"So the fact that someone might interfere with the election means nothing to you?"

Frank tapped his finger against the photo. "It's not possible."

"So you're going to ignore everything that I've just told you and hope it goes away?"

Chad took another bite of his fish and caught the worried expression on Frank's face.

"What do you want me to do?" Frank's bottle clanked against the table. "I have secure voter boxes with dozens of volunteers in place right now to ensure everything goes off like clockwork. I don't have time to chase a bunch of rumors right now."

"You can ignore this, but it's not going away. And somehow I don't think you want to be remembered as the man who threw this country into another civil war because he didn't pay attention to these 'rumors,' as you call them."

"That's not fair —"

"There's nothing fair about this entire situation." Paul glanced at Chad. "Tell Frank exactly what you've gone through this past week."

Chad's knife and fork hovered above the fish's head. He glanced at the two men, not sure he wanted to get involved in the discussion. A verbal black belt he wasn't.

A glance at the stack of photos reminded him of what was more important. He set the silverware against the sides of the plate and, as briefly as he could, explained what had happened. As he spoke, Frank looked through the photos Joseph had taken.

When Chad finished, Frank slapped the last picture against the edge of the table and shook his head. "And you're basing all of this on the word of a fifteen-year-old?"

"What reason does he have to lie, Frank?" Paul was clearly getting irritated.

"I can think of a dozen off the top of my head. Bribery, extortion—"

"Joseph's resting in the other room if you'd like to talk to him, but for now ..." Paul held up his hand. "These photos are for real. You can't deny that."

"Maybe."

"Then let's assume that what Chad just told you is true, as I believe it to be. What might the opposition be planning?"

"I don't know ..." Frank shook his head. "Anything from stuffing ballot boxes to changing votes to intimidation."

"What about an assassination?" Chad threw out.

"Or a coup?" Paul added.

"A coup ..." Frank's brow began to sweat.

"What kind of security does the president have at the moment?" Paul asked.

"That's not my department."

"Come on, Frank." Paul drummed his fingers on the table. "You're involved deeply enough in this election to know who's guarding the president today, and we need to look at all the options."

"Fine." Frank wiped the corners of his mouth with his napkin. "Here's what I do know. His security team is headed up by Ernest Ademola, who's worked for the president for over nine years."

"Is the man trustworthy?"

"As trustworthy as any other employee of a corrupt government."

"You're very reassuring."

Frank shrugged.

"What about the gala the president is hosting tonight?" Paul continued.

"Guests have been screened and will only be allowed inside the building with an invitation."

"What about the guards, the kitchen staff, the servers—"

"Again, you're talking to the wrong person. All I know is that security will be tight."

"Just suppose, for a moment, that all I've just said is true."

Frank paused. "If it is true, I wouldn't know where to begin trying to stop it. Logistically, I'd say a would-be assassin would have a dozen opportunities to do his work. President Tau doesn't believe in hiding behind the walls of his presidential palace. Despite our warnings, he has meetings set up all day, including a visit to a local orphanage and an afternoon press conference."

"None of the options we've discussed so far will go over well for any of us."

"So what are you proposing? That we work together on this one?"

"To put it bluntly," Paul continued, "I don't want to be stuck here in the middle of a civil war while my wife and daughters celebrate Thanksgiving and Christmas with my parents back in the States. And you don't want your reputation as an election official marred because of some crazy plot to take over the government."

Chad felt his shoulders tense. The whole situation was sounding far too real, and Natalie was still out there somewhere in the middle of it.

"Okay, so I admit you have a point." Frank rubbed his chin. "You're really convinced that someone is trying to take over the presidency?"

"After what I've seen the past twenty-four hours?" Paul asked. "You bet."

"So where do you propose we go from here?"

Paul took a sip of his soft drink. "I've been in contact with the president's staff and have promised to keep them updated with any new findings we have. But like I said earlier, the president's planning to keep to his schedule for now."

"What about security?" Frank asked.

"We only have half a dozen marines here. We're going to need all the reinforcements we can get. We're in touch with Washington, but the additional troops they're sending might end up being too late. At least to stop anything that's attempted in the next few hours."

Frank tapped his fork against the edge of his plate. "We've got roughly four hundred United Nations troops scattered throughout the country. A hundred of those are in Bogama, but they are all stationed at the various voting locations."

There was a soft rap on the door. It was Mercy.

"I'm sorry to interrupt, sir."

"That's fine. What is it?"

Mercy's gaze dropped to the floor. "I just received a call."

From the somber expression on her face, Chad wasn't sure he wanted to hear what she had to say.

She pressed her lips together. "Ernest Ademola, head of the president's security detail, was found in his apartment less than an hour ago. The man's dead."

FIFTY-SIX

FRIDAY, NOVEMBER 20, 12:05 P.M.
LENBO, SUBURB OF BOGAMA

Natalie stood on the sidewalk in front of a narrow dress shop and looked up at the hand-painted sign hanging lopsided above the door. *Malik's Number One Sewing Shop.* She'd assumed that the address Stephen had given her was for a residence, but a second glance at the number on the building confirmed that she was at the right place.

An older woman appeared in the doorway, her bosom as ample as her smile. "Can I help you?"

"Yes." Natalie shoved the address into her pocket. "I'm looking for a Mrs. Komaga."

"I'm Mrs. Komaga, but please, call me Malik. Everyone does."

"It's nice to meet you, Malik." Natalie hesitated. The long taxi ride had given her plenty of time to consider what she should do. In the end, she'd decided to trust Stephen. Considering the circumstances, she wasn't sure she had a choice. "I was sent here by Stephen Moyo."

"Stephen?" The broad smile on the woman's face faded.

"You know him?"

"Of course I know him. He was like family once, but it's been so many years now. I . . ." Malik pressed her hand against her heart and shook her head. "Please, come in."

Natalie followed the woman into a small workroom where a half dozen young women in tailored uniforms clattered away on old-fashioned pedal-style sewing machines. Finished dresses, in a rainbow of fabrics, hung from the ceiling on the sides of the room. In the front corner were sample photographs of outfits clients could choose from.

Natalie set her backpack on the edge of a table piled high with fabric, then ran her fingers across the sleeve of a colorful dress with an intricately embroidered collar. It was amazing how a tiny shop with no electricity in the middle of a rundown suburb could create something so beautiful. "This is stunning work, Mrs… Malik."

Malik's own loose-fitting blouse and skirt ensemble, made from traditional green-and-blue handwoven cloth, was just as beautiful, with its contrasting yellow embroidered stitches along the bottom of the skirt and sleeves.

Malik held up a photo. "All I need is a photograph and a few measurements, and I can create for you anything you want." She dropped the photo back onto the table and frowned. "But if Stephen sent you, you didn't come here in search of a new dress, did you?"

"No."

"It's been so many years since I've seen him." She pressed her lips together. "Why did he send you?"

"To be honest, I'm not sure …" Natalie glanced around the room, still uncertain of what she was doing here. "I'm in trouble. I guess he thought you could help, and that it would be safe here. I need a way to contact the U.S. Embassy."

"You need a phone?"

Natalie nodded.

Malik called in Dha to a young woman in the back of the room, then glanced at Natalie's shoulder. "If you ask me, you need more than a telephone. You've been hurt."

"It's not too bad."

"What happened?"

"I …" Natalie shook her head. "It's a long story."

Malik peeled off the edge of the bandage "Long story or not, it's infected." Her frown deepened. "I have a room behind the shop where we can take care of this."

"It's fine for now. Really." For the moment, all Natalie wanted was a shower, a clean set of clothes, and a decent night's sleep. That and Chad. She needed to let him know she was all right.

"You're as stubborn as my daughter, Camille, was." Malik grasped Natalie's hand. "Come. I've sent one of my girls to fetch my cell phone — my neighbor borrowed it this morning. For now, let me look at your wound."

Natalie followed her into a sitting room that opened up to a small courtyard. The cheap red-leather furniture filling the space could have been bought from one of dozens of street vendors sprinkled across the city. Instead of family photos or art, the walls were covered with glossy pictures of dress designs cut from magazines.

Malik scooted aside some pillows and motioned for Natalie to sit. "I'm saving to buy a house outside the city where I can plant a garden and watch my sister's grandchildren grow up."

"Does your daughter live here?"

"Camille? No ... She was murdered seventeen years ago." Malik's gaze dropped as she crossed the room. "Sometimes it seems like forever. Then there are days when I still expect her to walk into the room and eat supper with me."

"I'm sorry." Natalie sank into the couch.

Malik paused in the doorway leading outside. "I'm not the only one who suffered from her death. Stephen's carried the guilt of Camille's death all these years."

A moment later she returned with a bowl of water, a clean rag, and a small jar. She laid them on the end table, then sat down beside Natalie on the couch.

"How was Stephen involved in your daughter's death?" Natalie asked.

"He's never talked to you about Camille?"

Natalie tried not to wince as the older woman pulled off the bandage. "No. He's never spoken much about his private life."

"I heard he has two daughters now?"

"They're beautiful twin girls. Jahia and Nabilia turned seven this year."

Malik dipped the rag into the water, squeezed it, and began washing the wound. "The cut is deep, but it should heal."

Natalie debated on how many details she should divulge to the woman. If word got out that there was going to be an attempt on the president's life, she was certain panic would ensue. Camille's death might not have anything to do with what was going on today, but for the current crisis, she needed to know more about Stephen. Camille seemed to be the best place to start. "Tell me about your daughter."

"I lost Camille during the coup." Malik squeezed out the rag again. "She planned to marry Stephen, but she was always so stubborn."

"What happened?"

"We were told to leave the city if at all possible. We had a place for her at my sister's house, but Camille refused to leave. She worked for a local mission that had a home for street children. She loved those kids so much. I told her there had to be a way to get them out as well, but she didn't think things would get as bad as they ultimately did. She was an optimist. Convinced that things would turn out okay."

"But they didn't turn out okay."

"I wasn't the only one who lost her. They killed Camille in front of Stephen, and there was nothing he could do to stop them. He ended up blaming himself."

Malik slowly rubbed ointment onto the wound. Natalie eyed the scentless paste. "What is that?"

"A natural remedy my mother taught me how to make years ago from the African sausage tree."

While the medicinal qualities of the unique tree with its dark, bell-shaped flowers intrigued her, Natalie focused her thoughts on the situation at hand. "Why did he blame himself for her death? Because he couldn't stop it?"

Malik nodded. "He'd tried over and over again to get her to leave. Begged her, even, but she wouldn't. If Camille would have listened, she'd be here today, and I'd have my own grandbabies to take care of."

"So she was your only child?"

"The only one who survived past infancy. I lost my husband two years after Camille's death, and my sister six months after that. I took in her four children. I had an apartment, but eventually I started this place so I could have enough money to feed them."

"You've been through a lot."

Malik set the cream down and picked up the bandage Natalie had handed her from her backpack. "What I've been through is no more than every other person in this country. We've all experienced loss. Children, parents, husbands ... Life is hard. It's what we expect."

Natalie rotated her shoulder slowly and thanked the older woman. The reality of what had happened to her made her all the more grateful she was alive. In eighteen months she'd witnessed more than her own share of heartache.

A young girl entered the room and handed Natalie a cell phone. Thanking her, Natalie took the phone and flipped it open. She drew in a deep breath. Miles from the embassy and without enough money to get there, she dialed Chad's number and prayed that he'd answer.

FIFTY-SEVEN

Ernest Ademola was dead.

It took a few moments for the reality of what Mercy said to sink in. Chad noted the stunned expressions on the faces of the two other men. Their looks of disbelief mirrored his own feelings of shock.

"This isn't a coincidence." Paul spoke aloud the obvious. He smacked his fingers against the table. "If you had doubts, Frank, that this election was in trouble ... Well, I don't know what further evidence you need."

Chad glanced down at his half-eaten lunch. Rachel and Ademola were dead — both likely murdered by the opposition. And it seemed just as certain that Natalie was being held by the same people. He closed his eyes, afraid of how hard that thought hit him. How had her brown eyes and bright smile managed to capture his heart in such a short time? He couldn't erase her image ... nor the fact that she might not even be alive — because these people had no qualms in killing those who got in the way.

The pungent scent of fried fish filled his senses and turned his stomach. He pushed his plate away. More than likely when this was over — if they both managed to make it out alive — life would go back to normal. He'd finish out his commitment at the hospital, return to the States, and never see her again.

Except that's not what he wanted. Maybe it was only the intensity of the situation they'd been thrust into, but he could no longer deny the feelings he felt toward her. Nor the fact that for the first time in a long time he'd found a woman worth holding onto. No. He might not know what the future held, but he didn't want to lose her yet. Not this way, anyway.

"What are they calling his death? Murder or suicide?" Paul's question yanked Chad from his thoughts.

Mercy clasped her hands behind her. "An official statement hasn't been released. I ... I just thought you should know."

"Then how did you find out?" Paul's brow rose.

Mercy cleared her throat. "My brother has connections with several of the president's staff. I asked him to call if anything happened."

"Then well done."

Mercy smiled. "Thank you, sir."

Frank stood and moved to the window. "From what I've heard so far, I'm guessing that calling this a suicide isn't an option in this situation."

"But if they are calling it a suicide — " Paul began.

"Someone wants the situation to disappear." Chad finished for him. "Like the photos. Another loose end swept under the carpet and forgotten. At least that's what someone wants to happen."

"And I'm determined not to let that happen. We've got to do something." Paul scratched his chin. "I've got a hole in the west wing of the embassy, an American being held for ransom, and now a dead head of security for a president who's been targeted for assassination."

Chad groaned. "It's beginning to sound like some B-rated movie review."

"I wish it was. Then I could simply push the Off button so all of this would disappear." Paul glanced at his watch. "Mercy, let the staff know that I'll be holding an emergency meeting in fifteen minutes."

"Yes, sir."

She left the room, closing the door behind her.

Paul leaned against the table. "Your people should be here as well, Frank. If we're going to do something to stop this, we're going to have to work together to come up with a strategy. We're running out of time."

Frank nodded and pulled out his cell phone. "I'll get them here as fast as I can."

"Did you mention to the president Patrick Seko's possible involvement with the opposition?" Chad asked.

Paul took a sip of his drink. "Yes, but the problem is we still don't have any solid evidence at this point to back up those claims."

"What about the e-mails Mercy gave us?"

"While I think our case is strong, apparently the president doesn't believe it. We still need something more concrete."

"A dead president would be pretty concrete." Chad rubbed the back of his neck. "Do you have his detailed itinerary for the rest of the day?"

Paul glanced at the notebook in front of him and flipped back a couple of pages. "He's got a private luncheon at one, press conference at three-thirty, then a brief stop at the orphanage with the vice president before the gala at seven."

Chad rubbed his chin and ran the scenarios. "The press conference will be his most public appearance."

"True."

"And all they'll need is one sharpshooter."

"A scenario I'd probably dismiss, except for the fact that it looks as if we've got more behind this plot than just a handful of rogue mercenaries."

"What about the FBI attaché?" Chad grabbed another bottle of Coke from the table behind him and popped off the cap. While saving the life of the president was important, finding Natalie was his priority at the moment. He was tired of sitting around doing nothing.

Paul glanced at his watch. "I was told to expect them within the next two hours, but according to the latest memo I received, planes are currently being delayed both in and out of the country."

Great. Delays in this country might be commonplace, but he was ready for a bit of efficiency.

His cell phone rang. Caller unknown.

He pressed the button to take the call. "Hello?"

Static clogged the line.

"Hello?"

"Chad?"

"Natalie?" His voice caught at the relief that flooded through him at the sound of her voice. She was alive. "Are you okay?"

"Yes. I ... I managed to escape."

Chad gave Paul a thumbs-up, then said a prayer of thanksgiving. "Tell me where you are, and we'll come pick you up."

He jotted down the address she gave him. "Did they hurt you?"

"No, I'm fine. Really."

She sounded shaken, but who wouldn't be, given what she'd gone through the past few days? "You're sure?"

"Yes."

Her answer relieved him, but he wouldn't totally relax until he could see her for himself. He glanced at the address. "Where are you, exactly?"

"I'm with a friend of Stephen's. At her sewing shop on the south side of the city." There was a pause on the line. "But, Chad ... there's something else you need to know."

"What is it?"

"There's a plan to assassinate the president tonight. I talked to Stephen, and while I don't understand how he's involved, I believe he's telling the truth."

Chad frowned. At this point he trusted Stephen as much as he trusted Patrick. If this was another trap ... He swallowed hard. "You really think you can trust him?"

"Yes. I do."

"How does Stephen know about the plan if he isn't involved?"

"I don't know, but he told me it's going to happen tonight."

"Where?"

"At the president's gala."

"You're sure?"

"Yes."

"I'll make sure that this information is passed on to the right people, but for now, all I am concerned about is getting you here."

"Thank you." There was a pause on the line. "And, Chad ..."

"Yeah?"

"Please hurry."

FIFTY-EIGHT

FRIDAY, NOVEMBER 20, 1:15 P.M.
MALIK'S NUMBER ONE DRESS SHOP, BOGAMA

Natalie sat in the early-afternoon shadows of the dress shop and watched the passing cars for Chad. She knew that the last few days had set her nerves on edge, but even with that knowledge it was becoming more and more difficult to suppress the nagging fear that Patrick would find her here.

Lord, I sure could use an extra dose of peace right now.

She peered toward the busy street, past the colorful row of embroidered shirts hanging in the warm afternoon sun, but there was still no sign of Chad. Like every other day, the road was congested with dozens of taxis, cars, and motorcycles filling the air with their thick exhaust. Side streets were busy with the commotion of sellers and buyers, and while there had been no signs of any political rallies or demonstrations on her taxi ride to the dress shop, that hadn't alleviated her concerns.

The hum of the sewing machines buzzed around her as the young women worked. Malik had excused herself to speak to a client, leaving Natalie to watch for Chad — and to ponder another growing concern. How well did she really know Stephen?

While she'd worked closely with Stephen for eighteen months, the events of this past week had brought into question who he really was. She'd described him to Chad as organized, educated, and well respected. Malik, on the other hand, spoke of him like the prodigal son who'd yet to return home. A man haunted with demons, he'd never come to terms with his past.

While Stephen had never mentioned Camille to her, Natalie couldn't help but wonder if these ghosts from the past civil unrest had in turn affected his own marriage. Stephen had only hinted of problems between him and his wife, but Natalie hadn't seen Anna or his girls for weeks. The last she'd heard they'd come to Bogama for a visit with her parents ... and had yet to return.

But from what Stephen had told her in their brief exchange, she believed his inner turmoil went far beyond his family. Today Stephen had hinted at compromises he'd made, decisions he'd regretted making, and how he'd lost everything. Was it guilt that had made him willing to risk his life to save her? And if so, what else was he willing to risk?

Caution continued to prevail against logic. While she longed to trust Stephen, deep wounds from Patrick's betrayal still stung.

She unzipped the front pocket of her backpack and pulled out a piece of gum. Her conversation with Rachel on forgiveness replayed in her mind. It was easy to talk about, but granting forgiveness was the last thing she wanted to do at the moment. And if Patrick had killed Rachel, it would be even harder.

Five minutes later, a vehicle pulled up to the curb in front of the shop. Chad jumped out with a uniformed marine right behind him.

"Chad!" Relief flooding though her, Natalie rushed out of the shop and into the sunlight.

Chad caught her gaze and his lips curled into a smile. She stepped into his arms, and for the first time in twenty-four hours she felt safe. For a moment, neither of them said anything. Memories of the last time she'd seen him overwhelmed her. Part of her wanted to explore the feelings that had intensified while they'd been apart, but for the moment the fact that he'd found her was all that mattered.

He pulled back slightly without letting go of her waist and reached up with one hand to cup her cheek. "Are you really okay?"

"I am now."

"I've been so worried." He pushed back a wisp of her hair from her forehead, then wiped her tear away. "I'm so sorry you had to go through all of this."

She shook her head. "None of this was your fault."

"Maybe not, but wish I could have been there with you."

She buried her head into his shoulder again. "It's over now."

"Miss Sinclair?"

She turned to the officer standing beside them. "Yes?"

He cleared his throat. "I'm sorry to interrupt. I'm Corporal Wingate from the United States Embassy. Are you sure you're all right, ma'am?"

"Yes. I'm tired, but fine."

"Then I suggest we get out of here. It's not safe for either of you."

"Just one more minute, please." Natalie turned to Malik, who stood in the doorway, and hugged the older woman. "Thank you. For everything."

Malik reached out and grasped her hand. "Promise me that you'll tell Stephen I forgive him. I don't want pain haunting him for the rest of his life. And if he ever decides to stop by and see me ... I just want him to know that I don't hold anything against him."

Natalie nodded. "I'll tell him. I promise."

Corporal Wingate opened the back door of the car and waved them both inside. "Let's get out of here."

FIFTY-NINE

Natalie munched on a fry, then added some salt. Fatigue had masked her appetite — until the secretary set the hamburger and fries in front of her.

"Hungry?" Chad sat beside her, his blue eyes teasing.

"Starving." She picked up another fry. "I didn't realize how hungry I was. Malik gave me tea and fried biscuits, but this is fantastic."

"They're going to want to ask you some questions. Are you up to it?"

She nodded. "I think I've got enough energy left to push me through another few hours as long as I can crash afterward for the next month."

Chad shot her a wide grin. "I'd say you deserve a vacation after all this."

Natalie turned as a fortysomething-year-old man stepped into the room and shook her hand. "Miss Sinclair. Welcome to the United States Embassy."

"Thank you. And please, you can call me Natalie."

"All right, Natalie. My name is Paul Hayes. I'm the consul here at the embassy. I understand you've been through quite an ordeal."

Natalie chuckled at the understatement. "You could say that."

"I'm glad to see that you're all right."

"And I'm very glad to be here."

Paul dropped into the chair across from her and set his notebook and water bottle on the table in front of him. "I'm sure you're tired, but I need to ask you some questions, if you don't mind."

"Of course not. I understand."

"From what you told Chad on the phone, we have very little time to stop a possible assassination. Chad has been helping put some sense of order to the facts we do have, but anything you can add could potentially help."

"I'm afraid I don't know very much."

Paul unscrewed the lid of his water bottle and took a long drink. "Why don't you start by telling us what happened while you were in captivity? The more we know about who we're up against, the better."

Natalie squeezed her eyes shut for a moment, then started describing the kidnapping, the place she was held, and the guard. When she mentioned Patrick, she caught the startled reaction on Chad's face.

"You saw Patrick?"

"Yes."

"There ... there's something you need to know before we go any further." Chad reached out and took her hand.

Natalie bit her lip, afraid she knew what he was about to say. "What is it?"

"I wish I didn't have to tell you this, but Rachel's dead."

Natalie pressed her free hand against her mouth. Tears welled in her eyes. "He told me that he loved her, but that everything had gone wrong. He didn't admit to killing her, but he didn't deny it either. I've been so afraid that's what happened."

"I'm so sorry. I know you were friends."

"And you're sure it was Patrick?"

"No," Chad continued, "but at the moment, he seems to be the most likely choice. Officially her death is being called a suicide, but we're pretty sure she was murdered. Nick found her."

"Is he okay?"

Chad nodded. "He went ahead and flew back to Kasili."

Natalie pushed her hair from her eyes and tried to slow her ragged breathing. The white walls of the room pressed in around her. Nothing seemed real. Not the fact that she'd just escaped her captors, or that Rachel was dead ... "What about Joseph?"

"He's at his uncle's. We figured for now he'd be safer there than here." Paul took another sip of his water. "Listen. I'm sorry to have to keep on with this, but I need any information you might have on plans to assassinate the president."

"Stephen told me that they were planning it tonight at the gala."

"You're certain about that?"

Natalie nodded.

"Why believe him?" Chad asked.

"Because he could have killed me, but instead he let me go. Which is why I'm worried about him now. I have no doubt that if they find out he let me go, they'll kill him."

"So you think he's working as some sort of mole in Patrick's entourage?"

She shrugged a shoulder. "That's something I've been trying to figure out. The problem is that it all happened so fast, I didn't have time to ask him anything else."

Paul tapped a pen against his notebook. "Have you considered the possibility that the man fed you false information and then let you go on purpose?"

Natalie's head began to pound. Why did the questions always outweigh the answers? "Why would he do that?"

"I don't know, but it's an angle we have to consider," Paul said. "He knows enough about you to be able to play off your emotions."

Even though she'd considered the same thing, she didn't buy the reasoning. "What would be his motivation? It doesn't make sense."

"I don't know, but I've been doing some research of my own the past few hours." Paul flipped open his notebook. "Seven months ago, Stephen purchased an apartment in Switzerland and paid cash."

"Cash?" Natalie blinked. "I don't understand. Stephen was paid well, but not enough to invest in overseas property."

"That's what I thought."

The secretary tapped on the door, then walked in. "You asked for updates, sir."

"Please. Come in."

"It's not good news, I'm afraid." Mercy laced her hands in front of her. "The president has just named his new head of security."

Natalie felt her pulse quicken. It couldn't be—

"Patrick Seko has just taken over for Ernest Ademola."

The room fell silent. All Natalie could hear was the pounding of her heart and the rain splattering against the window. Paul shoved back his chair and marched over to look out at the soggy embassy grounds.

After a moment he turned back toward them. "I specifically told the president we suspect that Seko's involved in a plot against the president's life. What are they doing?"

Mercy fingered the hem of her shirt. "I don't know, sir. Apparently they don't agree with our evidence. Patrick Seko has worked as one of the president's trusted employees for years."

Natalie drew in a deep breath as she tried to put the pieces of the puzzle together. She needed to talk to Stephen. He was the one person she knew who had answers and would talk to her. The problem was she had no idea where he was.

She bit her lip and mulled over the only option she could come up with. "I need to go to the gala tonight."

Chad's brow narrowed at her announcement. "You've got to be kidding. Patrick will be there with plans to take out the president. For all we know it could be a bomb that wipes out the entire palace."

"I don't think so." Natalie shook her head. "He's no martyr. It will be something small and precise that takes out the president. Just think about it. I'm the only one here who knows both Patrick and Stephen. If Stephen is in on what's happening, I can get him to talk."

"You don't know that," Chad countered.

"Maybe not, but do you have any other ideas for finding out what's happening?"

"Showing up at the gala would be a huge risk." Paul sat back down across from them.

Natalie pushed her plate away and leaned forward. "Not going is just as big a risk. I've tried calling Stephen and his phone is off, which means I have no way of finding him. Both of you know that we can't wait until some sharpshooter takes out the president and throws this country into another civil war."

Natalie looked to Chad. He sat beside her, his brow furrowed. She knew he was only trying to protect her, but the last five days had taught her that nothing in life was certain. She had no desire to head off on some suicide mission, but if she could do something to make a difference she was ready to do it.

"What happens tonight is going to affect more than this country," she continued. "Malik told me this afternoon that unofficial reports were stating that the president has a strong lead. If the opposition is determined to win this, they'll do whatever it takes. Especially if they have the backing of some international cartel."

"So you believe Stephen's trying to play Patrick?" Chad asked.

"Stephen said he wanted to do something right, but going up against Patrick is more than he can handle. Which means while we might need him to get information, he needs us as well."

Chad fiddled with the saltshaker. "What if you're wrong?"

"What if I'm right?"

"You heard what Paul said. Stephen's got his hand on a small fortune, so as far as we know, he could be on someone's payroll."

While Chad obviously wasn't convinced, neither was she ready to back down. "When I talked to Malik this afternoon, I learned about another side of Stephen. He's living with guilt over something that happened during the coup seventeen years ago. I think he wants to make things right this time. That's why he let me go. And why he's managed to prove to Patrick that he's playing on his side now. If we can find out from Stephen exactly what's going to happen tonight, we can stop this."

Paul came back to the table and leaned against it. "As much as I don't like to admit it, she makes sense, Chad."

"I know. That's what I hate." Chad rubbed the back of his neck and shook his head. "What kind of resources do you have here?"

"Six marines. If we get lucky, we might have access to some of the UN soldiers overseeing the election, but not much else," Paul said. "At this point, I don't think even the FBI attaché is going to make it on time."

"We've got five hours to find Stephen," Chad said. "If we find him first, there's no reason for you to go."

"True, but if we don't find him by then, the gala is the one place I'm certain I'll be able to find him."

"There's one other problem," Chad continued. "What about invitations? Rachel told us it's going to be impossible to get in without an invitation."

Paul leaned back and folded his hands across his chest. "Give me a little bit of time, and I can get you both in."

SIXTY

Natalie reached for Chad's hand as she stepped out of the embassy car onto the circular drive at the presidential palace. Thanks to Paul, false names, and a few inside connections, they had gotten through the front gate. Hopefully their formal attire — a stark contrast from the blurred newspaper photo — would keep them here undetected long enough to accomplish their goals.

The monotonous chirping of crickets competed with the peppy jazz coming from the president's mansion. She'd heard comments about the leader's luxurious residence, but it was almost impossible to believe they were still in the Republic of Dhambizao. A magical backdrop of thousands of tiny lights lit up a waterfall in front of the columned entrance of the three-story white structure. Green and yellow flags blew in the breeze above a massive front staircase lined with the president's security force. Beyond the palace, manicured lawns spread out among exotic flowers and palm trees.

Wearing a pair of high heels she'd borrowed from one of the other American ex-patriots, Natalie took a tentative step forward on the stone sidewalk leading to the house. "This place is beautiful."

Chad offered his arm. "So are you."

Natalie felt the heat in her cheeks rise at the compliment. She did feel beautiful. After all that had transpired the past few days, a hot shower and the borrowed black-satin dress that swirled at her feet below a fitted bodice made her feel like Cinderella going to the ball. Its matching satin bolero added the perfect touch and made her wish that this was nothing other than a night out at an elegant party with a handsome man.

Chad stopped at the edge of the sidewalk leading toward the house and raised her chin with his thumb until she was looking directly at him. "I want you to promise me one thing tonight."

He was near enough for her to smell the spicy scent of his cologne and see the brilliant blue of his eyes. The moonlit sky hung over them, accompanied by a sprinkling of stars. The afternoon showers had brought out the sweet scent of tropical flowers.

If they got through this alive ...

She took in a deep breath. "What do you want me to promise?"

"I'm still not sure if we're doing the right thing in coming here tonight, but — "

"Chad." Her smile faded. It was too late for either of them to back out now.

"Wait a minute." He ran his thumb down her cheek. "All I wanted to say was for you to promise me that you'll be careful. And that you will stay with me."

She glanced up at well-dressed guests who were entering the heavily guarded entrance. "Despite all of Paul's precautions, I still don't think they'll do anything to us in there."

"They're planning to assassinate the president, Natalie. None of us will be safe until this is over."

At the intensity of his words, the reality of the situation she'd tried to forget swept over her. After an afternoon of strategizing, they'd arrived armed with nothing more than a handful of information regarding some of the players involved and a time line of the evening's events. Paul waited in an embassy van outside the palace gates with four marines. Paul's instructions had been brief: find Stephen and learn what was planned, avoid Patrick, and get out alive.

Chad's words of concern weren't the only things marring the evening. The stark reality of how the president lived compared to the rest of the country was impossible to ignore. Here there were no signs of poverty, high-density housing, or lack of basic necessities like water and electricity. It was this very fact that had many of the people skeptical about the president's true intentions behind his promises of a fair and honest campaign.

"Are you ready for this?" Chad's question yanked her back to the present situation.

She nodded. She'd do it for Joseph, his father, Aina, and all the families trapped within the horrors of slavery.

It took them fifteen minutes to find Stephen. He was standing alone toward the back of one of the large living areas. For a moment, she second-guessed every assumption she'd made about him. Government liaisons didn't receive invitations to presidential galas. Her hunch that he would be here tonight because of his association with Patrick had been right on. Her only fear was that Stephen had been playing her as well.

She and Chad wove their way across the crowded imported-tile floor. Guests mingled throughout the vaulted entryway and spilled into the two enormous reception areas on each side. An eclectic mix of European architecture and African art, along with heavily carved pieces of furniture, only managed to add to the distinctive ambiance. In other circumstances, the design choices would have fascinated her. But for the moment, all she could think about was the importance of getting Stephen to talk to her.

"Stephen?"

"Natalie. What are you doing here?" He stepped back against the wall, looking like a trapped animal. "It's not safe for us to be talking."

"Because of Patrick?"

Stephen's gaze flitted around the room. "If he saw me ..."

"We need to know what's going on," Natalie prompted.

"I can't." He shook his head and glanced at his watch. "I don't have a lot of time left."

"Please, Stephen, we need to know. We can help. If the president is killed, it will start something that none of us will be able to stop. Is that what you want?"

"That's why I'm here." Stephen pressed himself against the wall and lowered his voice. "He has to be stopped."

"That's why we're here as well," Chad said. "This situation is bigger than any of us. All we want to do is help."

Stephen didn't look convinced.

Natalie tightened her grip on the crook of Chad's arm. "I talked to Malik. She told me about Camille."

Stephen's eyes widened. Now she had his attention.

"She wanted me to tell you that she forgives you. She also told me about the guilt you've been carrying around the past seventeen years — guilt for not stopping the soldiers who killed Camille."

Stephen pressed his lips together and looked across the room at the jazz quartet that was playing a mixture of blues and African rhythms for the delegates, government officials, and ambassadors.

"Tell me how you're going to stop him, Stephen."

He shook his head. "We can't talk here. There is a passageway beyond the large staircase in the entryway that leads outside to a long, stone veranda. It should be empty. Meet me on the far north side in ten minutes."

Without another word, Stephen disappeared into the crowd as the ensemble switched to a more traditional African rhythm with drums and a flute.

Chad leaned against the wall. "I don't trust him."

"We have no choice but to trust him."

She glanced at her watch. It was already seven-forty. For safety concerns, the president had finally agreed to limit his appearance to a short speech at eight-fifteen instead of an hour mingling with the guests. Directly afterward, his entourage would escort him to an undisclosed location where he would stay until the results of the election were officially announced.

They waited ten minutes, nibbling on the vast array of food laid out across three tables, and tried to blend in with the rest of the guests. Imported cheeses, fruits, caviar, thin cuts of smoked meat, and wine filled the elaborately decorated tables. The president had obviously spared no expense for what might be one of his last meals in the palace.

Chad reached down and squeezed her hand. It was time. Silently they made their way toward the back of the house. Natalie turned to go down the wide hallway, then stopped short.

Patrick blocked their way.

SIXTY-ONE

"Patrick?" Natalie caught the look of surprise in his expression, though she wasn't sure who was more startled. Chad drew his arm tighter around her waist.

"Natalie. I have to say that you're the last person I expected to see here tonight."

"I suppose if I'd hung around in that shack you'd have disposed of me by now?"

"Now I don't know why you'd say something like that." He took a sip of his wine from the tapered glass he held. "Makes me sound ... barbaric."

"Maybe I should clarify for you, then. I'll start with kidnapping and holding an American citizen for ransom," Chad threw out.

Patrick's brow rose. "I'd be happy to turn the tables back onto you with the evidence I've recently gathered on your involvement with embezzled aid funds."

Natalie's eyes widened as she looked at Chad. "Embezzled funds?"

"Didn't your boyfriend tell you?"

"Don't listen to him, Natalie," Chad countered. "It's nothing more than a bunch of lies."

"It's enough to have you arrested right now if I wanted to."

"If that were true, then you wouldn't have hidden me away in some godforsaken shack in the middle of nowhere. They're lies and you know it," Natalie countered. "Like the suicide of Ernest Ademola, for example."

"His death was unfortunate, wasn't it? Thankfully, the president had enough sense to commission me to take over once again as the head of security."

Natalie felt her chest constrict. "What do you have planned, Patrick?"

Patrick glanced at the front door. "I think it's time I called security — "

"Mr. . . . Seko." A balding gentleman who, according to his slurred speech and foul breath, had already had too much to drink, interrupted them. "I've been looking everywhere for you."

"Mr. Abega, I'm sorry but — "

Chad nudged Natalie with his elbow. She pressed her lips together as he pulled her through the crowded entryway and they made their escape. She had wanted to confront Patrick over Rachel's death, but Chad was right. Her losing her temper wouldn't get them anywhere. Neither would their getting arrested. Their priority right now had to be to get to Stephen.

They rushed out the front door before Patrick had a chance to call security. She hurried down the marble staircase beside Chad, who pulled out the walkie-talkie Paul had given him. Once they were a safe distance from the guards, he clicked the Call button.

"What have you got?" Paul's voice crackled from the other end.

"We have a problem. We have a meeting with Stephen now, but Patrick saw us. I don't know how we're going to be able to get back in and meet with Stephen without Patrick having us arrested."

"Where were you planning to meet him?"

"On the north side of the veranda that runs along the back. He should be there right now."

Natalie stood beside Chad, hidden in the shadows of a small grove of trees in the front yard as they waited for Paul's advice. "If you can't get to Stephen, then we need to get Stephen to you."

"And how do we do that? We're running out of time, and the president's due to give his speech soon."

"I want you to leave now. I'll send the car back to the front of the house to pick you up."

Five minutes later they were outside the gate in the back of the embassy van where Paul waited with his surveillance team.

"What did you mean when you said we need Stephen to come to us?" Natalie asked.

Paul set his walkie-talkie on the bench beside him. "In exchange for extra security, the president is allowing my marines access to the palace. With the description Natalie gave us this afternoon, they should have no problem bringing Stephen in."

The back of the van opened again. Two marines thrust Stephen into the vehicle.

"What's going on?" Stephen jerked his arm away and sat down hard against the bench lining the side of the van.

Paul nodded to Natalie.

"We ran into Patrick," she began. "We couldn't get to you."

The veins in Stephen's neck pulsed. "The president's getting ready to give his speech in ten minutes. I have to be there."

"So that's when they're planning to shoot him?"

"No."

"Come on, Stephen." Natalie clasped the bench. "We're on your side. Tell us what's going to happen."

Stephen's expression was marked with defeat as he stared at the floor. "It's not during the speech. It will be afterward, as the president leaves."

"Okay, now we're getting somewhere. How? A car bomb? A sharpshooter?"

Stephen hesitated, then nodded. "There's a sniper set up on the third floor of the palace. I'm planning to take him out before the president leaves the building."

Paul's eyes widened. "Take him out? Now you're sounding like James Bond."

"With the threat neutralized, I'll drive the president's car—which will be the third in line in a convoy of seven—as scheduled."

"Then you'll be free to get the president to safety."

Stephen nodded.

"And with the sniper in custody," Chad added, "Paul should have enough leverage to bring in the others."

"I can do this myself." Stephen eyed the closed door. "But I'm running out of time."

"Plans are changing a bit. We'll take care of the sniper; you drive the president out of here as scheduled. We'll have reinforcements meet you outside the palace gates." Paul signaled to the other end of the crowded van. "Are you boys ready for some more action?"

The two fatigue-clad marines who'd brought in Stephen waited for their orders.

"Did you have any problems getting into the palace earlier?" Paul asked.

"None at all, sir," one of them answered.

Stephen still didn't look pleased. "You know you could get into a lot of trouble for this. There are those who will do anything to ensure the president's death."

"From what we've heard, if we don't go in we could get in even more trouble."

"There is one more thing you should know going into this."

"What's that?"

"The opposition isn't who's behind this attempted assassination."

"It's not Bernard Okella?"

Stephen shook his head. "Bernard Okella will be lucky if he captures a quarter of the votes. He was never the competition."

"Then who is?"

"General Dumasi."

Natalie tried to digest Stephen's words as she watched the two marines whisk him out of the van. The general's involvement with the election put an entirely new light on the situation. It wasn't the first time a military leader had attempted to take over the government in this vast continent. Coups and attempted coups had ravaged Africa from Nigeria to Madagascar to the Central African Republic. The continuous cycle of corruption, coups, and countercoups was a difficult chain to break.

Even President Tau's less than ethical takeover a decade and a half ago was still fresh in the minds of the people as they wondered whether or not he was going to keep his promises of the first fair election this country had ever seen. One thing was certain: if the general had the backing of the military and a foreign investment group, the impending uprising was going to be worse than any of them had imagined.

Natalie edged forward on her seat. "Do you think he's telling the truth?"

Paul shrugged. "I have to say it makes sense in light of all that's happened the past twenty-four hours. What if the riots and following negotiations by the general were not by chance, but a well thought-out and executed plan?"

"Helping General Dumasi win the people's favor and giving him an even greater chance to take over the country."

Paul tuned in his radio to the local station so they could listen to the president's live address, which was being broadcast across the country. While the polls had officially closed over an hour ago, the president thanked the people and assured them that each one of their votes would count.

He sounded confident. Too confident, in her opinion. No one had forgotten how the president had taken over his office. How much had President Tau really changed? Enough to be willing to step down from office? And what if the general forced him to step down?

From Natalie's vantage point in the van she could see the long driveway leading up to the house. The massive structure itself was partially blocked by a row of towering palm trees. She checked her watch. If they were still on schedule, the president would make his exit within the next five minutes. Already the presidential motorcade had begun to line up along the circular drive.

Paul's walkie-talkie clicked and he picked it up. "Go ahead."

"We've got a problem, sir. We're here on the third floor, but there's no sign of a sharpshooter anywhere."

"Are you sure?"

"We've checked every room on this side of the house."

Paul's gaze snapped to Natalie. "Stephen was lying to us?"

"I don't know. I ..." She stared out the window of the van, unsure what to think.

"The cars are in position," Paul said. "We don't have much time."

"It looks as if the president is leaving the palace and heading for his car."

"Keep your eye on him."

"We'll try, but I'm not sure we can. The crowd is heavy and they all want to shake his hand. It's chaos, sir."

"Well, at least the sniper's going to have problems picking him off."

A burst of static filled the line. "I'm sorry ... sir ... we've lost him."

Paul grabbed a pair of night-vision binoculars and stepped out of the van.

A flash of light lit up the night in front of the presidential palace, followed by a deafening bang. The explosion shook the ground.

"What just happened out there?" Paul shouted into the walkie-talkie.

Natalie grabbed a set of binoculars and jumped out of the van behind Chad. She counted the cars through the smoke. The president's car was engulfed in flames.

SIXTY-TWO

Chad jumped out of the van and stared in disbelief at the black-and-gray smoke billowing from the president's car. A sick feeling washed over him. All their efforts to save the president had just blown up with one well-timed explosive device.

Natalie stumbled beside him, and he tightened his grip on her forearm.

"Stephen lied to us." Her voice was barely above a whisper. "And now the president's dead."

Paul shouted into his walkie-talkie to the marines who were still on the third floor of the palace. "I want a play-by-play from your position of what's happening on the lawn. Once you see us drive in, get down there as fast as you can. I've got UN troops on standby that I'm calling in now. Everyone else, let's go."

Chad helped Natalie back into the van, then jumped in behind her and slammed the door as the driver started the engine. Centrifugal force slammed them against the side of the van as the driver spun around and headed for the palace. Paul signaled to the driver to stop at the security gate, where he flashed his identification at the guard. After an intense minute of arguing, the man finally opened the gate.

Chad stared ahead at the smoldering car that sat on the other side of the drive. Stephen had played them all by sending them on a wild goose chase.

In the lights of the entrance, he caught Natalie's glazed look and squeezed her hand. "You okay?"

"Yeah. I'm just ready for this to be over."

When the van stopped, he jumped out, then quickly covered his mouth with his sleeve. Smoke poured from the vehicle, obscuring those who'd been injured from the impact of the explosion. The charred vehicle was completely destroyed and had clearly left no survivors.

A quick assessment of the grounds revealed complete chaos. They'd be lucky if they didn't find more casualties among the injured. Guests ran across the grass toward the front gates, apparently afraid another bomb might detonate. When all this was over, they were going to have more to deal with than just the physical wounds. In this situation neither position nor status mattered; trauma would affect all of them.

Paul barked out orders to the marines on the ground, then turned to Chad. "I need you to deal with the injured. I'll try and see if there are any other doctors here."

"I'm on it."

Chad knelt down beside a man in a three-piece suit with burn marks on his face. Natalie and one of the marines crouched down beside him.

"What can we do to help?" Natalie asked.

"We need to treat the more serious patients first, which is primarily going to be burn victims and those hit with shrapnel. See if you can find some room-temperature bottled water and pass it out to any of the responsive victims. They need to use it to flush any burns and then drink the rest to ensure they stay hydrated, which can be a concern with burns. Get whoever you can to help you, because I'll be sending you more victims."

He pointed to a clear area a good twenty-five feet from the blast sight and addressed the marine as he moved onto the next patient. "We need to get these injured people away from here in case there's another explosion. Anyone who is injured but still able to get up needs to go with you there. I'll deal with those who can't move."

While he didn't expect chemical or biological agents to be involved, he wasn't taking any chances. Even without them, there would still be large quantities of particulates in the air.

"Excuse me, sir?"

Chad looked up from a twentysomething-year-old in front of him who was having trouble breathing to see one of the uniformed presidential guards. Maybe Paul had managed to find a medic. "Do you have medical experience?"

"No. I need you to leave the grounds immediately. I have orders to secure the scene and remove all nonessential personnel from the premises."

"You've got to be kidding. I'm a doctor and I'm treating this woman."

"General Dumasi is in charge of this situation now, which means you and the marines need to leave immediately."

Chad ignored the man as he unclasped the woman's bracelet from around her wrist in case of swelling. Bureaucracy was bad enough here on a good day. He wasn't leaving these people behind because of some general's lust for power.

"Sir, I'm asking you to leave now. If you don't, I'll be forced to place you under arrest."

"You just don't get it, do you?" Chad stood to face the man, using the six inches he towered over him to his advantage. "There's got to be at least two dozen people here who were just injured in a blast that killed your president. I'm not leaving until I know everyone has been taken care of."

The guard reached for Chad's arm, but Chad jerked away before he could grasp it. "Don't even try it."

Paul appeared from behind the man. "What's going on?"

"Apparently Stephen was telling the truth about one thing." Chad spoke above the growing clatter. "General Dumasi thinks he's in charge now and doesn't want our help."

A UN-marked helicopter whirled above them, drowning out any further arguments as it prepared to land on the palace grounds.

Chad went back to work on the woman while Paul dealt with the guard. "We're dealing with dozens of foreign delegates and other government officials here, and I can promise that you don't want to see your face splattered in newspapers all over the world as the one responsible for their deaths."

"I'm under strict orders to — "

"I don't care what your orders are." Paul stood his ground. "We're going to care for the injured and evacuate as many of the delegates as we can by air and get them somewhere safe."

A UN officer dressed in fatigues and a blue helmet jumped from the helicopter as the rotor blades began to slow. With the guard seemingly put in his place, Paul hurried off to coordinate the evacuation.

A car door banged shut behind them and Chad glanced over. At first he focused on Natalie, who was walking toward him. Then his attention shifted beyond her to the car directly behind the charred vehicle.

President Tau stood beside the car looking dazed.

Chad blinked his eyes and shook his head. It couldn't be the president. He was dead.

Natalie caught his shocked expression and looked behind her.

Someone shouted.

Chad hollered for Paul, then darted toward the car with Natalie right behind him. They had to get the president to safety.

President Tau slumped against the car.

Chad heard the shot a split second before the president dropped to the ground. Adrenalin surged through his body and he shifted toward Natalie. There was a sniper and she stood less than ten feet from the president. "Natalie, get down!"

He pushed her to the ground, then ran for the car. Several shots rang out as the marines sighted the sniper and opened fire.

Ignoring the danger, Chad dropped to his knees to examine the president, who was still conscious. His unexpected move as the shooter took aim had probably saved his life. "My name is Dr. Talcott. I'm here to help."

"It's my leg."

"I want you to lie still so I can evaluate the extent of your injury."

Chad ripped off the pant leg and found where the bullet had lodged. He pulled off his shirt and tore off a strip. Using it as a bandage, he pressed it firmly against the wound.

"Are you hurt anywhere else, sir?"

The burly leader shook his head and attempted to sit up.

Chad pressed gently against the man's shoulder. "Not yet. I'm going to see that you get out of here as soon as possible, but until then I need you to lie still and relax."

Keeping pressure on the wound, he studied the sloping grounds that led up toward the palace, where shadows played against the walls from the outside lights. His breath caught. The marines had taken down the shooter and were now leading him across the lawn.

Patrick.

Paul appeared above Chad. There'd be time to absorb the implications later. "How is he?"

"Lucky," Chad said. "The bullet went through his leg. He's lost a lot of blood, but he'll live if we can get him out of here."

Paul called over two of the UN soldiers. "As soon as you've got him stabilized, Chad, I want him on that helicopter."

Five minutes later, Chad watched as the two men carried the president to safety. He then took a quick look inside the car the president had been in, but it was empty.

Natalie stepped up behind him. "We've passed out all the water, and those who are able to are helping to dress wounds. Three were killed when the bomb exploded, but all other injuries appear to be only burns and shrapnel wounds. It was a miracle that it wasn't — "

She stopped midsentence.

Chad ran his hand down his arm. "You okay?"

"I don't know."

He followed her gaze to the charred vehicle. "What is it?"

"I haven't had time to stop and figure out what happened until now. Stephen said he was driving the president's car, which was supposed to be the third car."

"And the third car is the vehicle that exploded."

"But the president wasn't in the third car."

She was right. He hadn't had time to examine the situation closely either, but the president had obviously not come from the third car. He'd come out of the car behind it.

"What if Patrick had planned to take them both out at once, but in the confusion of the crowd the president got into the wrong car?" he asked.

"But if that's true, where's the driver of this car? And where is Stephen?"

"I don't know, Natalie."

Chad walked to the smoldering car, fearing what he was going to find. The backseat was empty, but in the driver's seat sat a charred body.

SIXTY-THREE

Gabby pulled off her tennis shoe and rubbed the heel of her foot. She'd have preferred a run in the quiet neighborhood, but had decided it was a risk she wasn't going to take. The dusty treadmill had been the next best thing.

Sabrina entered the living room, still clad in her favorite plaid flannel pajamas. "Don't you think it's a bit early — and cold for that matter — to be exercising?"

"Nope." Gabby placed her hands on her hips and shot her friend a grin. "Forty-five minutes on the treadmill, and I'm a new person."

"You know I hate mornings. Especially early mornings." Sabrina picked up the bowl of popcorn from the movie she'd watched last night with Michael and chomped down on a popped kernel. "How are you feeling?"

Gabby pulled off her other shoe. "Are you referring to my sprained wrist, the scrapes across my shins, or the cut on my head?"

"I think it's time you took up another career."

Her cell phone interrupted their conversation. She turned down the music on the stereo and answered the call. "Gabby Mackenzie speaking."

"Miss Mackenzie, this is Mickey Chandler. I just wanted to call and see how you were feeling."

Gabby gaze focused on the candles sitting on the stone hearth. How quickly was one supposed to recover from being carjacked, threatened, and almost kidnapped in the scope of one week? She'd yet to find a rulebook on that one.

She pressed her lips together. "I've still got some scrapes and scratches, and a few nightmares, but I'm going to be all right. Still trying to convince my mother that she doesn't need to hire a bodyguard for me."

"She may not have to."

Gabby's journalistic instincts kicked in. "What do you mean?"

"A lot of the information you passed on was able to help solidify the government's case against Alexis Yasin. He was arrested last night for money laundering, attempted murder, and alleged terrorist ties, to name a few. "

"Wow. That's wonderful." Gabby sat down on the couch, drawing one of the loose cushions into her lap. Maybe his arrest would be the start of freedom for many. "I have to say, I'm going to sleep better tonight."

Mr. Chandler cleared his throat. "There's another reason I called. I thought you might like to know that U.S. troops found the first occupied slave camp in the RD this morning."

Gabby scrambled for the notepad she kept on the end table and started scribbling notes. "Where?"

"About 350 miles west of the capital. They're going to need someone to tell their story. I thought you'd be the perfect person. If you can get to Bogama, I'll personally arrange transport to the site for you in one of our military helicopters."

Gabby dropped her pen. "I don't know what to say."

"After reading your articles, I believe you have plenty to say. Don't let anyone stop you from telling the truth."

"I won't, sir. That I can promise you."

Gabby hung up the phone, her mind spinning with all the details of what he'd proposed. She had her passport and visas. If she left today, she could be in Bogama tomorrow night.

"Gabby?" Sabrina plopped down on the couch beside her. "What's going on?"

Gabby pulled up her knees beneath her. "That was Mickey Chandler with Interpol. I'm going back to Africa."

SIXTY-FOUR

Chad started to knock on the door of Natalie's office, then paused. She sat at her computer, completely absorbed in whatever she was doing. She'd pulled back her hair with a clip, leaving a few stray wisps around her neck that fluttered in the breeze from the ceiling fan. The sleeve of the red T-shirt she wore only covered half of the bandage on her shoulder — a blunt reminder of everything they'd been through the past week. He'd been amazed at how well she'd held up the past three days, enduring hours of interviews as both the UN and the Dhambizan government worked together to sort through what had happened. And what the future of this country held.

He rapped lightly on the door frame. "Hey. Are you about ready to go? Joseph's waiting for us."

Without looking up, she held up her hand for him to wait. "Give me another second or two."

He stepped into the tiny office where she'd managed to add a few personal items to transform the space into something both functional and warm. His gaze stopped at the collage of photos hanging above her desk. Paris, Egypt, England, Rwanda, Brazil ... He hadn't realized she'd visited so many places. Which was only one of the dozens of things he still wanted to learn about her.

She swirled around in her chair and shot him an apologetic look. "Sorry."

"You're not supposed to be working today." He sat down across from her in the other chair. Because of the tight quarters, they were so close that their knees touched. Not that he was complaining. He leaned forward and squeezed her leg. "How are you feeling?"

She pulled the clip from her hair and ruffled the back before securing it again. "Besides trying to endure this heat wave?"

"Yeah. Besides the heat."

"Well, thanks to the sleeping pills you prescribed, I'm feeling pretty rested. And I have to admit that it was good to be back home in my own bed last night even though I have a mountain of work to do to get everything cleaned up from the break-in. I just wish ... I don't know." She started playing with the edge of a chipped fingernail. "Paul called me a little bit ago and told me that the police have confirmed that it was Stephen's body found in the bombed vehicle."

He reached for her hands and held them between his. "I'm so sorry. I know that while it doesn't come as a surprise, that's not what you wanted to hear, either."

"I guess I kept hoping that somehow there had been a mistake." Natalie pulled away from him and turned back to her computer. "And there's something else, Chad."

She held up an envelope while he scooted his chair beside her. "I received a letter this morning. He must have put it in the post last Friday afternoon."

Chad tensed. "What does it say?"

"There are letters he wanted me to give to his wife and daughters if anything happened to him. I know it won't change anything, but I'm hoping it will help."

"So he had this planned all along?"

She nodded.

"So his death wasn't an accident?"

"No, and I guess he wanted me to know that once it was all over.

When he found out about the car bomb, he didn't know how to stop it, because Patrick was keeping a close watch on him. He decided that the only way to save the president was to ensure that the president wasn't in the car. It was crowded that night, and he bribed the man assigned to drive the president to switch to the fourth car. It was a gamble, I suppose, but since President Tau was used to simply following the guard into the vehicle, he didn't question anything. I'm sure Patrick was counting on that."

"And then Stephen drove the car with the bomb."

"Exactly. He was assigned to drive one of the decoy cars, making the switch even easier."

"So he was trying to make up for the mistakes in his past?"

"And apparently he made a lot of them. He bought the house in Switzerland with money skimmed off the books from aid organizations. I guess he's been doing it for years, but until lately he was too afraid to spend it."

"So that's how he bribed the driver?"

"Yes, and for him, this was the only way he thought he could finally be at peace. I guess he lied to us that night because he didn't want to take a chance of anything going wrong."

Chad tapped his fingers on the desk. "Paul's going to need to see these."

"I know. I'm planning to send him copies right away." She turned toward him. "The only good thing about all of this is that his letters bring about some closure. He might have made a lot of mistakes, but at least I don't have to wonder anymore which side he was playing on. He did what he thought he had to do to save the president."

"And he did save him, Natalie. Which in turn helped stop what could have been a horrid civil war."

A lone tear rolled down her cheek. "But we could have found another way to stop it without him dying."

"Maybe for him, that's what he had to do. On the bright side, they've arrested Patrick, as well as General Dumasi, who allegedly was being backed financially by Yasin so that he could take over the country during the upcoming elections." He drew out a low whistle. "There's nothing like a few hundred million dollars worth of natural resources as motivation."

"Which means that this won't be the end of trouble for this country."

"At least the UN is claiming Tau's victory was fair. Other than a few angry protestors, things have been fairly quiet."

"And that's not the only good news. The helicopter will be here in five minutes. Do you think you can make it?"

Natalie's smile reached inside his heart and tugged. "You know I wouldn't miss this for anything."

SIXTY-FIVE

An hour and fifteen minutes later they were airborne above the vast mountains of northern RD in the transport helicopter. The vast expanse of green forests spread out beneath them. Joseph peered out the window across from him and Natalie. Seven days ago, they'd left Kasili together for the capital. Today, the three of them were finally back together again. This time, thankfully, they were on their way to a celebration. While further searches would still be conducted in the coming weeks, using demographic reports and satellite photos, U.S. troops had already found two slave camps high in the mountains. Joseph's family had been kept in one of them. It was time to bring them home.

"What exactly are they mining down there?" Chad shouted above the noise of the helicopter to the officer leading the mission.

"From our briefing," the officer explained, "I was told that four months ago, columbite-tantalite, or coltan for short, was discovered. It's a dull metallic ore found in major quantities primarily in the eastern areas of Congo."

"How is it mined?" Natalie asked.

"It's collected much like gold. When it's refined, it becomes metallic tantalum, a heat-resistant powder that can hold a high electrical

312

charge. Coltan has become a vital element in creating capacitors, the electronic elements that control current flow inside circuit boards."

"So what do they use it for? Cell phones?"

"Exactly. Cell phones, laptops, pagers, and scores of other electronics."

The helicopter set down on a small clearing a hundred yards from the mines. Joseph was the first to alight onto the area that had been secured by UN and U.S. troops working together after the arrest of the thirteen Ghost Soldiers who'd been guarding the compound. His family stood in the clearing, waiting to leave, while Gabby, who'd arrived earlier, snapped photos of the poignant reunion.

Chad watched the scene unfold before them. It made the past week worth everything they had been through. The horror of what Joseph's family had endured wouldn't be erased overnight, but at least they had survived and would be returning to their village.

Joseph broke away from the group and walked toward them between his little sister, his mother, and his father. "Dr. Talcott ... Ma'am. I want you to meet some of my family."

Chad shook the older man's hand with one hand while clasping his forearm with his other hand as a sign of respect. "Eh fo banda."

"Eh fa."

Joseph couldn't stop beaming. "They have promised my father medical care in the capital until he's well."

"That's wonderful news." Natalie knelt down in front of the little girl and pulled something from her pocket. "I believe I have something that belongs to you."

The little girl's mouth dropped open as Natalie held out a handmade doll with tiny black beaded eyes and a crooked smile. Aina's face lit up as she pressed the doll against her chest, then fell into Natalie's embrace.

With her arm still around Aina, Natalie glanced up at Joseph. "You've proven yourself to be a man, Joseph. I'm proud of you."

"Thank you, ma'am. And … I did what you said." Joseph looked from Natalie to Chad. "I prayed to Jesus. And He heard me."

"Yes, He did." Natalie stroked Aina's hair. "No matter what the circumstances, He cares for both of you."

Someone shouted from the helicopter. It was time to start boarding.

"Go on." Chad motioned to Joseph and his sister. "We'll be there in just a minute."

Natalie stood and watched them walk hand in hand to the helicopter. "It's a miracle, isn't it?"

"Yes, and I want you to see another miracle."

He took her hand and led her through a clump of bamboo with its long, spear-shaped leaves to the edge of a deep precipice. A thin, white mist covered the fertile valley below them, while farther in the distance Mt. Maja, an inactive volcano, rose proudly from the earth.

"I thought the view was incredible from the helicopter, but this is amazing."

He caught the enthusiasm in her voice as an eagle soared across the valley below them. It was the same passion he'd seen in everything she did.

For the next few moments, they stood side by side and listened to the chatter of birds competing with the thick hum of insects.

"I haven't had a chance to tell you everything yet." Natalie broke the comfortable silence that had settled in between them. "The president has agreed to work with the UN in reestablishing homes for those forced to work in the mines, and my organization has agreed to additional funds and will prioritize aid to the victims. They want me to be in charge of the project."

He wrapped his arm around her and felt her snuggle against his shoulder. "I'd say they found the perfect person."

"I haven't said yes. So much has happened that I told them I needed time to think and pray about it. "

"I've certainly been doing a whole lot more of that lately. The past few days have taught me at least three important things."

"What are they?"

The wind blew a strand of her hair against his face and he gently brushed it away. "One, there are still a few good men left in this world, like Stephen. He might not have been perfect, but then neither am I. And in spite of all his faults, he was willing to give his life to save his country."

"It's humbling, isn't it?"

"Yes, and it reminded me of number two: the even greater sacrifice made by Jesus Christ."

Neither of them said anything for a moment. The thought struck even harder after Stephen's death. Christ had given up His life so that they might have an abundant life.

"What about number three?" Natalie prodded.

"Number three?"

"You said you'd learned three things."

He swung her around until she faced him. The panoramic view of the valley and mountains spread out behind her, but all he could see at the moment was the woman he'd fallen in love with. "I've decided that a week wasn't near enough time for me to get to know you."

"Really?" She giggled as she looked up at him.

"I was thinking we needed to do something about it."

"Did you come up with anything?"

"Personally, I've never liked the nightlife of Kasili."

Natalie laughed again as the blades of the helicopter began to rotate. "What nightlife?"

He glanced behind him. They were still loading the last of the refugees, which gave them a couple more minutes. "We need to go, but I was thinking dinner and talking under the stars in your backyard."

Her smile widened. "I think I can manage that."

He ran his finger down her cheek, then tilted her chin toward him. "I don't know what the future holds, but I don't want to lose you."

"I've been hoping you would say that."

Chad kissed her gently, then paused to take in one final glimpse of the magnificent view in front of him before heading back with Natalie toward the helicopter — and their future.

ACKNOWLEDGMENTS

As with all novels, it takes a village to complete a manuscript, and there are so many friends and colleagues to whom I will be forever grateful for taking this journey with me. For Sue Brower, who first believed in the idea for my series along with the incredible Zondervan team who took my manuscript and helped shape it into what it is today. Thank you Jackie, Joyce, Karwyn, Bob, Leslie, Matt, and all of you who were a part of bringing this longtime dream to life.

My wonderful friend and agent, Joyce Hart, along with my fabulous crit partners and writer friends who have laughed and cried with me each step of the way: Susan Paige Davis, Darlene Franklin, Lynette Sowell, Elizabeth Goddard, Ronie Kendig, and Ellen Tarver.

My incredible husband and precious kids who let me get lost in another world and still love me!

My panel of experts who are willing to answer all of my questions, allowing me to bring depth to my stories. Thank you Randy, my pilot and arms expert, and Faith and Paul, my medical sources. Any and all mistakes are mine!

I love to hear from my readers!
E-mail me at contact.harris@gmail.com
or visit my blog and website at
http://myblogintheheartofafrica.blogspot.com
www.lisaharriswrites.com